THE
CON

KAREN WOODS

Harper
North

HarperNorth
Windmill Green,
Mount Street,
Manchester, M2 3NX

A division of
HarperCollins*Publishers*
1 London Bridge Street
London SE1 9GF

www.harpercollins.co.uk

HarperCollins*Publishers*
Macken House,
39/40 Mayor Street Upper,
Dublin 1
D01 C9W8

First published by HarperNorth in 2023

1 3 5 7 9 10 8 6 4 2

A catalogue record for this book
is available from the British Library

ISBN: 978-0-00-859210-3

Printed and bound in Great Britain by
CPI Group (UK) Ltd, Croydon

This book is produced from independently certified FSC™ paper
to ensure responsible forest management.

For more information visit: www.harpercollins.co.uk/green

To my mother, my queen, Margaret Price. You have given us memories we will never forget. I will make you proud and do all the things we spoke about. You will be missed by all your family, rest in peace. Love you Mam x
In memory of Christine Price and Maureen Orman, always missed.
To our Daz, my brother, my friend and my angel. Love you always.
For my son Dale, goodnight God bless x

Prologue

Zara Makin remembered exactly how she felt when she first held her son: like she'd walk through fire to protect him. She'd never known love like it – and she knew then it would never change. And she remembered how he looked: vulnerable, pure and – most of all – innocent. If only he had stayed the same …

Chapter One

Tyler Makin stood in the dock at Manchester Crown Court and snarled over at the prosecution, his hands cupped together tightly, a look set deep in his eyes that told you this man was dangerous. Judge Vickers was getting ready to sentence Tyler and his crew, to get them off the streets, to rid Manchester of their crime wave and keep the community safe. Tyler was constantly licking his dry, cracked lips as he waited, ready to know his fate. He eyeballed the judge next, trying to work him out. The old fella looked like he was in a mood today, with a face like a bulldog chewing a wasp.

Tyler had stopped hoping for the best as the judge had summed up the case earlier. Maybe his luck had finally ran out. It hadn't sounded good, even he knew that. And most of the people gathered here in the court weren't on his side anyway. It was clear in their faces what they felt towards him: hate. A room full of people who wanted justice to be served here. They were looking at him as if he was some master criminal. It was all minor stuff in his eyes, fuck all to get upset about, if you asked him. This was real life, how people earned a crust where he was from. It was pretty much the norm to sell drugs in his neighbourhood these days, everyone was doing it. What the hell did the government think men like him were going to survive on, anyway? A poxy two ton a fortnight payment from Universal Credit, if they were lucky? It was a joke, barely enough to live on, let alone leave anything for even a taste of the stuff that made life sweet: a meal out, some new clothes, a bit of luxury.

These jossers here today were making him out to be some kind of psychopath. 'A danger to the public,' the prosecution had told the courtroom earlier. Was he having a laugh or what? Tyler had never hurt anyone who hadn't deserved it. Well, maybe a few, but they had taken the piss, tried to have him over, disrespected him. He had his name to defend, a reputation to keep. Tyler was fair, firm and the people who knew him well would have told anyone that, he reckoned. He was a good guy, he felt, maybe even a lovable rogue. But he knew now he'd got sloppy and let things slip, his head not properly in the game. A few beers too many sometimes didn't help. He'd made some daft mistakes, sent text messages that made him sound like he was at the top of the ladder, that set him up as the main man on this conspiracy charge to supply class A drugs.

He'd got too used to the life, he could see that now. When everyone around you is in the same line of business, you think you're untouchable. But nobody was bigger than the law and he should have known that, sooner or later, the dibble would be booming his door down, taking everything he'd grafted his balls off for. His car, watches, designer clothes: the police would take the lot. Money bought a lot of things, but safety wasn't one of them. Tyler hated to admit it, but even being on remand in Strangeways had taken its toll on him. When he'd looked at himself this morning, there were dark circles under his eyes, cheek bones showing in his once rounded, tanned face.

Strangeways was notorious for good reason. Set in the Cheetham Hill area of North Manchester, it was more than a jail, it was a meeting place for criminals from far and wide. It wasn't only lads on drugs charges like Tyler. There were murderers, armed robbers, and people traffickers residing there too. And they might have been – temporarily – off the streets, but they were all out to make a name for themselves in the big city. In fact, most of them wanted to land at this jail, to let all the other grafters in the area know that they were at the top of their game and willing to risk everything to have their names in everyone's mouths. Prison life was hard, a dog-eat-dog world, but it could also make your reputation, build your contacts and teach you some new tricks.

Tyler dropped his gaze to the floor, thinking. This prick needed to start talking again instead of fucking about with the paperwork. How hard was it to read out the sentence; it wasn't rocket science, was it? Tyler turned his head slowly and growled over at the public gallery, at the press. Scavengers, they were, pens at the ready, waiting on a story that would shock the nation. A story about a gang who'd been taken off the streets, making them safer for the average Joe and his family. Bullshit, pure fiction they would write. Why didn't they interview him and ask him the full story?

Yes, he would have put them right, then. The police had stitched him up, made it all sound way bigger than what it really was. They had found fuck all at his gaff when they raided the joint, yet they called him the General of the operation. Were they having a laugh or what? If that was the case, where was his dosh, his luxury lifestyle?

Tyler lifted his head and his eyes widened as he looked over at his mother, Zara. He tried to smile despite the feeling inside his chest like a brick had been tied around his heart and dropped from a bridge into a deep river. His whole life, she had always been there, always made him feel better about himself, told him everything would be alright. But today her expression told him her hands were tied and she could no longer protect him from the dangers he was facing. He knew his mother would take on anyone for her boys. She'd fight tooth and nail, warn them that, if she needed to, she would go to jail herself to protect her boys. But it wasn't her in the dock.

He felt terrible as he saw his mother's eyes flooded with tears, her nostrils flaring, her face flushed and her lips trembling. He knew she was trying to hold it together and he watched as she quickly turned her head away from him: she needed to be strong, show no signs of weakness. She'd brought her boys up that way too, to never let anyone see when they were hurt. She'd drummed that into them from an early age. Big boys don't cry, she'd told them. Tyler quickly turned away too now, and, remembering her words, gritted his teeth and shot a look at the guard stood at the side of him. He was clearly bored, barely paying attention and, if they'd been anywhere other than here, he would

4

have been a sitting duck. Tyler rolled his shoulders back out of habit, trying to show he could take him down with one punch if he needed to.

The guard didn't give him any eye contact, just carried on looking straight in front of him and pretended Tyler wasn't even there. Feeling slighted, Tyler looked instead to his left at his two co-accused. He couldn't catch his mate Tony's eye, but he smirked at Barry Golding. Smidge, as he always called him, had been his boy for over ten years now – his right-hand man, the pair of them brothers in arms. Thick as thieves they were: if you fought one, then you fought them both.

Tyler brought his hand up to his mouth and spoke through his slim, fanned fingers in a whisper, 'This judge is doing my head in, what the fuck is up with him? He's been reading the fucking files now for time. I bet he's got a dirty mag hidden behind them. That's what he's doing. Pervert.'

Smidge sniggered and hung his head low. Usually, he would have been laughing his head off at the comment, but today he had lost his mojo. He kept his voice low, 'It is what it is. I just want it over with now.' He shot his eyes around the courtroom, stretching his neck. 'That bitch never turned up to court, did she?'

Tyler shook his head. Smidge's girlfriend Becks had a reputation and he'd told him time and time again that the woman was nothing but trouble. He'd heard enough rumours about her putting it about, knee-tremblers at the back of the pub, but there was no way he was telling Smidge that. No, no way. It would have broken his friend, sent his head west. 'Nah mate, didn't think she would. She's never been there when you needed her. Waste of space, that one is. Bin her. I told you, mate.'

Smidge swallowed hard. 'Fuck her, I won't be in jail forever and when I get out you watch this space, pal. I'll fucking show her when I have a new bird on my arm. Yes, you just watch.'

Tyler patted his hand on his mate's leg. 'You sure will, mate. You always bounce back.'

The guard clocked Tyler's movement and flicked his head to show something was about to go down.

At the front of the court, the judge looked at them all from over his gold-rimmed glasses, shuffling his papers, ready to sentence the men. He had a serious look and sat back in his black leather chair, sipping on the cold water he'd just poured.

'Showtime,' Tyler whispered under his breath.

Papers were rustling, journalists rolling their pens between their fingers, eager to get a headline story.

The judge addressed the men. Tyler was the first to be sentenced. He stood tall, shoulders back, heartbeat doubled. A quick look over at his mother, then he locked eyes with the judge, showing he held no fear of what he was about to say next. Smidge was shaking next to him, and Tony had hardly said a word since he'd come into the dock – although he was always like that, a man of few words.

Tyler's hands gripped the cold, brass rail in front of him and his ears pinned back. He mumbled under his breath again, 'Come on, fucking sentence me and get this over with.'

He hated someone having this power over him, acting all high and mighty, when in reality he reckoned a lot of these judges were as bent as a nine bob note. Yeah, Tyler had heard a few stories about these bigwigs; stories about affairs, kinks, power games in their chambers when everybody had gone home. Dirty bastards, they were, highly paid wankers who didn't know shit about the real world and what people like him had to do to get by. He'd tell him that too, given half a chance. Fuck him and fuck the so-called justice system.

'Tyler Makin, you are a danger to society and a man who has caused much misery to families in and around this area. You preyed on the vulnerable and lined your pocket. Money and power are all you sought. I will not stand for men like you who think they are a law unto themselves. I have a duty of care to protect our streets and our children from criminals like you. I hope the time you spend behind bars helps you mend your ways and enables you to think about all the lives you have ruined to satisfy your own greed. Tyler Makin, I sentence you to five years imprisonment.'

There was whispering in the public gallery, sobbing from somewhere. Journalists' heads down, scribbling. Tyler nodded his head slowly. He couldn't let anyone see him flinch, so he ran his tongue over his pearly white teeth. He loved his smile. After a good earner, he'd taken himself off to Turkey and got a makeover. And on the few occasions he found himself lost for words, a flash of his whiter than white, Hollywood smile usually did the trick.

Tyler sat back down and listened as his friends got the same sentence as him. Smidge wasn't taking the news well – he was well known for being a snapper. There was no stopping him, he practically had steam coming out of his ears, fists clenched. He roared at the judge, 'Listen, you cock-sucking, bent bastard, you know nothing about me. It's twats like you who need locking behind bars. You won't think about me when I get dragged out of here – but I'll remember you. Don't you forget that.'

Tyler sniggered. Fuck it, what did he have to be quiet for now, anyway? This old guy had already slammed them. He better not let Smidge get all the limelight. If he was going down, he had better give the journalists something decent to write about. Tyler pointed at the prosecution, the vein at the side of his neck pumping with rage. He spoke through clenched teeth. 'It was a set-up and you know it. Five years. It's a joke. But we'll be home soon, and you lot should watch your backs.' He pointed his finger around the courtroom at the public gallery. 'I never forget a face.'

The judge wanted these men gone from the dock as soon as possible and he made sure the guards got extra staff to get the thugs out of his courtroom. Zara cringed as she heard Tyler screaming while the guards manhandled him.

Then a woman's voice cut through the noise. She was sat at the front of the public gallery, shouting over to the judge. 'He's seen my face. You heard him, he will come looking for us. I want protection. Did you see the look in his eyes? No, I didn't sign up for this. I only came here to do some research for my studies. But he knows me now, he'll find me and then what?' The woman was hysterical, and the usher was quickly by her side. But that wasn't good enough for this woman, no, she was furious. She stood up and pointed her finger over at Zara. 'Is he your son? Because if he is, you have let him down. How can he turn out like that? I blame the parents, no control over them, no bleeding morals.'

Zara stood up too. How dare this daft cow judge her? She didn't know her story, her life, her past. The usher could see this was going to kick off and he summoned two police officers over to split the two women up. Zara was calm, though. 'You know nothing about me or my son, so keep your smart comments to yourself, you toffee-nosed bitch.' Everyone could see she meant business and, when she felt the officer take her arm to escort her out of the courtroom, she turned to face him and looked him directly in the eyes. 'Take your hands off me. You have just witnessed that woman was the one who started firing insults, not me. I'll ask you again, take your hands from me,' she hissed. The officer backed off, aware she was ready to explode. Zara flicked some invisible dust from her shoulder and walked out of the courtroom with her head held high.

She knew she looked good today and it gave her confidence. Tyler had sorted her out with a few quid, and she'd been to Primark to kit herself out with a nice suit for court. Her son said he wanted the judge to look at her and see he was from a good family, that his mother was respectable. Shame not everyone had felt that. She could hear the other woman behind her still causing a commotion, but she never turned her head back once.

The press was at her side now. 'Anything to say, Mrs Makin? Come on, how do you feel about your son, one of

Manchester's biggest criminals, being jailed? Are you going to miss him, will you go and see him?'

Zara barged passed them and headed down the stairs and outside, where she gulped lungfuls of the cool air and walked quickly away. She hid a few yards from the entrance and watched the press running one way then another. There would be no interview with her, not now, not ever. Tucked away from view she dug her hand into her red leather bag and pulled her fags out with shaking hands. Popping one into the side of her mouth, she sucked in hard as she flicked her lighter underneath it. Then she pulled her mobile phone from her pocket and looked through her contacts.

'Hello, it's me. He got five years, gutted I am. You should have seen him in the dock when he got sentenced. He was going sick. Fucking nightmare he is when he's like that. I hope they haven't tuned him in when they took him down. You know what these screws are like, snidey bastards.'

The voice at the other end of the phone was speaking, but it was clear she wasn't really listening to what they had to say. Her boy was banged up and that was the end of it. How would he cope? And how would she manage now, pay the bills, keep the family home? The shit had hit the fan big time, and she needed a plan to keep her head above water until her eldest came back home.

Zara ended the phone call and flicked her cigarette on the floor. She widened her eyes when she spotted the woman from the courtroom earlier walking her way. Zara made her move quickly. She gripped the woman and dragged her out of view, pinning her up against the wall with one hand. All her fear, all her worry for her son poured out of her. 'If you ever, *ever*, speak about me or my family like that again, I'll scratch your bleeding eyes out. Do you hear me?' Zara was nose to nose with her victim now.

'I'm sorry, I got scared. Please, I just want a quiet life, let me go, please?'

Zara stared at her for a few seconds more and knew this woman would give her no more problems. She released her grip and watched as the woman sped away. It was out of character for her to react like that, but her nerves were shot after today. She mumbled under her breath as she watched her leave. 'I thought so. If you have a big mouth, you should always be able to back it up.'

That was one of Zara's rules – most of the time she kept her lip buttoned, but anyone around her knew that when she spoke, she meant it. She'd learned from an early age how to fight back. She'd had to, otherwise she would have been a goner. But she thought she'd left that part of her life behind – and it was a shock to find she was back on her own, back fighting for herself.

Chapter Two

Zara sat staring around the front room in silence. Her heart was low and no matter how hard she tried she couldn't bring herself to get ready today. She didn't often sit in her pyjamas dossing all day, watching catch-up TV, not managing to concentrate on anything. Usually, she'd be busy working out when she would next be out on the razzle. Normally, once Zara got a phone call from one of her friends, she'd get her glad rags on, a bit of slap and she'd be out the front door as fast as could be, no questions asked. She hated sitting in staring at four walls, but right now all she could think of was where Tyler was.

Maybe it was time to think about leaving this place. She'd thought about moving, upping sticks and starting afresh, before. But something kept her tied to this part of Manchester. And now it was her boys' home. Maybe she should have got out when they were kids, the first time she thought about getting away.

She supposed Rod Stewart was right when he sang that song *The First Cut is the Deepest* because, after her kids' dad Max betrayed her, she had never really felt heartache like that again. Yes, in the years since, men had come and she'd cried after they'd gone, and after a few gins with the girls she was back to her normal self, on the hunt for the next Mr Right. But her story always ended the same: a few dates, sex, then she never heard from them again. No one serious had come along since the boys' father.

Max Makin had been the love of her life and even today when she spoke about her ex-husband she always choked up at what he'd done to her. Screwing her best friend was the lowest of the low and something she could not forgive him for – forgive them for. When she'd found them in her bed together her world had fallen apart. The trust she'd given him, the love they shared, the plans they made together, all destroyed in a single moment. Sandra Pillington had been her best mate but at least she'd had the sense to do a runner. Sandra hadn't shown her face since it happened all those years ago, and even now Zara said she couldn't promise not to rag her if she ever saw her. That woman had ruined her life, taken a father away from his children, and for that she would never forgive her. Straight after, Max had tried to get back with Zara after she'd uncovered his affair, but she couldn't forget, couldn't unsee what she had seen in her own bed. Sometimes, you just had to move on, however much it hurt.

Maybe she should have expected it. Max had always been a Jack the Lad, dodgy, always up to something hooky.

But he was a charmer with it – good at whatever he did because his pockets were always lined. Not that Zara had ever seen any money from him since she threw him out. No child maintenance, no visits or gifts for his children: he had just pissed off into the sunset. She'd heard a few rumours of his whereabouts and from what she'd heard he'd gone downhill since she told him it was over. Small mercies, she thought, at least she didn't have to sit back and watch the wanker doing well. She wasn't one to forgive and forget. No, she prayed for him to hurt like she had – prayed that he would get his comeuppance one day for her broken heart.

The living room door opened and in walked her middle son, Rico. He could tell instantly that she was miserable. He plonked down next to her and placed his warm hand on her shoulder. 'Stop worrying about our Tyler, Mam. He's a big boy and he can look after himself. Plus, you've got me to look after you still. Every cloud and all that.'

She let out a laboured breath, sick to death of going over stuff in her head. Problems, problems and more bleeding problems. 'But he's not alright, Rico. He's never been to jail before, and you know what he's like even more than me. He hates anybody telling him what he can do and can't do. He's not as big as he makes out.'

'That's jail for ya, Mam. He'll adapt to it in no time. Listen, Tyler will have that landing boxed off in days. Once he finds his feet, he'll be smashing it in there. Already, he's got a few parcels being dropped in there for him. I'm all over it. Our kid will be sorted.'

Zara was immediately alert. 'What do you mean, parcels?'

Rico sighed and sat back on the sofa with a cunning look in his eye, the one he often had when he was up to no good. 'Mam, you're not thick, you know how it rolls in jail. You need to run everything in there if you're going to stay on top. That's the way it is, always has been. Sure, I only did six months in the big house, but I'll tell you now there are more drugs in jails than there are on the streets. Fact.'

Zara brushed her hair back from her face. Bloody hell, more for her to worry about, as if she didn't have enough on her plate. 'Oh, like he *needs* to start dealing in jail. The idiot. If he gets caught, he'll get more time. For crying out loud, don't tell me anymore. I can't take it.'

Rico sat scrolling through his phone and froze as he looked at a photograph of his younger brother online. 'Where's our Brian? Is that little bastard here or what? He was on the balloons again last night. He's put photos all over Instagram, the fucking tool. How many times do we have to tell him about embarrassing us like that?'

Zara looked like she had the world on her shoulders. 'I'll have another word with him. I'm sick of him getting high on those bleeding balloons. I've heard of kids being rushed into hospital, not being able to walk because of the nerve damage it causes. They look harmless, but it's nitrous oxide not fizzy pop. Honest, the side effects from them things are horrible. You can lose your memory too, or even choke to death. I swear, once that idiot gets up out of bed,

I'm laying the law down. Can't you have a word with him too?'

Rico squirmed. 'Nah, Mam, that's your job. I've got too much on. Now our Tyler's in the chokey, it's up to me to keep things moving.' Rico licked his teeth and gave his mother a cheesy smile.

'Don't you be fucking things up, Rico. I know what you're like when you think you have a bit of power. Just ask yourself, what would Tyler do?' Zara played with her fingers, cheeks going red, mouth dry as she plucked up the courage to ask him for some money. 'Did Ty tell you to give me some money? He always helps me out with the bills and that. He knows I struggle.'

Rico grimaced and sprung to his feet. 'Nah, there'll be no more handouts, Mam, at least not for a while. Man needs every penny. You get your benefits so you will have to make ends meet from the legit stuff. Sorry, Mam, if there is any spare when everything's been paid out, I might be able to give you a bit of dosh, but right now the pot is empty.'

Selfish bastard, he was, always been the same. Zara snarled at him, 'Yeah, whatever. I'll speak with the organ grinder not the monkey. Just wait til I get my first visit to Ty. I don't know why I wasted my breath even asking you.'

Rico went up to the silver mirror on the wall and started playing with his hair. 'No wonder all these women can't leave me alone. Right, I'm off. Don't forget to word that prick up. If I see him doing balloons, he's getting floored, end of. Sick of people telling me about him, it's a joke.' Rico walked out of the living room. Zara sat back, reached over to her black leather purse and opened it. It was empty.

Rico pressed the fob on his key to open the silver GTI Golf. What a mint motor this was, his brother's pride and joy. He checked himself in the reflection from the tinted windows and opened the door. He sat back in the driver's seat, tunes on, windows open. He wanted everyone to feel his presence, look at him and admire him. This was *his* show now and he'd prove to everybody in the area that he was more than Tyler's younger brother. He was the man, the main man. He knew a lot of the guys in his area were haters of him and his older brother. Their family had lived in Collyhurst since he was a small child, and these streets, this patch, was pretty much the only stable thing he'd ever had in his life. Home was where the heart was, and he loved that his mother had stayed in the same house and never moved away, even after all the heartbreak she'd had. His mum was always threatening to move away after a breakup. How could she walk down the street and see them with someone else on their arm, she'd cry? But Zara always seemed to pick herself up after her relationships broke down and put on a brave face for her boys.

Rico flicked the engine over and revved it. It roared like a caged lion. The younger kids across the road stood watching the car reverse and he smiled in his rear-view mirror at them, watching them buzz from his manoeuvre. The teenagers in the area looked up to the Makin boys and they all wanted to be like them when they were older. They had it all, in their eyes: nice whip, girls, money. Rico had been licking shot in the area since he was sixteen years old. It was a family business and one his older brother had worked hard to set up. The fights were endless back in the day, and he'd done some nasty stuff to help his brother take over the drug scene in the area. Secrets the two of them would take to the grave. But right now, with Tyler banged up, it was all down to him.

Rico jerked his head as the Aitch and Ashanti song, *Baby*, came on the radio. He started to sing along. Rico claimed he used to chill with the singer when he was growing up, and he always told everyone that when one of Aitch's songs came on the radio. Rico was a born liar, always stretching the truth, but he loved the story of the local lad done good. Aitch was just a normal kid like Rico and, if the artist could make it big out there, then so could he, he figured. Rico wanted the dream too, a nice house, decent bird on his arm and money behind him. That's all he'd ever wanted. He didn't sell drugs for the fun of it. He did what he did to change his life and eventually take him out of this rat race. Collyhurst was home to a lot of known criminals, each of them searching to become the next main man, to have more power than the next man. It was a dangerous world that you only stepped into if you were willing to risk it all. Rico had always lived in his brother's shadow and, now that Tyler was locked up in the big house, it was his time to shine. This was his show now and he was going to run things the way he deemed fit. Fuck listening to Tyler and his rules, he was upping his game, taking more chances to fill his pockets and make his dream a reality.

Rico bibbed the car hooter outside a house on Collyhurst Village, a council estate not far from where he lived. Old bikes lay on grass verges, graffiti sprayed on walls. The area was ripe for regeneration, and it looked like it was more than overdue. Zara had told her son that when she was a young girl she used to live in the exact same place where these council houses were built, back when there used to be flats there. Collyhurst flats were where a lot of families lived back in the seventies and even today his mother still stayed in touch with some of the residents who used to live there. They were the good old days, she told him, times when you could leave your car unlocked, windows open and nobody would touch anything. A lot had changed since then. Nowadays thieving bastards were lurking everywhere you looked, ready to take anything that wasn't nailed down. No morals, no respect for the working-class people, his mother always told him.

Rico peered out of the car window. His girl, Clara, walked down the path and smiled at him. She looked like she'd just stepped out of *Love Island*, small white shorts and a bright pink belly top, deep-tanned skin. Rico took in every inch of her as she walked past him to get into the passenger side. He quickly rubbed at his crotch and smirked. This was his woman, and he was as proud as punch when he got her on his arm. So what he was in his brother's car? It was his now. Just like his brother's empire was. His mum didn't like Clara though, called her a gold-digger, just after a Makin boy to buy her a new set of tits and a smile makeover, she told him. He didn't mind – he was young and having fun.

'Yo, you look mint, babes,' he said as she sat down next to him, her sweet perfume tickling his senses. It was a scent he'd forked out over a hundred quid for. I mean, she had to smell good for him, didn't she?

She pulled down the mirror and started applying her candy-pink lip gloss as she replied to him. 'I always make the effort to look nice for you, Rico. That's why you love me. If I was one of those girls wearing saggy black leggings and a big t-shirt you would cart me without a second thought. I'm what you call a classy chick. I like to keep my man happy in and out of the bedroom, as you know,' she giggled. 'Where are we going anyway? Please say we are going for food, because I'm starving. My mam's not been shopping yet and there is nothing in the fridge until later. Well,' she sniggered, 'there is, but I couldn't be arsed cooking it. I'm not into all that processed shit anymore. I want to eat proper food.' She flicked her long honey-blonde hair over her shoulder and closed the mirror. Her lips looked plump – maybe the lip-filler he'd paid for only last week had been a good investment. He had told her she didn't need it, but she'd insisted.

'We can go out to Uppermill if you want. There are a few nice country pubs up there that serve decent grub.'

She squirmed at him and fanned her nails out in front of her. 'Ew, I don't fancy that. It stinks of cow shit in the hills. No, it's not for me. Can't we just go into town and get something there. Maybe San Carlo's? We can even do a bit of shopping after it. I've seen a nice Gucci cap I wanted to show you. I swear, I've not stopped thinking about it. It would look great on me. Parklife is next week, and it will go nice with my outfit.'

Rico rolled his eyes. He supposed women like Clara came at a price. 'Anything that makes you happy, baby girl. I need to get myself something decent to wear too. I've got us VIP weekend tickets so it's going to be a mad one.' What a melt he felt like. Where were his balls he thought to himself as he listened to the words leave his mouth. He knew he should turn around and tell her to take a running jump. He liked it up in those country pubs around Saddleworth and he should have told her straight, for once, that's where they were going, end of. Wasn't a relationship about giving and taking, not give, give, give? But he knew if he didn't agree with her she would leave him, tell him it was over right there and then, and move on to someone else in a heartbeat – someone who could dig deeper into his pockets and give her heart's desires.

And Rico wasn't ready to let her go yet. No way. The thought of losing her gave him anxiety and so the moment she said *jump*, he said *how high?* Pathetic really. Rico was the envy of all his boys, and he'd never admit to any of them that he was jumping through hoops to hold on to this beauty. No way in this world. He always bigged himself up and told his lads she was the one who was doing all the running, but they all knew Clara was a high maintenance chick.

———

Clara sat down in the restaurant and looked around. She was impressed and couldn't wait to take a photograph and update her social media. She puckered her lips and moved her head next to Rico. 'Smile, babes.'

And there it was, the first of many photos that would hit her Snapchat today. He had no time for that stuff. What a load of lies. Trying to show your friends that you had the perfect life. He knew Clara didn't really have many close friends. They were false, braggers, all about what they had or what they were getting. Who'd want a friend like that? Rico ordered his food and waited as Clara scanned the menu. He knew what was coming next, she never ordered anything cheap. He was sure she looked at the prices and ordered the most expensive meal just so the waiter would look at her and think they had loads of money. Rico tried to cover his anxiety. Already he was dipping into his brother's stash that he'd left him with strict instructions how to spend. It was money that was supposed to be used to look after Tyler while he was locked up, money to pay their foot soldiers for dealing and moving gear if their cash flow hit a bump in the road, money to help their mam out when she was struggling. But he'd earn good cash soon he figured and he'd put everything he owed back, he told himself.

Rico's mobile started ringing. He looked at the name on the screen and smirked as he answered the call. 'Yo, man like Harley, what you saying?'

Clara frowned at his street talk. What the hell was he talking like that for when they were eating out in one of the best restaurants in Manchester? She didn't want him showing her up like this when she wanted everyone around them to think she was like them, had money, a cushy life. She looked around the restaurant and smiled. She would eat here every day if she could. The people just looked rich. They smelt rich too, expensive perfumes and aftershaves lingering in the air.

Rico finished his call and reached over. 'I've got some stuff to take care of after we have finished here. A couple of hours, tops.' He could already tell by her face she wasn't happy.

'I thought we were going shopping. Rico, if we are going to stay together, you need to start putting me before your boys. I don't want a part-time boyfriend, I want someone who is with me all the time, because that's how a relationship works, isn't it?'

He could see she was fuming. He needed to make her smile again, get back in her good books. 'Babes, you know how I roll, I need to sort some important stuff out. Our Tyler is sweating his back out in the slammer and it's up to me to make sure everything runs smoothly. This is my chance to take over shit around here, show them all I'm not just Tyler's younger brother. I want my own reputation.'

'What does it even matter who runs things? I'm sure Harley or Tex can man the fort until you get there.'

She just wasn't getting it, wanted everything her own way. He dug his hand into his pocket and pulled out a wad of cash. 'Here, there's three ton for you. Go and buy that hat and some other bits, some nice underwear for later.'

Now he was talking. The corners of her mouth started to rise, this was music to her ears. She placed her palm onto the side of his cheek and spoke in a gentle tone – of course, she picked up the money first and secured it in her handbag.

'Babes, I miss you when we're not together. Thanks for the money, but it still doesn't get past the fact that I will be shopping alone. In the future, will you just tell your cronies to piss off? Tell them you are spending time with me. They must understand, they both have girlfriends, right?'

'Yeah, Harley has been with Samantha for time. But he's like me, he has to graft, earn some readies. Sam understands.'

She snarled through her white teeth. 'So, I don't understand, then? Thanks a bunch, Rico. I thought me and you were on the same page, but I must have got that wrong.'

He panicked, gripping her hand tighter. 'Of course, we're on the same page, babes. I've told you how much I love you. Fuck me, if it's causing this much trouble, I'll get on the blower and tell Harley I can't make it.' He watched her carefully from the corner of his eye, hoping she would change her mind. Clara knew without asking that graft meant more money, more nights out, weekends away, new clothes. Was she really going to piss on her own parade?

She started to smile again, money tucked away nicely in her bag, already thinking about what she could buy. 'No, I'll be fine on my own shopping. You do what you have to do, and we'll meet up later. We can do something nice. Maybe book a nice hotel and we'll have a romantic night in together.'

Later that afternoon, Rico was sat with Harley and Tex in the Clarendon pub. It was situated in the middle of the

Monsall estate and was a place he felt safe talking about anything. The landlord turned a blind eye to a lot of the things he'd see, and Rico often backhanded him a few quid for keeping his mouth shut.

Harley was a tank of a man, a body built from hitting the steroids. His arms looked hench and his chest was twice the size of Rico's. Harley was a gym-head and loved the way he looked. Fuelling his body was his religion – he always preached to Rico when they pulled up at Maccies that he was filling his body with crap. Harley had his food made fresh each day. High protein and low carbs, macro this and slow release that. It wasn't Rico's scene.

Tex brought the drinks to the table and plonked down next to Rico. He had a cheeky face and a look of mischief in his eyes. The three had been friends for a long time, bonded by having been through some tough shit together. But, first and foremost, Harley was one of Tyler's boys, and he was here to make sure Tyler's younger brother wasn't fucking things up. Any decisions about the business had to be put through Harley first, to make sure he was alright with it. Tyler had given him instructions to watch his younger brother like a hawk and, judging by his face, he was doing just that. Ty might have named Rico as choice, but he wasn't leaving him unobserved.

'We need to pick up some gear later on and get it bagged. Tex's mam said she will bag it up for us. We just need to pay her market rate. You know the score.'

Tex sniggered. 'Yep, she won't do it for fuck all. I'm sure she had a few cheeky bumps from the last lot too. I've never seen her so happy. On my life, she was full of the joys of spring when I went to pick it up. I better keep my eye on her, don't want her ending up a fucking sniff-head, do I?'

Rico chuckled. Tex was *his* right-hand man and he wasn't into this life as much as the others was. The time he'd spent in jail a little while back had done his head in big time and he openly told them that he would never ever go back there again. But here he was, still dabbling in the drug world. Round this way, it was hard to walk away from a world you didn't want to be involved in, really hard. Tex was living on Universal Credit, and was always short at the end of the 'every' month. He found a few days straight work cash-in-hand every now and then, but it was never enough to get him the things he needed, even less the things he wanted.

Rico rubbed his hands together as he spoke. 'I've had a tip-off for a right few quid to be earned, if you're both up for it. Marsy from the Manning estate put me on to it. A guy drops money off for gear once a month and he said he should be carrying over one hundred and fifty grand.'

Tex's ears pinned back: he was listening now. That kind of money could change his life, get him a new motor, get his jewellery out of the pawn shop.

'I say we surprise the fucker, throw him in the boot of the car and take his fucking money,' Rico said.

Harley wasn't saying much, clearly uncomfortable with what Rico was saying. 'Who's he dropping money off to is the question. Because, if it's down these ends, then it will be somebody who we all know. And if it's big money, then it's a big fish. Do we really want to step on somebody else's toes and cause beef? Because, if that's the way you want to play it, we're talking heavy shit in revenge. I mean guys with guns, machetes coming through our doors if it ever gets out we were the ones who did it.'

Rico rubbed at his arms and a cold chill ran down his spine. Yes, it was dangerous, but the pay-out was a big one and money he needed to properly make his name, show everyone he wasn't just holding the fort for his brother. Plus, he'd have some spends for the fun stuff. He could take Clara to the Maldives, buy her a nice car of her own. Yeah, the prize was bigger than the fear of whoever it belonged to – for now.

Tex rubbed his hands together, already thinking of retiring and setting himself up somewhere nice out of the area. One last gig. 'Fuck 'em, Harley. We are the big boys around here and, if we all keep our mouths shut, then the job's a good 'un. We will keep it on the low and have the bastard over the next time he's down these ends.'

Rico was waiting on Harley's response, one that wasn't coming as quickly as he wanted it to. He knew he was debating it in his head. Rico had another shot at him, trying to win him over. 'It will be like taking candy from a baby. No one will know it's us. It hurts me to admit it, but now's the perfect time – folk won't be expecting anything from our operation – I know they think I'm just a caretaker. We've got surprise on our side. We just need to keep our traps shut, especially you, Tex.'

Tex's mouth dropped open. 'Me! I never tell anybody fuck all. Ask anyone, I keep my business to myself.'

Harley rolled his eyes and knew what was coming next.

Rico playfully punched him in the arm and reminded him of past events. 'So, when you were banging that bird from Harpurhey you never told her nothing about what you were involved in? Because I know one hundred and ten per cent that you told her it was us who took Gary Perkins' grow away. She was telling everyone.'

Tex knew he couldn't come back from this, and his cheeks went bright red. 'I might have let it slip to her, but apart from that my mouth is shut.'

Harley still wasn't smiling. 'Nah, it's too close to home. It doesn't sit right with me. I'm giving it a wide berth. And you should do the same, Rico. You have plenty of work on our patch. Don't be getting greedy and fucking things up for us all.'

Tex had a rethink. Maybe Harley was right, and this job was too risky. He had a family, kids he wasn't willing to put at risk. 'Maybe you're right, H. I keep saying I want to get out – not get back inside.'

Rico slumped back, thinking. If he wanted to do the job, who were these muppets to tell him he couldn't? But he kept that thought to himself.

Harley changed the subject. 'Tyler phoned me last night. He seems to be adjusting to prison life. He's on B-Wing and said he'll have it boxed off in a few weeks. There are a couple of faces he knows there already, so he shouldn't have a problem. I need you to get Nitty Dawn to do a drop in the jail too. Tyler said he will sort out a visit with some other inmate and she can go and see him and pass the parcel over. Two ton she charges, so wait until he sorts out the details and we'll nab Dawn to go to the ways on a visit.'

Rico nodded his head. 'Dawn? I've heard she will do anything for money, the old baghead. I heard she's been seeing men for twenty quid at the back of the pub. Bleeding shame, it is. She used to be a nice girl years ago, before she got on the smack. On my life, she's got about two teeth in her gob and she looks eighty years of age.'

Tex nodded his head in agreement. 'Yeah, rough she is now. She sits outside Asda begging all day with that rat of a man she's with. Honest, I feel heartbroken when I look at her. Sad, isn't it, when people get caught up with heroin? Look at our John. It got a grip of him, and he was all skin and bones when he died.' Sorrow filled Tex's eyes. There was a pain in his heart that he couldn't hide away. It was only last year when his brother overdosed on smack, and it hit him hard when he got the news that he had passed away. Over the years he'd tried everything, even locked his brother away to make him go cold turkey, but nothing ever worked. It was another reason he had to get clear of this world. For all the talk of money and buying the life you wanted, you didn't have to look far before you saw the flip side – people whose lives had been taken away by this stuff, families who had a hole left where a loved one should have been.

Harley checked his wristwatch and stood up. 'So, meet me about half six, Rico, and we'll sort that parcel out. Tex, tell ya mam about eight bells we'll drop the gear off. Sort the grafters out and load them up as soon as. Send some to Blackley too. We've got a new kid licking shot up there and he's been doing well. He's only fifteen but he knows the score. Eager to impress, he is.'

'Just the way I like it,' Rico chuckled. Tyler had lots of grafters in surrounding areas. Each of them eager to earn money. Teenagers mostly, willing to risk it all to get cash for new trainers, new designer gear, to put their name on the map. Despite the risks, there were always kids ready to step into this world to change their lives. Teenagers living on the bread line, kids who had nothing in life. The older lads always sold the dream to them, told them about the riches they could have, told them they would be like a new family. Yeah, they lapped it up, couldn't wait to get their fingers into the pie and have a piece of luxury. Rico never told them the darker side, though, never told them they could end up in jail. That wasn't the worst of it either. Every day there was a risk of them getting attacked, stabbed up, put in wheelchairs when somebody bigger than them found out they were carrying money and drugs. Yes, it was a dog-eat-dog world in this game and no one should enter unless they were willing to risk their life.

Chapter Three

Zara pulled up outside Strangeways prison. It loomed over her through the pouring rain, big grey clouds hanging low in the sky. Just the look of this place gave her the jitters. The jail stank of misery. Dark-brown brick walls with barbed wire crawling along every wall, warned the public that, whatever lay behind these walls, they did not ever want to see. An eerie silence was lingering, even the birds were quiet today, as if they were afraid of waking the inmates. She sat in the car, smoking, looking over at the prison, thinking. It had been a long time since she'd been here. Max, her ex, had been banged up in here quite a few times when she was married to him. He never served a long sentence, but it was often enough for her to tell him that, if he ever got proper time, she wouldn't be standing by him anymore. Yeah, she told him straight, there was no way she was being a life prisoner's wife, wasn't raising boys to think it was normal to do time. His gambling habit had landed

31

him in there the first time. Unable to pay debts, he'd ended up robbing to fund his addiction. And once you'd met guys on the inside, that was it: you had a job for life that paid more than anything down the job centre.

Zara sucked hard on the last bit of her fag. She knew she wouldn't be having one for at least another hour and she wanted to make sure her nicotine level was high enough to help her get through the visit with her son. This first visit after he'd been sentenced would be the hardest. She would be able to see the pain behind his eyes, the feeling of hopelessness, knowing there was nothing she could do to help him out of this mess. Someone else controlled him now, told him when and where he could go. He was under lock and key. She looked up at the large tower that was the land-mark of this prison. It pointed high up into the sky, looking down over all the other buildings. A message to all the crim-inals in the area that it was watching them, waiting to welcome them if they broke the law – or rather, if they got caught. Even driving past this place, you couldn't help but wonder what lay behind those strong thick brick walls. Men, laughing and joking, getting through their sentences and planning their next jobs, or broken men who were pledging to themselves that they would never end up here again? Men too scared to sleep in case they were set on by rival gangs? Zara flicked her cig end out of the window, got out of the car and made her way to the visitors' centre with her head low. Zara knew the script here and knew she'd have to wait about twenty minutes in the first room before she could go over to the main jail. She'd made an effort today. She looked fresh in her white skinny jeans and red blouse, shoes matching too. She knew the kind of people who came here and, if her luck was in, she might even get talking to a man, somebody visiting a friend in the nick. She was never one to miss a chance of meeting a new fella and earlier this morning she had got up extra early and washed and blown her hair.

Zara booked in for the visit and handed in her son's gifts at the small office. Two pairs of tracksuit bottoms, four t-shirts, two pairs of shorts and seven pairs of socks. She sat down and looked around the centre. What a grubby place it was, contrasting fiercely with most of the people. It was as if the visitors were determined to make up for their drab surroundings: young girls dressed to the nines, make-up, hair done, all ready to go and see their loved ones. Girls who would find out the hard way that being with a bad boy was not what it was made out to be. To the right of her was a woman who looked to be in her early forties and was keeping herself to herself. You could tell this was a place she didn't want to be and the way she looked at some of these young girls told Zara that she'd learned some lessons the hard way. Zara picked up a newspaper, not your normal rag but a paper written by the prisoners – stories and poems from inmates. She started to read it, immediately engrossed in some of the stories from the men behind bars. People who'd never touched this world forgot the inmates were human after all and that they had their own sad story that had landed them in the chokey. Tales of poverty, stories of hardship where they had no other options. She wished more folk had a chance to hear these voices, but most people felt losing your freedom meant you also lost your voice.

A young child was at Zara's side now, touching the arm of her leather coat with her sticky fingers. She quickly looked for the child's mother.

A voice from across the room, a strong accent: 'Aw Chardonnay, what have I told you about hassling people you don't know? Sorry love.'

Zara was pretty good at nailing down someone to their postcode with their voice. She pulled a tissue from her pocket and quickly rubbed the melted chocolate from her sleeve as the child toddled off. Zara looked over at the other woman sat near her, who looked anxious.

She managed a smile back at Zara. 'They should have a play area for these young ones. How do they expect them to be quiet for however long it is and not get bored?'

Zara agreed. 'Tell me about it, love. Did you see the state of my jacket from that kid? I wouldn't mind, it's a new coat that I've only worn a couple of times. It wasn't cheap either. My son bought it for me for my birthday.'

The woman introduced herself as Jane and moved seats to sit closer to her.

Zara knew the drill but still she hated being made to wait. 'I've been sat here for over half an hour. Is your visit for two o'clock too?'

'Yes, they are never on time here, no rushing with them, is there?' Jane sounded defeated by the system already.

'You can say that again. I've only been here a few times and it makes my stomach turn every time I step foot inside the place. It's not the nicest of places to come, is it? My son just got sentenced and it looks like this will be my second home for the next few years. You never think when you're wiping their noses and helping them blow out their birthday candles that one day you'll be visiting them in a place like this.'

'Oh, I'm sorry to hear that. I'm here to see my son too. I still can't believe it, two years he got for fighting when he was drunk. I knew nothing about it until I got the phone call he was in here. He didn't even tell me he was up at court,' Jane sighed. 'Probably because he knew I would have kicked off.'

Zara recognised a mother's broken heart. 'Mums have to stand by their kids, no matter how many times they mess up, don't they? It's just part and parcel of the role – just one you hope you'll never to have to resort to. Where are you from, around here?'

'Chorlton, not that far really. Do you know it? About a twenty-minute drive when the traffic is good. What about you?'

Zara flicked her hair and sat back in her seat, more relaxed now, the anxiety receding. 'Collyhurst. It's not far, ten minutes or so in the car. I'm just glad they haven't shipped him out, because I'd hate travelling around the country to see my boy. It's expensive too. They don't understand, do they, how much it costs to come and see them. I mean, you have to fork out for petrol money and then you need money to buy them food on the visit. It isn't a cheap do, either.' Zara folded her arms in front of her, aware that she shouldn't give too much away without knowing who Jane's son really was.

The screw finally stepped out from his office with a sheet of paper in his hands. He shouted names out and Zara sat on the edge of her seat getting ready to stand up to make her way to the main jail. This was a part of the visit that she hated most. Being searched, frisked from head to toe, showing her ID, a sniffer dog running around near her feet. It made her feel like a criminal too.

Zara walked with Jane over to the main jail wondering if they might become friends over the times their boys were serving their sentences. She knew that at times like these you need all the friends you can get – if only she could find a way of checking that Jane's lad wasn't one of Ty's rivals.

Zara stood on a wooden box with her arms stretched out fully while the female officer frisked her with her blue disposable gloves on. The screw gave her a look that told her she was doing a proper job today, making sure no contraband got inside the jail. She even lifted Zara's hair up, checked her cuffs, the heels of her shoes, everywhere she thought someone could stash anything. Zara was clean, much to the disappointment of this officer. She walked away, sat down and grabbed her shoes to put back on her feet, still hissing over at the screw. Once she was ready, she stood at another set of doors and waited for them to open. She thought prison's job was to stop people getting out... but it was almost as hard to get in. Eyes watching you from every corner.

Zara made her way up two flights of stairs and found another waiting room where she had to give her son's name in at the next desk. It was so much hassle to get into the main jail. It wasn't just a case of passing one checkpoint. Even after you were frisked, ticked off the list and let through, you couldn't move unless an officer was closely behind you. They treated everyone like they were criminals too, no respect for the friends and family visiting – no matter that they had never broken the law. Zara prepared to give her son's details again when the man from behind the desk smiled at her. He was dishy, in his mid-forties with piercing blue eyes and a great smile. She checked behind her to make sure he was smiling at her and nobody else, then turned back to face him. Her luck was in. He was still staring. Zara pulled her shoulders back and smiled slowly. She was never one to miss an opportunity. Her flirting mode was now switched on.

'Good afternoon, Miss. I've not seen you here before. How are you finding Costa Del Strangeways?' he chuckled.

Zara was tempted to give him a full list of all the things that were wrong with the jail, but it was that rare to find a staff member in here with a sense of humour, that she didn't want to upset him. Plus, those baby blue eyes were mesmerising her. Come-to-bed eyes, she'd go as far as calling them. 'I have been to nicer places but, as far as jails go, it's up there with the best of them.'

'Glad you like it. Are you here to see your hubby?'

Zara blushed, delighted she'd got a chance to tell him she was single. She batted her eyelashes. 'No, it's to see my son. I don't have a husband.' And there it was, the ball was in his court, she was fair game.

'What, a beautiful woman like you has not been snapped up?' he smiled.

Oh, this was good. Zara started to relax. She knew the score with men like him and made sure her blouse was down just enough so he could get a glimpse of cleavage. 'How long do we have to wait now?' she asked.

'Erm, shouldn't be long. What's your lad's name again? I'll have a butcher's at the list and see if he's on his way over to the main jail.'

'Tyler Makin, he's on B-Wing.'

The officer walked away and checked the computer. He made his way back to her. 'You will be next. I'm a bit gutted really, I would have liked to talk to you a bit more.'

Zara smiled, playing it cool. 'You can catch me on the way back out if you're still on duty.'

'That's a good idea. Yes, I'll see you in a bit then. The name's Mike, by the way.' He quickly checked behind him, making sure none of the other screws were listening. There were strict rules about not dating inmates' relations. He'd get the sack if anyone got wind of it.

Jane was next in the queue, and she seemed flustered that she'd had to wait to give her son's details in. She rolled her eyes.

Tyler's name was called out and Zara jumped up from her seat. 'Right, that's me. See you soon,' she said to Jane. She walked away and Mike leaned forward over the counter slightly to get a better look. He nodded his head and again checked nobody had clocked him. Zara could have sworn she heard him mutter 'Nice arse' as she passed.

———

The visiting room had lots of table and chairs in it. A canteen to the left of her. All the inmates wearing red bibs, like a footy squad no one wanted to belong to. Bloody hell, there was so many of them. How was she supposed to find her son among this rabble? The officer on the door had said table number 12 to her, but where were the numbers? She stood scanning the area, eyes drawn to the five screws sat up higher than the rest of the visitors behind a wooden desk on a platform at the back. Then she saw a hand waving in the air at the far right of the room. She squinted. At last, she'd found him. With haste she rushed to his table.

'Christ on a bike, you think they would have bigger numbers displayed on the tables so you can see which one's which! My eyes are not as good as they used to be, I'm blind as a bat. Now come here, you.'

Tyler leaned over the table separating them and hugged his mam. His eyes closed tightly, never wanting to let her go. His mother was his comfort blanket. Whenever anything was going wrong in his life, she was always there to pick him up and put him back together, to fix him. But there was none of that today, she could no longer wave a magic wand. It was down to him. He was riding solo.

'Should I go and get you some food before the queue goes massive?' Zara knew a bit of scran was the highlight of a visit.

Tyler shot a look over at the canteen and nodded his head. 'Yeah, get me a butty and some crisps and a bit of chocolate. A coffee too, would you, Mam?'

Zara took her coat off and hung it on the back of the chair. She took the twenty pound note out of her pocket and made her way to get him some grub. Prison food was grim, or so her son said, and visits were a great time for inmates to get filled up on some treats, things you couldn't get normally. Zara stood in the queue and shot a look back at her son. He looked stressed, eyes darker underneath, and he'd definitely lost a bit of weight. But he was always like that when he was stressed: the weight fell off him and he never slept properly. Before he was sent down, many a night she would find him still downstairs at daft o'clock, watching television, unable to sleep when he had things on his mind. He was a born worrier – although not without cause. In a business like his, you had to watch your back.

Zara carried the food over to the table and sat down. Tyler started to eat his egg mayonnaise sarnie straight away, speaking with his mouth full, sauce gathered at the side of his mouth. 'It's a shithole in here, Mam. I was padded up with a smackhead last night. You should have heard the bastard rattling, going cold turkey. I kicked the fuck out of my door and told them, if they didn't take him out, I would do the twat in. Honest, I was fuming. What's their game, throwing a baghead in with people like me? The scruff stank as well.'

Zara shook her head and ran her finger around her white plastic cup of coffee. 'Oh, you don't need that, do you? They should have a special place for junkies when they are coming off the hard stuff. I feel sorry for them, though. They're just people who have got lost and ended up in a world they can't get out of. Remember that, son, they all have stories behind them. They weren't born bad, life made them bad.'

Tyler let out a sarcastic laugh. 'What? You think they'd let these guys swap prison for a rehabilitation centre or something? They don't give a fuck in here. It's every man for himself. You can't get fuck all from the screws. I've been shut up behind my door most of the day. A fucking hour they let us out for, said they were understaffed. Like that's my bleeding fault.'

Zara looked around for an officer. She needed to say something. Her son might have been banged up, but he still had human rights. How dare they cage him all day.

Tyler knew what she was up to. He reached over and touched her warm hand. 'Mam, just leave it. I'm a big boy and I don't need you putting in any complaints about the service here. It's prison, not a bleeding hotel. Don't start fucking things up for me in here. It's the last thing I need, you getting on your high horse and shouting the odds out.'

Zara dropped her head: he was right. It wasn't like the time she went to Spain, and she'd asked the hotel for a sea-front view and, when she got there, she looked out of her window facing a bleeding brick wall. She'd gone ballistic, straight to reception and kicked up a fuss until they swapped her room. Even a bit of flirting with Mike wasn't going to get Tyler the holiday camp treatment.

'How's Rico doing? Please tell me he's doing things the way I've told him. You know what he's like, Mam, you'll have to watch him like a hawk and make sure he's not fucking things up.' Tyler was straight down to business.

Zara spoke in a low voice, checking around her to make sure nobody could hear her. 'He said he's got to keep a tight grip on the money. I only mentioned I was struggling, and he told me in his own words that I wasn't getting a carrot.'

Tyler growled, head moving nearer to her. 'Tell him to give you fifty quid a week, is that enough? If you need any more, let me know and I'll word him up. He better be looking after my car. I swear, I don't even know why I let him talk me into letting him drive it around while I'm in here. I should have sold it and had extra money or, better still, let you have it.'

Zara let out a laboured breath. 'I still can't believe it. I can't get used to you being in here. The house seems dead without you pottering about. Rico was fuming about Brian being on them balloons again, said he was going to deck him if he carries on.'

Tyler sat back in his chair, arms stretching above his head. 'Mam, everyone's on them – it's not that hardcore – and anyway, how can Rico say anything? Because he's on them too when he's on a bender. Don't let him pull the wool over your eyes. Our Bri is just having a buzz. As long as he's not on them every day, then it's sweet.'

'But he seemed really bothered. Said Bri is having them all the time. And I'm not dim, I've seen the news – you can land yourself in the ozzy if you have too many.'

'Tell you what, he might listen to me. I'll have a word with our kid when I get a phone of my own sorted. Fuck me, I need to get one in here as soon as possible. I can't stand not being able to talk to everyone when I want to. Hard it is, Mam. I'm sick of borrowing one from one of the others – or even worse, using on the landing where everyone's listening.'

Zara rubbed at her arms. She knew he was not allowed a mobile in jail and, while she knew messages got in and out, she thought he'd be keeping his nose clean at first. 'How can you get a phone in here?'

Tyler winked and smirked. 'When you have money, Mother, you can get what you want in this place. I only need to suss out what's what and I'll have everything I need. Give me a few weeks and I will be fine.'

Zara decided there were some things she'd rather not know – and she knew well enough that any time she gave Tyler a lecture it only made him doubly sure not to do what she said. So she pushed it to the back of her mind and made small talk. 'One of the screws downstairs was flirting with me. Probably wants my number.'

'Fuck that, Mam, a fucking screw! Are you for real or what?'

She'd spoken without thinking. 'He could be a good man to know, especially with you needing things in here, so keep that in mind before you go jumping the gun and putting the dampeners on it.'

Tyler digested this and chuckled. 'I'll keep that in mind, but Mother, come on, you don't want a guy who works in a nick, do you?'

'I'm not exactly spoilt for choice at the moment, son. And, if I'm being honest here, I could do with the company. Bri and Rico are out all the time and I sit there staring at four walls.'

Tyler chuckled and sighed. 'Quit the sob story, Mam, you're never bleeding in. One phone call from the girls and you're out in the boozers.'

She started smiling. 'Well, you don't get no bleeding medals for staying in the house, do you? Life's too short to sit watching television each night. I am still in my prime, you know, not a bloody pensioner yet.'

Tyler looked at the clock then scanned the visiting centre. It was a chance to get a look at some of the inmates he didn't usually see. There were a few familiar faces here today, local lads he'd had dealings with in the past. Nothing he couldn't handle.

The visit was due to end, and Zara could see inmates gripping their loved ones and kissing them, getting some human contact before the screws stepped in. Suddenly these men – supposedly the hard men of Manchester – looked vulnerable. Fear was in their eyes, knowing they had to go back into their pads for hours on end. It was a time for over-thinking, crying, wishing they hadn't ended up here, missing their mums, kids, wives.

Zara thought that was something. At least her boy didn't have a girlfriend he'd left behind. In fact, Tyler had never had a proper girlfriend. Always said he didn't need the stress of some woman nagging him. He was no saint, she knew that much – he was always in some girl's bed – but he would never make it official with them: he liked the single life too much. And she bet he was glad he'd made that choice after hearing what he said about some of the lads on his wing. Half were moaning about their other half giving them a hard time while they was locked away, demanding cash to keep waiting for them, and the other half were worried about who their girlfriends were seeing while they were doing time. No, he didn't want a girlfriend, he told Zara again. Too much of a headache. Plus, he had enough on his plate with making sure the business kept running without him. Added to that, loving a girl was weakness in his eyes. It gave your opponents a jugular to attack.

A screw walked up to the table and patted Tyler's shoulder. 'Finish your visit, lad.'

Tyler squirmed and shook his shoulder. He shot the officer a look that told him he didn't feel comfortable that he'd touched him. Tyler never liked anyone touching him without him saying so. Zara peeled her coat from the back of the chair and stood up. She hated goodbyes and her eyes were already filling with tears. She swallowed hard and reached over to her son. 'It will be all over soon, son. The time will fly, just you watch.'

He hugged her and he had a tear in his eye. 'Mam, keep an eye on things. If that tool so much as steps out of line, let me know and I'll land on him like a ton of bricks.' Tyler released his grip. Time to pull his shoulders back, expand his chest, and walk back to his landing with his head held high. These screws would never break him. He knew he couldn't let his guard down. This was a time when you were a sitting target, open to a knife attack, a fist coming from nowhere landing on your chin. There were plenty of guys who could be bought – they'd happily be paid for an attack, even with the screws watching. He gave his mam a nod and strutted off like he owned the place.

Zara walked off, still looking behind her, waiting for her son to give her a last wave before he disappeared. And there it was, she could rest now.

Zara's heart was low as she walked down the stairs. It was the worst, leaving her son behind, knowing what he was facing. Her anxiety was through the roof and she decided that, as soon as she got home, she would be cracking open a bottle of wine and inviting a few of the girls around. Zara could see Mike at the desk now. He was busy talking to Jane. Fuck, fuck, and double fuck, there was no way she could go over and start talking to him with other people listening, that would be begging for it, too eager. Reluctantly, she walked past him and headed to the exit. If he was that keen, he'd keep for another day, she told herself.

Chapter Four

Tyler stepped onto the landing, looked one way and then the other. Smidge and Tony, who everyone knew as Rhino, were in pads on the other side of the landing, facing him. The screws loved having the power to choose where to put people. On his first night, Tyler had asked for Smidge to be padded up with him and immediately got a lecture from the officer. Tyler had told him straight that, if that conversation had been on the outside, he would have one-bombed him, said he was just a prick wearing a uniform. He had known it wasn't a good start to his sentence, but there was no way he was having some self-important wanker shouting the odds out at him.

Tyler stood with his back to the wall and surveyed everything that was going on around him. This place was never quiet, always some prisoners shouting, some druggie rattling. His nostrils flared as he got a glimpse of a new lad who had been padded up next door to him. He'd overheard the screws saying he'd been moved from a few doors down and this was the first time he'd seen him out of his cell. A tank of a man he was, definitely been tanning the juice. His arms were ripped, and his stomach was flat, he probably had a six-pack under his tight white t-shirt. Useful to know. This was still learning time for Tyler, to see what the crack was on this wing, work out who was the muscle, who was the brains, and which guys just wanted to get their heads down and stay quiet. From the corner of his eye, he spotted Smidge coming out of his cell. He whistled over, relieved to see someone he knew.

Smidge waved his arm in the air. 'Meet you downstairs. Just going for a dump. Sack shitting in my pad, going to use the communal.'

Tyler nodded his head. Any excuse to get out of your pad was valid. The guy from next door was at his side now. He could smell his aftershave, clearly not prison-issue.

'How do you like Hotel Strangeways, pal? You can reserve a sunbed by the pool if you hurry up,' he chuckled.

Tyler raised a smile, still not sure about this guy.

'Name's Johnny Thompson.' He held his hand out to Tyler.

They shook hands and stood together looking about the jail. Every day you had to read the mood of the place. You didn't have long to suss out what was what and where you wanted to spend what little communal time you got.

Johnny's eyes scanned the landing as he spoke. 'So, let me tell you about this wing. All your crackheads are down at the bottom. Never, ever leave fuck all about near them.

Scruffy twats, they are. Have your eyes out and come back for the sockets, given half the chance.'

Tyler shot a look to the bottom of the wing and shook his head slowly. 'Let one of them step foot near my pad and I'll fucking do them in. They tried banging some raging baghead in with me when I first landed, and they got told. Honest, fuming I was. I banged at the door until they opened it, told them if they didn't get him out of my pad, I would do the rat in.'

'Yeah, good move. You've got to show the screws you're not a pushover. I've only been here a few months and I've had a few arguments with them already. They keep moving me because they think I'm trouble.'

Tyler still kept his eyes facing forward. 'So, what's the rest of the script on this wing, then? Who's got what, who's the man to talk to?'

Johnny kept his voice low, eyes watching every nook and cranny for anybody listening. 'As far as I know, Big Sam Vickers is the one calling all the shots. He had a few parcels in here and he's the one raking all the cash in.' He rolled his eyes as he continued, 'He's got a few muppets round here running about for him too. Lick-arses they are, you know the sort. Do you know him?'

Tyler knew it was too soon to talk business with Johnny, he'd just met him, knew nothing about the guy. He'd talk to his own boys first, men who he knew he could trust.

Johnny seemed unbothered. He patted his shoulder as he started to walk away. 'If you fancy a session in the gym, I'll be down there. Come along and I'll introduce you to a few of the lads. Sorted, they are.'

'Yes, will do after I've caught up with my mates.' Tyler nodded at him.

Johnny walked down the landing like a man of steel, the muscles in his shoulders rippling. Tyler had noticed that about the prisoners in here: they all stood with their backs to the wall, never leaving themselves open, sitting ducks. Then when they moved they either went in packs or, if they were built like Johnny, walked around like they expected people to get out of their way.

Rhino was walking towards Tyler now, his head dipped low. He wasn't really coping with prison life and, every time he met up with him, he was always moaning and telling Tyler that he wanted to go home. If only it was that easy. Prison life was an eye-opener. You were no longer your own boss. The screws told you when and where you could go, when you could eat, when you could use the bog. It was barely a life behind prison walls and some of the stories the inmates told you in this place would curl your toes. Stories about lads getting done in, stretchered off the wing, stabbed up, face smashed in. No wonder Rhino wasn't loving it.

He was at Tyler's side now. 'Are you going down for food or what?'

Tyler started walking towards the stairs before he answered. 'Yes, the meals are shite, but a man's got to eat, doesn't he?'

Rhino patted his belly with a flat palm. 'I feel like I've lost a few pounds already. I swear my boxer shorts are hanging from me. What I'd give for a greasy-spoon breakfast now. Black pudding, mushrooms, egg, bacon, beans, the works.'

Tyler smirked. 'Losing weight will do you good, Bruce Bogtrotter. How many times on the out did you say to me that you wished you could lose a few stone? Be careful what you wish for!'

Rhino let out a chuckle. 'I didn't fucking mean lose it in the pen, though. I'll be thin as a rake by the time I get out of here. I swear I'm always thinking about food. A nice curry, Nandos, a kebab. The things I would do to get a kebab delivered here is unreal. See that podgy screw over there? I'd bang her for a donner on a naan with hot sauce on it.'

Tyler burst out laughing and started to edge down the stairs. 'Stop thinking about food. Anyway, banging that screw doesn't seem such a bad idea. She's better than some of them birds you've been up on the out. Remember that Mona Lewis? Eww, she was below you, man.'

Rhino sniggered. 'She was a good lay though – Mona by name…'

Tyler made his way down the stairs, still aware of who was behind him, to the side of him, coming into his personal space. Bloody hell, the noise was deafening down here, loud laughter echoing from the bare walls, shouting, things being thrown about. One thing never changed in this place, though: eyes were everywhere. The cons were watching each other, and the screws were out in full force. They knew if any beef was going on, this was the time it would be sorted out. Tyler admitted to himself it was a dangerous job and probably not even worth the pay. Sure, there were some people who took a job in the jail for the power, but they weren't all bad. That Hargreaves guy he'd spoken to on his first day stood out.

Keith Hargreaves had worked in here for over ten years and he always told the new recruits that you needed eyes in the back of your head in this place, and he was right. Anything could happen in the blink of an eye. Keith took his job seriously and had a name for himself amongst the other staff. He'd been in the army in his younger years and seen some things a man his age was never supposed to see: dead bodies, friends blown up right in front of him, gun shots. He'd told Tyler this was a walk in the park for him, but still, he said he was never off guard.

Tyler couldn't see him on the wing today and carried on straight to the canteen and queued up for his food. He looked down at his blue plastic tray and shook his head. So, this was the best thing he had to look forward to all day. Had he been a reader the time might have gone a bit faster, but he'd always struggled to hold his concentration for longer than a few minutes, so reading was a no-go area for him. Maybe he could do some art, some portraits. He had been good at drawing at school and his teacher had told him that he had a talent for capturing people in his art. Still, he knew he had work to do clocking the rest of the wing and figuring out who ran who, before he turned his hand to other things.

Tyler watched what the other inmates were doing and followed suit. He held his blue plate out to the server and waited until they'd banged some food on it. They just slammed it down on the tray, no please thank you or kiss my arse. Tyler made his way down the queue and listened to Rhino arguing with the server in front of him. 'Come on pal, slap a few more slices of bacon on there, I'm a growing man. That won't feed my left bollock what you've just given me,' he growled.

The server completely ignored him and carried on serving. Tyler nudged him from behind and whispered in his ear. 'Just move along, keep a low profile for now and, in a few weeks, we'll live like kings in here.'

Rhino was deflated. The food he had wouldn't have fed a small child let alone a grown man. He snarled over at the server again and made a note of his face. A few more weeks and he'd make sure the next time he asked for more food he would pile it on his plate.

A silence crept over the room. Guys who'd been shouting a moment ago were whispering now, hanging their heads low as a new inmate walked into the canteen. Tyler clocked him straight away and eyeballed Smidge who was in front of him. This was Big Sam, he knew that much. Big Sam never queued, ever. He walked straight up to the server and nodded his head at him. Without uttering a word, this man got the works on his plate, nothing like Rhino's measly rations. The prisoners separated as he walked past them to sit down, none of them saying a word to him. Tyler watched Sam with eager eyes. So, this was his competition? Good to know. Sam was around six foot tall, thick black hair, and Tyler wondered if he belonged to the travelling community.

Tyler walked past him with Rhino and Smidge at his side. He sat down facing his pals and started eating. Rhino was finished in a few minutes, already looking at his mates' plates for anything they were leaving.

Tyler's voice was low. 'He's the main man on our wing. Johnny who is padded up next door to me filled me in before. He's the one we need to take down if we want to run the wing and this jail.'

Smidge looked up and clocked the men around Sam. 'Give it time and we'll have him. Those muppets with him will jump ship the second we kick fuck out of him. You can tell just by looking at them: an ounce of burn and a few spliffs and they'll do anything, I can just tell.'

Tyler pushed his plate away and sat back stretching his arms above his head. 'He's a big bastard, I'll give him that. We need to do our homework before we go in all guns blazing, find out where he's from, who his boys are, who he answers to outside. The last thing we need in here is beef we can't handle.'

Rhino agreed. 'I'll ask a few questions, find out where he's getting his parcels from, who's supplying him.'

Smidge sighed. 'When is Dawn coming on one of her drop visits? Have we got someone sorted yet for her to come and see?'

Tyler rocked about on his chair and replied, 'It's all in hand, boys. I've got a baghead on our landing ready to go out and see her on a visit. It should be here by the end of the week if it all goes to plan. We get our supply, then the shit will hit the fan when we start selling. I don't think Sam over there will like us pissing on his doorstep, but aye, it is what it is.'

Smidge tilted his head to the side. 'So, what's the deal with your Rico? Is he running our shit via Dawn and sending us some cash in each week? Because I need money regularly. My old queen hasn't got a pot to piss in and I wouldn't expect her to use her pension money to send me postal orders, so he better be on the ball and not fuck about.'

Tyler sat cracking his knuckles. 'He knows, I've told him the script time and time again. He puts one foot wrong and I get wind of it, he's fucked. I'll have the lot took off him and get someone else running the show til we're back out.'

Rhino agreed. 'Yes Ty. It's on your head if it goes wrong. You know we were against Rico running the show. It was you who gave him your backing, telling us it would be sweet. I hope you're right and he doesn't let us down. Money is one thing I don't want to worry about while I'm locked up in this shithole.'

Tyler never replied. His eyes were still on Sam and what was coming next. If you didn't strike hard and strike fast, you'd never get ahead in this place.

Chapter Five

Brian Makin lay on the sofa, wearing his shorts and a t-shirt, as his mother walked into the room. He clocked her looking at him and cringed. He knew what was coming and prepared himself for a lecture. He didn't have to wait long either.

'Oi you. What time did you come in last night? I'm sick of you waking me up, where is your bleeding key?'

Brian rolled on his side and yawned. He was a double of his eldest brother Tyler, same colour eyes and a similar hair-cut. 'Mam, don't start moaning at me. I've got a banging headache, and pins and needles in my hands. I'm sure I'm dying or something. I've googled it and it said I should go and see my GP, it could be my heart.'

Zara plonked down on the chair facing him and let out a sarcastic laugh. 'Funny, you say that every bleeding week-end after you've had a skinful. If you're that bothered, I'll book you in the doctors to get checked out. You can tell them about all those balloons you think I don't know you do.'

Brian chuckled. 'I wouldn't go that far, Mam. I'm just saying, that's all. How was Tyler when you went to see him, was he alright?'

Zara ran her fingers through her hair. 'He looked thin, worries of the world on his shoulders. You know he doesn't like new places. He's a home bird, always has been.'

'He'll settle in, Mam. He has no other option, does he? Because, let's face it, he's there for the long haul, not a few months. I'm going to go and see him next. I cheer him up, he always tells me that.'

'Yeah, that would be nice. Book a visit for you and Rico. He wants to see him, anyway, to tell him about not giving me any money.'

Brian grabbed a cushion and placed it in front of him. 'I think he's dropped the ball letting Rico manage his shit. We both know what Rico is like, and it's only a matter of time before he brings trouble to our door. He's a dickhead. But,' he paused and rubbed his arms as he continued, the hairs on his arms standing on end, 'he hasn't got Tyler and the crew backing him anymore. The word is out that Tyler is in the chokey, and you'll have all the clowns from different areas coming around here trying to tax him, take over his graft. Next thing you know, they'll be knocking on here.'

Zara shook her head. She got by most of the time by not thinking too closely about how the boys earned their money. She didn't want to know the details, but she sure as heck wasn't going to let some toerag bring trouble to her front step. 'So, Tyler better word him up then. If any tossers come here trying to boom my door down, they should know I keep a hammer stashed in the hall and I'm not afraid to give someone a belt.'

Brian burst out laughing. 'Whoa, calm down, woman. These men are dangerous, not kids acting tough.'

'Like I give a flying fuck about that. You've seen me when I'm premenstrual: I'd tackle anyone. I'm like a raging lunatic.'

Brian smirked over at his mother. He knew she talked a good game. He nervously started playing with the edge of his red Nike shorts. 'Eh, I saw Uncle Ben the other day. He was asking how we all were.' He cringed, waiting for her reply, knowing she would never have a good word to say about anyone connected with his father's family.

'What's he asking how we are for? He's never given a shit all these years, so why act now like he cares? He didn't say a word when his brother fucked off and left me, did he?'

Brian let out a laboured breath. 'Mam, Ben has always been there in the background. It's you who told him if he ever came near me and my brothers you would stab a knife right through his heart, are you forgetting that?'

'And I stick to that. The whole damn lot of your father's family are a shower of shite. When we first split up, they all blamed me, told me to have him back even though he was the one screwing around. It was a fucking 'mistake', they said, and I should take it on the chin. The cheek of them! Imagine any of them doing that. No, they can all rot in hell for all I care. I've never asked them for anything, and I never will. Wankers, the lot of them.'

Brian sat up, ready to defend his relations. 'Mam, it wasn't Ben who slept with your best friend. It was my dad. You're forgetting Ben is a good bloke and maybe it's time you knew that – yes – we have seen him over the years. He's always bunged us a few quid too when he sees us. He doesn't agree with what my dad did and hates him for never staying in touch with his children. He told me that himself, so what do you make of that?'

This was news to Zara, and she was taken aback that her boys had been seeing Ben all these years. Where were their family loyalties? The tears she'd cried, the endless sleepless nights, re-building her life on her own without any support from Max? And all the time they'd been taking backhanders from Max's brother. She digested what Bri had said and reached over for her cigarettes. She lit one quickly with shaking hands and licked at her lips. She wasn't calm yet, nope, not when that twat's name was mentioned. 'So, did he say where your dad is these days? Because, let's face it Brian, since the day he walked out he's never been within a mile of our front doorstep. He could have easily posted fifty quid through every now and then to support you all. Come on, you tell me why he's never done that. I get why he didn't want to see me, but to walk away from you three, his own flesh and blood, is on another level. He's a dickhead, nothing more, nothing less. Probably gambled all his money away like he always did. Wanker.'

Brian was still fighting his corner. 'Yes, agreed. I'm not here to defend my dad, mam. I don't know why he bailed on us when he did the dirty on you, but we're talking about Ben here, not my dad.'

Zara mumbled under her breath, the pain still there in her heart, the days when she cried endlessly still fresh in her mind like it was yesterday. Since her boys had been little, she'd never had a good word to say about their father. Every time she spoke about him was with venom attached. Maybe it would have been nice if she had told her boys about when the times were good and about the love they shared before Max had the affair. Even she could admit he'd had some good traits, otherwise why did she marry him in the first place?

Brian hunched his shoulders. 'Like I said, Ben's not been in contact with my dad for years. The last place he heard of him was in Liverpool, banged up with some new chick.'

Zara cringed, the grip on her fag tightening, imagining it was his neck. She took a deep breath, trying to speak in a calm tone, trying not to show that just the mention of his name made her blood boil. 'Well, as long as he's not near me, I'm not arsed.'

Brian continued, 'So, anyway, Ben knows about Tyler and said he would like to go and see him. No problem in that, is there?'

Zara squashed her cig out in the ashtray. Ben was a decent man back in the day and maybe her son was right, he wasn't the one who had wronged her. But, if she let him into her boy's life, that might mean her seeing him, talking to him again. What if he asked her if she still loved Max? What if he could see in her eyes that she still wasn't over him?

'Do whatever, Brian. All I'm saying is, as long as your dad doesn't come near me, then we should be sweet. Anyway, I need to start looking for a job. I'm on my arse and, now Rico is holding the purse strings, I won't be getting a penny. You watch, I'll tell him what Tyler said about giving me some money and he'll make some excuse as to why I can't have it.'

Brian shrugged. 'Yeah, our kid is as tight as a fish's arse, Mam. He'll be spending it all on that money-grabbing Clara. Honest, when he's with her he's like a different person. I went over to see them both last night in the club and it was like he didn't even know me. I told him straight, told him to do one treating me like that.'

Zara shook her head. She knew what Rico was like, obsessed with his own image, with status. 'Well, I'll have a serious word with him when he comes home. Blood is thicker than water and all that. Anyway, if I do that, you'd better sort out those balloons he's said you are on all the time. Knock it on the head before it gets too much.'

Brian burst out laughing. 'Me? What about him? He's worse than me. Fucking grassing me up like I'm some kid. Mam, it's harmless. A quick buzz you get from them, that's all. It's not like smack or crack. I'm not going to get addicted to them, go in rehab.'

Zara looked unconvinced but she knew not to push him too far – he had to decide to quit them rather than feeling like it was his mum banning him from them. She opened the newspaper on the table and started to look in the job section. Zara had never got a good education, no GCSEs. Back in her day, she'd been given precious little encouragement. School had written her off and she'd accepted it. Instead, she learned life skills, how to survive. Then she met Max Makin. Max had always looked after Zara when she was younger.

When she was with him she felt cared for, never short of money, always provided for. Maybe because they'd got together young, she'd accepted things as they were – never questioned the path he was taking. Before she knew it, Max was an armed robber: shooters, big money jobs. She'd loved him, trusted him, and she never complained while the money was coming in. Round her way, no one was making ends meet without some hustle, it was just that Max ran a bigger hustle than most. And so, bit by bit, the life got her. And when the boys came along, she was so busy she pretended she never knew where the money was coming from. But she'd washed the blood from his clothes, no questions asked, given him alibis when the dibble come knocking at the door. She was as bad as him back in the day.

Zara circled a job she'd found in black ink. Was it too late for her to go straight? She kept her head down as she spoke to her son. 'There's a job here working behind the bar in The Fox. I could do that, pulling a few pints?'

Brian darted up from his seat, blood red. 'Nah, that's not happening. No mother of mine is working behind the bar. You'll have those pissed-up blokes leering at you.'

Zara chuckled. 'You think? A few of my mates have done bar work before and they loved it. Great tips too.'

'Not happening, Mother. You're a Makin, and when I tell Tyler he'll tell you the same too, so find something else. A bit less public. How about a cleaning job or something like that.'

Zara snarled over at him. 'Aren't I doing enough skivvying at home?'

'Oh Mam, you know what I mean, stop being touchy. I'll ask about if there are any jobs going for you. Mr Patel at the offie is always looking for staff.'

'You can piss off if you think I'm working for that perve. Forget the drunks at The Fox – he's ten times worse. That randy old sod is well known around here for flirting with the women. May Mellor from down the road worked a month for him and she said he was hovering around her all the time with his old man erect in his trousers. I can't look at him anymore after she told me that about him. He knocks me sick.'

Brian laughed as he headed upstairs. 'Go on, Mr Patel, God loves a tryer.'

Zara stared a few minutes longer at the jobs section, then screwed the newspaper up with both her hands. 'I'm Zara Makin. And no man is deciding my future,' she hissed.

Chapter Six

Rico sat low in the passenger side of the car as they watched a house facing them. He was still, eyes fixed on the property across the road from them. He checked his watch and sneered over at Freddy. 'Not long now lads, just be ready when the prick pulls up. We need to grip him before he goes into the house. If we don't, then we've fucked it.'

Freddy kept his eyes on the house too and spoke in a deep voice. 'You better be right about this job, pal, because I've put my neck on the line for this. I don't usually graft new jobs unless I've set them up myself. Too many cocks in this game getting things wrong and causing me shit.' Freddy had a large scar on his cheek, his neck covered in tattoos. He was a mean-looking tank of a man. He looked in the rear-view mirror at his wingman. They'd been grafting together for a long time and never got it wrong. 'Isn't that right, pal?'

Wayne nodded his head, never replied. His head was in the game now, his hands clutching the silver claw hammer he was ready to use on anybody who got in his way.

Rico rubbed his hands together, still eyes on the job. 'When I overheard the convo about this job, I knew you two were the right men for it. My boys are sound, don't get me wrong, but a chance like this? It needs experienced men on the case. That's why I got in touch with you two. Like I said, this guy picks up the money from wherever he's been and keeps it in his house until the morning when the big boys pick it up. I've watched for a few weeks now and every time it's the same script. He pulls up, unlocks the gates, and then drives the van inside. We need to make sure as soon as he steps out, we're on him. No fucking about.'

Freddy growled over at Rico. 'Mate, stop going on like we're some kind of fucking amateurs. If anything goes wrong, then my little friend comes out of my coat and ends any nonsense.' Freddy patted the side of his coat and Rico swallowed hard as he clocked the butt of a silver pistol sticking out from it.

'Yeah, I never said you were, I'm just thinking out loud that's all. This is big money, lads, if we pull it off. One hundred and fifty grand, I reckon.'

Freddy's eyes widened. His grip on the steering wheel tightening. 'Music to my ears, if it is. That's the kind of money I get out of bed for. Nice little name-maker for you, too, while you're minding the graft for your brother.'

Wayne popped a fag into his mouth and opened the window slightly. He'd been smoking like a trooper since they'd pulled up here and he was forever fidgeting about, itching. Rico knew when to be quiet and this was one of them times. They had to clear their minds, be on point, precise.

Rico felt his heartbeat surge as the white transit drove past. This was it. Small beads of sweat started to form on his forehead. Had he really thought this through? Doubts flooded his mind, but it was too late to turn back. 'Showtime,' he whispered under his breath, still apprehensive.

Freddy had his hand on the door handle, and it was all systems go.

They'd been over this hundreds of times and everyone knew their place. The van driver turned the engine off and Freddy sprinted towards him. The man was put on his arse before he knew what day it was. So quick, no time to fight back. Wayne jumped into the driver's seat and started the van up. They already had a lock-up ready to empty the money from this van, but they couldn't risk the driver following them. Freddy's face was covered by a black bala-clava as he picked the man up and headbutted him. The man didn't stand a chance. Freddy booted him within an inch of his life and didn't stop until the man remained still. Rico made himself watch, willing himself to hold it together. His hands were shaking, and he was looking one way then the other, not sure where his oppo was.

Then Freddy sprinted back to the car. 'Fucking drive!' he screamed.

Rico screeched off and kept checking his rear-view mirror, but nobody was behind them. Freddy pulled his balaclava off and threw it onto the dash, hair stuck to his face with sweat. 'Why didn't you cover your face, you wanker? You don't ever take chances when there is big money involved, you know. I hope for your sake nobody clocked you on the street? Fucking prick, that's how people get caught.'

Rico kept his eyes on the road. 'I had my scarf on. I pulled it up over my mouth and nose. Nobody will identify me, stop flapping. It all happened so fast. Calm the fuck down, will you.'

Freddy looked down at his blood-stained knuckles. 'That prick won't be talking for a while anyway. You always have to give it them big time to make sure they don't get back up. I made that mistake a long time ago when I twatted some guy and thought he was out for the count. More fool me. He got back up and fucking smashed me over the head with a brick and sliced my face. I'll never make that mistake again, let me tell you.' Freddy ran his fingers over the deep purple scar on his cheek and growled, still upset he'd left himself open.

Rico gulped, his heart still racing inside his chest. 'Let's go and see what cash there is. Seeing the green makes it all worthwhile, doesn't it?' He tried to keep his voice level, determined not to let Freddy see how shaken he was.

Freddy nodded his head. 'Yep, it sure does. If it's right what you're saying, I'm booking a flight tonight and heading to the sun for a few months. Fuck staying around these ends in this shithole. I need sun and sex. I can get a couple of brasses over there, no worries.'

Rico agreed. 'Yeah, I might join you, take my bird away for a few weeks. It would be nice to chill.'

Freddy looked at him through the corner of his eyes and scowled. He didn't look like he wanted company.

———

At the lock-up, Freddy swung the hammer at the black safe in the back of the van, drilling away at it, thumping the lock repeatedly. They'd been there for over an hour now. 'Fuck me, I should have dragged that prick with us and made him open it. I feel like I've been in the ring for twelve rounds with Tyson Fury. Look at me, I'm fucked.'

Rico took another hammer and started to smash on the same spot Freddy had been targetting. Wayne stood over them both and waiting his turn to try to crowbar their way in. The money was in there, they could almost taste it, hungry to hold it. Like a dodgy pinata, they would make it surrender the goods, come hell or high water.

———

Four hours in total it took to get the black box open. They all looked exhausted. Rico had only just managed to stop the others from trying to shoot the lock off. Even round here, some nosey sod would come looking if they heard shots fired. Instead, they'd eventually beaten their way in and now it was the moment of truth. All eyes were on the box.

Freddy's large hand went inside. Bingo, he smiled. He was pulling out wads and wads of cash. Wayne started to dance about, rubbing his hands together. Rico couldn't take his eyes from the money. He knew he should be celebrating like Wayne but there was another side to this too. They all knew this was drug money – bad money earned by bad people, bigger and tougher than the local grafters he was used to buying and selling with on the streets of Collyhurst. This was a lot of money for someone to lose and he knew without a shadow of doubt that heads were going to roll when the driver told his people what had happened. They would probably turn on him first – suspecting the van driver to be in on it. If he had nothing to tell them, Rico suspected they'd torture him, or threaten his family until they were sure he was nothing to do with it. Everybody in this world was out to make a few quid, nobody could ever be trusted, and most people would suspect an inside job.

Tyler had warned his brother about jobs like this one, ones over their pay grade. He'd told him to never ever step into this world, because he knew more than anybody it was a dark world, a place you very rarely come back from. There was no honour amongst thieves. But Rico didn't want honour. He wanted cash, lots of it, and fast.

Freddy counted the money out and looked over at Rico. 'We've given you thirty grand and sixty each for us.'

Rico growled and went to get up from his seat, but Freddy pushed him back down with a flat palm. He eyeballed him and spoke through gritted teeth. 'We took the risks, not you. You're lucky to be getting that, if I'm being honest.'

Wayne stepped forward too and both of them towered over him.

Wayne spoke now. 'I drove the van, Freddy twisted the clown up and you just drove us back here. No risks you had, not like us, and that's how we work out the wages. You're good with that, aren't you, sunshine?'

Rico bit down hard on his bottom lip, from the corner of his eye he could see Freddy touching his coat pocket, ready to pull a shooter out and end his life if he argued. And thirty grand for a night's works wasn't that bad, was it? It was more than Tyler's deals usually got. He gulped, trying not to show any fear. 'Yeah, whatever, but I thought we were all equal. I was the one who sorted the job out and all that, but it is what it is.' Rico knew he wasn't safe and wanted out of here as soon as. These two were a couple of head-the-balls and wouldn't have thought twice about slicing him up and feeding him to the pigs. Rico reached his hand out to Wayne to shake hands, to end the beef and get gone. There was something in Wayne's eyes that didn't sit right with him and the moment he stood up he made his way to the door, determined to get out of here as fast as he could. 'You two can torch that van somewhere, make sure it's out of town too. We don't want any roads leading back to us, do we?' And with that Rico was gone.

Rico made sure his bedroom door was locked and spread the money out on the bed like a rainbow. He took a photograph of it and held a cheesy smile on his face as he included himself in the snapshot. The further he'd got from the lock-up the more his confidence had come back. He'd not only planned this all, he'd faced down Freddy and Wayne, and come home with more money than he'd ever had his hands on. This was a decent till, the kind of money he could have a seriously good time on. His flat palm stroked across the cash, admiring it, thinking what he could do with it. After a few minutes, he placed the cash in an old trainer box and stashed it under his bed. First thing in the morning he was going to book a holiday, jet off to the sun and let things calm down round here. He lay on his bed with his arms looped under his head. He looked out into the night sky and smiled at the moon. 'Everybody will know my name soon, fucking *everybody*.'

Chapter Seven

Tyler stuck his head out from his pad and surveyed the area as he sucked in the cold northerly wind from outside. What chance did he have of a lie-in when all he could hear was shouting and screaming? He could have done with some more sleep – today was a big day. Big Sam was getting taxed today. Smidge and Rhino had his back to make sure everything went to plan. Tyler knew, if it was a one-on-one, he didn't fancy his chances much. Sam was a beast of a man. One wrong move from Tyler and this guy would flatten him, biting him, stabbing him up, poking his eyes out. No, this had to be a team effort.

Tyler walked onto the landing and waited until he spotted his boys across the way. A quick nod told him they were ready. His ears pinned back, and his chest expanded. Time for some fresh blood on this wing. The screws were at the bottom of the landing. He had them clocked, making sure they were nowhere near Sam's pad. This was the only way to play it. The moment the screws took their eyes from the ball for a single second the inmates would strike. No hanging about. Tyler's nostrils flared as he marched down the landing, his boys meeting him on the other side. There was no room for mistakes today, they had to be in and out. Tyler booted the door open and, seeing Sam stood near his window, he went straight for him, pulling the iron bar he'd got from another inmate from his trackies. Without any hesitation, he whacked it over Sam's head, his face creasing with anger with every swing. 'I'm the boss on this wing now, you tosser, do you hear me, or do you want some fucking more?'

Sam held his hands up, shaking his head, spitting blood. They'd caught him off guard. Sam had been inside long enough to know the score, and he'd got complacent. He'd let himself trade off his reputation, and had got lazy, letting his guard down. Smidge gripped Sam's cellmate by the scruff of the neck and went nose to nose with him. The guy hadn't sprung to Sam's defence, clearly out to save his own skin.

'I want any phones you two clowns have got, and any gear. Don't make me wait, bro, because I'll end your fucking life.' Smidge barked out his orders.

Rhino was rummaging about in the pad too, looking in all the nooks and crannies, anywhere they could have stashed the drugs.

Tyler had to step it up a gear and dragged Sam to his feet. 'I swear to you now, if you have me stood here any longer, I'll break every bone in your bastard body. You'll leave here in a body bag unless you start fucking talking.'

Sam spat out a mouthful of bright red blood, his legs buckling underneath him. 'In the pipes, check the pipes.'

Rhino had his hand down them in seconds and pulled out a plastic bag. 'Job's a good 'un. Tyler, come on, get the fuck out of here.'

But Tyler held his ground. He had to make sure these clowns kept their mouths shut. He bent down and eyeballed Sam. 'You keep that fat fucking mouth shut, prick. One whisper you've been throwing my name into the mix with the screws, and I'll be back. And next time I'll finish you off. If not me, then I'll find someone who will end you. You know how it works.' Tyler winked at his victim. His words were firm, and Sam nodded his head, unable to speak.

The boys were out of there. The job was done.

Tyler came to his door as the siren went off on the wing. The screws were team-handed as they stormed into Sam's cell. Shouting, things being thrown about, the medical team rushing past to get to the injured party. One screw came and stood outside the pad and shot a look over at Tyler. He snarled at him and never lost eye contact. But the screw had nothing on him, and he knew it – suspicion wasn't proof. Sam would keep schtum. He knew the law behind bars and to grass would more than his life was worth.

Sam and his boy were stretchered out of the pad. Both were in a bad way but nothing that they hadn't dealt out to other inmates in days gone by.

But this was the start rather than the end of it. The screws were shouting now, screaming at the tops of their voices, 'Get behind your fucking doors now, fucking now!'

This was the usual protocol when something had kicked off. Each prisoner in turn would be questioned about what had happened to Big Sam. It was a pointless exercise, and the officers knew it, but they had to follow the rules, make sure they interviewed everyone who might have seen something.

Tyler stepped back into his pad and plonked down on his bed, waiting until he was called. This was water off a duck's back for him, and doing someone in was just part of his everyday work. In fact, he felt more like his old self, having got back to what he was used to – a show of force to show who was boss. It was how he earned his patch on the outside, and he knew the same skills would work in here. Tyler was strong. He spent hours in the gym, ate well, touched no fast food, and as a result had the body of a Greek god. He had always trained every day on the outside and, once he'd found his feet in this jail, he'd hit the gym and do exactly the same thing here. Putting wankers like Sam in their place was just a part of business. It wasn't something he enjoyed – he wasn't a head case like some of the lads he ran with – but he was used to it by now, and it got results.

Tyler flicked his TV on, though he could still hear all the commotion on the landing. Inmates were booting at their doors, screaming to be let out. This was their social time and now, just because some prick had been done in, all of them had to suffer and lose their association time.

'Shut the fuck up,' Officer Hargreaves yelled as he stood outside a prisoner's door. The job was getting to him and some days he didn't know why he even bothered turning up for work. Same shit different day, he supposed. There was never a day without drama in this place. Always fighting to tackle, someone at war with someone else, thieving from each other, inmates taking their own lives. Hargreaves walked slowly along the landing and stopped when he got to Tyler's door. This was an inmate he'd not really met before, but he'd read his file and knew from the moment he'd stepped onto this landing he'd have to keep a close eye on him. He lifted the metal flap on the door and sneered inside.

Tyler didn't move, kept his eyes on the TV, aware he was being watched. Keys jangled outside his door then it creaked open slowly and the screw stepped inside, one hand resting on the frame of the door. 'What was the score down at Big Sam's pad, lad?'

Tyler never took his eyes from the TV screen as he replied. 'Seen nothing, boss. I keep myself to myself, just want a quiet life.'

Officer Hargreaves checked behind him before he spoke. He knew the score and this arsehole knew more than he was saying. 'So that's the way you're playing it. Listen prick, just a few words for you to digest. I can make this place a nice place for you to stay or it can be a living hell. You're forgetting, I hold the keys to this door, not you.'

Tyler sat up on his bed, rage bubbling inside him. Who did this tosser think he was talking to? If this was on the outside, he would have jawed the fucker by now, put him on his arse. 'I've told you I want a quiet life, so do yourself a favour: close my door and go about your business, old man. I won't bother you and you don't bother me. Happy days.'

Hargreaves sucked hard on his gums, fist rolling into two tight balls at his sides. 'Your card is marked and, once I've told my workmates that bit of information, you can expect to lose that cocky attitude.'

Tyler didn't want to listen to this lecture and, although he should have kept his mouth shut, the anger inside him took over like it always did when he faced confrontation. 'I have mates too, ones who will stick a blade in you for a quick bag of smack. So, when you're throwing smart-arse comments about, remember who you are dealing with here. Like I said, dickhead, do one.'

The screw swallowed hard, looked over at the buzzer and debated pressing it for back-up so he could run into this pad and use his baton to knock some sense into this new kid. It was tempting, but he didn't know if he had the energy to start a vendetta. Not without doing a few background checks on this Makin kid first.

Tyler sat on the edge of his bed, ready to jump into action, aware this screw could strike at any moment. He spoke in a firm tone. 'Like I said, fuck off and close the door behind you. No bother for you, no bother for me. Simple.'

Their eyes locked together and for a few seconds neither blinked.

Then the officer backed off, never taking his eyes from Tyler, never leaving himself open. 'Your card is marked. My eyes are all over you from now on. I know you have something to do with Sam being done in, and now I'll do my homework and prove it. Watch your back, because I'll only ever be a few steps behind you.'

The door closed and Tyler released the breath he barely realised he'd been holding in. 'Prick, fucking prick,' he mumbled under his breath as he punched his clenched fist into his pillow.

───────

All the landing was talking about Big Sam. The screws might not have any proof who'd done it, but word spread instantly around the inmates. They knew who the main man was now and, as Tyler walked out from his pad, he was greeted by new friends, prisoners suddenly ready to do anything to get in his good books. The word was Sam had kept his mouth shut along with his wingman. He was on the hospital wing and waiting to be taken to the hospital for x-rays and brain scans.

Rhino came to Tyler's side and winked at him. 'Fuck me, I thought they were never letting us out. They can prove fuck all, it's sweet. I need to find a decent spot for our stash too. Sod leaving it in the pads. We'll be getting spun every fucking two minutes, knowing our luck.'

Tyler nodded. 'I've had that idiot Hargreaves at my door shouting the odds out at me, ballooning. We need to watch him carefully. Snidey bastard, he is.'

Rhino dragged his fingers through his hair. 'We need to set our stall up fast. At least we got a couple of iPhones too. We can sort shit out at home now and make sure everything is running alright.'

Smidge gave a knowing look to Rhino, both of them convinced Rico was too green and couldn't be trusted. He'd always been a liability and, if it wasn't for Tyler, none of them would have given him the time of day, let alone left him running the show.

Chapter Eight

Zara peered at herself in the mirror. Her skin looked older than it used to. Lines around her eyes left her feeling old and tired. If Tyler had been here and seen her like this, he would have bunged her some money. 'Go and get a facial, Mam, and cheer yourself up. Go and get a new dress.' But those days had gone. With no money, there'd be no facials, no little pick-me-ups, no new dresses. Maybe she should have stashed some cash, put it away for a rainy day, days like these when she was skint and on the bones of her arse. She lifted her hair up and sucked her cheeks in. Empty, they were, deflated just like her mood. Her make-up stood unused on her dressing table and she knew she would have to make an effort today to look half decent. She looked deep into her eyes: small red veins, scattered all over. Maybe she'd drank too much last night, had a few too many. But, in her defence, she had been on her own, with nobody to keep her company but her bottle of wine. She'd got pissed, listening to old tunes, tempted to go through her contact list and phone one of her exes. At one point she stared at a number, and it was only the sound of her Bri coming home that stopped her ringing her ex-boyfriend and making a fool of herself. She always got like this, ringing anyone who would talk to her when she was drunk, even though she'd be talking gibberish, telling them that they should try again, make it work this time. She knew she sounded desperate when she was in that kind of mood. She hated that side to her, but she knew in her heart she was lost. Zara was so lonely. She always denied it but, even when she went out to the pub with the girls, she would look around at the couples and wish she could find someone to share her life with.

Her mates had tried everything in the book to help her find love, but she knew they had conversations about her behind her back. 'It must be her. She must be too needy. How can all these men never want to go out with her after a few dates?' they would say.

And, if they were saying it, it must be true. They were her friends, after all, the people who spent the most time with her. Night after night, her friends listened to her pouring her heart out. But they had lives, someone in bed with them every night to snuggle up to, not like her, cold and alone. They would never understand how it felt to have a big void in your life, an empty heart, like she did. What was wrong with her? she wondered.

Molly was Zara's best friend and even she had given up any hope of her friend ever finding love. Lately she had been distant herself too. And, in truth, Zara suspected why – Molly didn't trust her near her man. A long while back she had kicked up a right fuss, thinking she'd seen Zara coming out of his car late one night. Molly had followed the woman, but never managed to get her hands on her. Yet she was convinced it was her best friend. Zara denied it, said she had been at home all night long. She couldn't even bear to admit to herself what she'd done behind her best mate's back when she'd had the same thing done to her. She knew she was capable of some dark deeds – but this was something she still lost sleep over. Zara had been tempted to ask Molly why she stayed with her man if she thought he had wronged her, but she knew that would only make things worse between them. Maybe she was scared of starting again, finding someone new and putting effort into another relationship, getting to know someone from scratch.

Zara slowly applied her make-up, hoping a new woman would emerge as she did her face. Her mobile phone started ringing and she flicked her hair behind her shoulder before she answered the call. 'Hi Molly, you've just caught me on a bad day. I'm off to see our Tyler at the nick again. I'm missing him something rotten.'

Zara looked at her reflection in the mirror as she carried on with the conversation with her friend. 'Right, give me a few hours and I will bell you when I get home. I could do with a good night out. Money's tight but once I've had a word with my son he'll sort me out. He's a good lad you know, underneath it all. He looks after his own.'

The call ended and Zara sat staring into space for a moment before turning back to her make-up. Every movement was effort today: she had no motivation. She had better get her game face on before she saw Tyler.

———

An hour later, outfit on point, hair and make-up spot on, Zara went up to the waiting room in the main jail and made her way to the desk. She knew the script this time. Jane, the woman who'd she met on the previous visit was back too, and smiled at her as she went to sit down. She looked perky today, full of the joys of spring. And there, behind the desk was the same screw. Mike was staring at her, all over her like a rash. She quickly smoothed her hair and wandered over.

'I thought you were giving me your phone number the last time you were here?'

Zara played the fool. Trying not to show how interested she was. 'Oh, really, did I say that?' She giggled.

Mike was clearly a chancer and a quick look over his shoulder told him it was safe to turn on the charm. He reached over, got a piece of paper and passed her a pen. 'There you go, no flies on me, love. Give me your digits and we'll go out for a few drinks later, if you're up for it?'

Zara gulped, looking at him in more detail. He wasn't her usual cup of tea, and in all honesty she could have done with him being a bit thinner, taller maybe, more hair, but beggars couldn't be choosers. And anyway, if she didn't take a shine to him, he could still prove to be useful. She took the pen from him and rolled it about in her long slender fingers, still not sure. 'I don't usually give my phone number out to anyone. I'm not sure about this: you could be a stalker, or some kind of murderer.'

Mike rolled his eyes and chuckled. 'Come on, look at this face, face of an angel. Anyway, all the bad boys are on the other side of this door. I'm one of the good guys.'

Zara blushed, trying to play hard to get. Between each number she scribbled down she looked up at him, letting him know he was lucky. Mike snatched the number as she finished writing it and folded it up into a small square and shoved it in his back pocket.

'Right, as soon as I get off my shift, I'll have a shave and that, and dust my swagger down. I hope you like dancing because I'm like John Travolta's brother when I get moving.'

She sniggered and raised her eyebrows. 'Ring me about eight o'clock. And, if you're lucky, I will be ready.'

Zara wiggled back over to her seat smiling like a Cheshire cat. The black cloud hanging over her head seemed to have lifted. She had always questioned why she felt she needed a man in her life to make her happy, and she could never find the answer. Maybe she should have started with self-love and feeling better about herself before she started putting all her eggs in one basket with any man who crossed her path. She knew her boys were sick to death of her crying about men. All their lives it had been the same old story. When the latest guy turned out to be another loser, the wine would come out, Whitney Houston would go on full blast, and Zara would be back to square one, crying her eyes out. Rico and Brian never really cared. It was same day different shit in their eyes. But Tyler always thought he could fix his mother, show her she didn't need a man when she had her sons. He wanted to make her happy with money, gifts and weekends away, all paid for by him. And it did make her happy for a short time, or at least until the next man let her down. It was a vicious circle.

———

Zara sat down with the tray of canteen food and smiled over the table at her boy, glad the wait had been shorter this time. Tyler looked like his dad, and she always told him that when she was in a good mood.

'Mam, I've tried ringing Rico a few times now and he's not answering my calls. Tell him I've got my own phone now, so he better start answering me. Honest, where is that kid's head at? He's a right pillock sometimes, but this is meant to be his time to grow up, show me he can take care of business. I want him working hard.'

'He's not been in that much. He's all loved up with that Clara, isn't he?'

Tyler blushed slightly and the corners of his mouth started to rise. 'Been there and done that, Mardukes, he's welcome to her,' he chuckled.

Zara's jaw dropped. Gobsmacked, she was. 'You kept that quiet! When did that happen?'

'About a year ago. The girl was all over me and I told her I'm not the settling down type. Next thing I know our kid is seeing her. I'm sure she got with him to be near me. Honest, once they've had a taste of this right here,' he pointed at his body, 'they always want to come back for seconds.'

'Bleeding hell, well, keep that to yourself: he'll do one if he ever finds out. He's smitten with her, always running here and there for her, you know what he's like. I've nicknamed him "Buddy Love".'

They burst out laughing. A secret they both shared now. Zara kept her voice low and leaned over the table. 'Eh, I've got a date with that screw I was telling you about. I've just given him my number. I'll be out with him tonight if he calls.'

Tyler looked at her in disbelief. 'For fuck's sake, Mam. You know what you're like when they let you down. I don't know why you put yourself through it all the time. You're a glutton for punishment.'

She folded her arms tightly in front of her. 'A bit harsh, Tyler. I'm just an all-or-nothing kind of woman. I don't have time for head games. Go big or go home is my motto. Anyway, if we get on, it might be sweet for you, getting the inside line on this place.'

Tyler started eating his food and Zara busied herself looking around the visiting centre. She fanned her fingers over her mouth and kept her voice low. 'What's he in for?' She shot her eyes at a large man with a big bushy beard.

'I think he's in for assault. He's one of them Hell's Angels. I've heard he's a right snapper. Chinned a few on his landing, he has.'

Zara looked at another inmate and asked the same question. Tyler blew a hard breath and said in a sarcastic tone,'Fucking hell, Mam, stop being so nosey. I don't know what he's in for. I'm an inmate in here, not a bleeding screw.'

Zara rolled her eyes. 'Only asking. Put your dummy back in, mard-arse.'

He sat munching on his chocolate bar and spoke with his mouth full. 'So, what's new at home, anything else bar your love life?'

Zara looked reluctant to say. 'Did you know that Brian still sees Ben, your bastard father's brother?'

Tyler nodded. 'Yeah, he's kept in touch with us all, over the years, Mam. I've often had a pint with him if I've seen him in town in the boozer. He's decent, still talks about you and how much he respects you.'

Her voice got higher. 'What, he *respects* me?' She didn't look convinced. 'If he was that full of respect, he would have made his brother pay some bloody maintenance.'

'Well, he's always singing your praises. He knows my dad was in the wrong and never tries to defend him.'

'How could he defend him when he knows full well what he did? And not just to me – but abandoning his own flesh and blood. That's low. Really low.'

'Mam, chill out, will you, and listen properly. I said, he doesn't agree with what my dad done. He's not his keeper, is he?'

Zara's back was up, and she screwed her mouth up. Just the mention of Max's name made her heart beat faster, rage bubbling up her windpipe, words getting ready to spit from her mouth. But she paused, not wanting any beef with her boy. Especially when she wanted to tap him up, get a few quid for a night out. She rested her head in her hands and opened her eyes wide: he knew she was on the borrow.

'Rico's still not given me a penny, you know. I hate bringing it to the table, but you did tell me to tell him. I did just that and he fobbed me off.'

Tyler gritted his teeth together and raised his eyebrows. 'You tell him I said to sort you out. I'll be on the blower tonight to him anyway, so if he picks up, rest assured he'll be put in his place. I might be in the nick, but I can still have him put in the boot of a car and mashed up if he starts taking the piss.'

Zara shook her head. 'No, it won't need any messy stuff. Just word him up. That's all it will take. He's flashing the cash about like nobody's business at the moment. Fucking Rockefeller, he is.'

Tyler looked unbothered. 'Like I said I would, I've found my feet in here now and I'll be getting money out to you to stash.'

Zara's eyes lit up. 'Oh, how's that happened?'

He tapped the side of his nose and winked over at her. 'Ask no questions, tell no lies,' he sniggered.

Zara knew her boy would land on his feet; he always came up smelling of roses. True, this life wasn't what most mothers wanted for their kids –if she had the choice, she'd want him doing something straight, something safe. But choice was never something she or her boys had the luxury of. And if you had to walk on the wild side, you may as well be the king of the jungle, she figured. She sat back like a proud parent, just like she had when she watched him in the school play when he was a nipper. He had bagged the part of Aladdin and every night after school she had helped him learn his words for the show. She'd cried at the end of the performance, stood up and clapped and clapped and wolf whistled her son. She couldn't have imagined then what that lad would grow up into. But one thing was constant: her love for him was as fierce as ever, and whatever he did, she had his back.

Tyler might have been taking over the place, but she could still see a softer side to her boy. There was a look in his eye that she knew well. A look that told her he was missing home, missing his family. He was never good at being away from home. Even when he went on holiday, he was homesick after a few days. He went on a lad's holiday to Ibiza and on day four he was on the phone telling his mother he couldn't wait to be back home to his bed. He had even moved out once, got a flat with his friend, but he didn't last long. After a few months, he was back home saying he missed his home comforts, telling her his mate was a scruffy sod and he was sick of picking up after him. Any excuse really. She never believed him. She knew he just missed the security of being at home and knowing she was there. And, in fairness, Zara missed him as much as he missed her.

Zara clocked the screw walking up to her and looked up at him as he told her to finish the visit. He was a big tower of a man, probably ex-military. No messing with this geezer. Zara reached over the table and held her son's hand tight. 'I'll make sure Rico answers his phone when you ring. The last thing you need is stressing about him.'

Tyler clocked the screw looking at him now and pulled his hand away. He knew he couldn't let them see where they could hurt you. If an inmate was giving them any jip they would stop their visits, put them on twenty-four-hour bang-up, stop their mail. He wasn't going there.

Zara reached behind her and grabbed her coat. She swept her hair back over her shoulder and smiled at her son. 'Be good, eh, Tyler? No trouble, keep your neck clean and get this sentence over and done with.'

He nodded, looking over his shoulder at an inmate two tables to the right of him. He gave him a wink and nodded his head slowly. Zara was oblivious and hadn't clocked that this point of the visit where everyone was shuffling around, putting coats on or holding hands one last time, was when most of the illegal stuff would be passed over: drugs, phones, you name it, these inmates had it. It only took the blink of an eye and switches were made, packages traded without the screws spotting a thing.

A quick kiss on the cheek and Zara plodded out of the visiting room. She looked at all the other people leaving and wondered how they were feeling, if they were feeling like she was. She looked at a young girl walking next to her. Three kids she had brought today, all under the age of seven. She had her hands full, that much was clear. Zara listened as the girl spoke to her children. 'Daddy works here now. In a few months, he will be home and he'll have plenty of money for us all.'

Zara rolled her eyes, knowing it was a big fat whopping lie. But what do you tell the kids who come to see their fathers in here? You can't tell them the truth, can you? Imagine their faces if you told them their dad was a criminal, a lying cheating, thieving bastard. No, she could see why it was better to let them believe a story.

Zara was out of the prison and in a rush to get home. She dug her hand into her handbag and pulled her fags out, popping one into her mouth. She lit it. She fished her car keys out of her bag and started to walk to her car. Her mobile rang and she frowned as she looked at the screen: no caller ID.

'Hello, who is this?' She turned around quickly, and her eyes squinted as she clocked a man waving from the top window in the building behind her. It was Mike, keen to check she hadn't fobbed him off with a fake number. Once the call ended, she smiled to herself and opened the car door. Mike seemed like an eager beaver, no head games, a straight talker. She was going to look her best tonight, show this man what he'd be missing if he didn't snap her up. Maybe he was the one, her Prince Charming. Could it really be that Zara Makin, mother to the hardest lads on this side of Manchester, could find her happy ever after with a prison officer?

Chapter Nine

'I'll slice the fuckers up. The cheeky bastards, don't they know who they are fucking with?' Jacob Watts chewed the ends of his knuckles and watched as they started bleeding. He looked at the pooling blood and smeared it across his hand. Looking up at his wingmen, Tommy and Peter, he said coldly, 'Get around to that useless driver's house again and bring him here to me. I don't care what state he's in. Bruised, battered or concussed, I'm not believing he's not in on it until I hear it from the horse's mouth. Nah, nothing makes sense. Get someone to go to him and drag the fucker here to me. Check on the street too if any houses nearby have one of those doorbell cameras. Chances are we can get a bit of info from one of them. I swear to you now, these men are dead men walking. Who the fuck in their right head would mess with me, with us? It makes me think it's grafters from out of the area, chancers, just pricks who targeted the van not realising what they were starting.'

Tommy nodded his head. He'd been around on the scene for a few years and knew most of the criminals in the area and agreed with Jacob that no one in their right mind would ever step on their toes.

Peter plonked down on the sofa, gutted that proper money had been lost. 'It's fucked my plans right up, this has. The Mrs was all ready to book us a holiday. You should have seen her kipper when I told her it wasn't happening.'

Tommy smirked. 'I thought you was getting rid of her, pal. Every week all you do is moan about her, say she's a lunatic, bi-polar. What's changed your mind this week?'

Peter raised his eyebrows high and retaliated. 'She's my baby-mama, I can't just fuck off and leave her and the kid. Plus, she has already told me if she ever finds out I've been shagging about she will cut my crown jewels off.' His eyes were wide open. 'And she'll do it. The times that woman has pulled a knife out of the kitchen drawer and ran at me is unreal. I sleep with one eye open when she is on one, let me tell you.'

Jacob was staring at the wall, thinking hard. 'Get the word out on the streets: ten grand reward for anyone telling us who it was. They'll be singing like fucking budgies when they know there is money on offer. Peter, I want you to go and see all the main boys in the surrounding areas: Harpurhey, Collyhurst, Miles Platting, Blackley, Newton Heath.'

Peter sat down next to Jacob and patted his knee. 'Relax Jake, you know all comes to those who wait. If any names are thrown into the mix, I'll promise you now I will destroy the fuckers one by one until we get to the truth. Who the hell do they think they are? I will make an example of them, the full works.'

Peter watched Tommy on the blower. Soon, it was sorted and the driver was being dragged to Jacob's. He was on his way.

Jacob Watts had lived in New Moston all of his life. His uncle was one of the main heads in the area when he was growing up and he was the one who got him licking shot when he was still a kid. Selling drugs was always the fastest way to earn money, line your pockets, no questions asked. But it meant a life of always watching your back, never crossing into someone else's patch alone, and facing up to the chance of getting shot, stabbed, your house torched, or being caught and sentenced to years in prison. Jacob had started his drug career as a runner, just bits of weed to start with. But he had a keen eye and watched his uncle Bernie like a hawk, listened to his phone calls and who his suppliers were. It was only a matter of time before greed got the better of him and he wanted a bigger piece of the pie. The stories about what he did to his uncle were still told. He'd given it to him good and proper, put him in hospital, where he stayed for at least two months. Everybody still whispered behind his back. 'If he could do that to his blood, imagine what he could do to someone who he didn't know.' Jacob was six foot two, brown eyes like chocolate, and built like a shit-house door. He trained like a gladiator every day like all the top dogs did.

Soon after, there was a knocking at the front door. Jacob picked his iPhone up and checked the doorbell footage. He nodded over at Peter. 'Sorted. It's Dingo and Sassy. Let them in.' Jacob sat back in his chair and smiled over at Tommy. 'You know the score and what needs to be done. If this dickhead of a driver is in on it, we need to break him. Get the drill plugged in ready.'

Tommy stood up and followed instructions. Drilling holes into people's body parts was something he'd done before. It gave him his name, the Driller, and let people know what he was capable of when his feathers were ruffled. He wasn't a big guy like Jacob, so he had to use his vicious streak to earn his reputation.

The inner door opened. Dingo and Sassy stood holding a man, grabbing an arm each. The carrier was called Les. He'd done a few jobs before for these lads and up to now he'd never given them a problem.

Dingo eyeballed Jacob. 'Where do you want him, mate?'

'Sling him on that chair there and then you two can get off. Cheers lads, sort you out later.'

Dingo stood tall and said, 'There are a few houses near this prick's house. If you can get to see the footage, I'm sure you will see exactly what happened. There is a house facing that should have a full view.'

Jacob rubbed his hands together and watched as Les was flung across the room to sit shivering on the armchair. His teeth were chattering together, and the poor fucker looked like he was going to have a heart attack. He was still covered in cuts and bruises from the night the safe had been nicked, but they were the least of his problems now.

Tommy had plugged the drill into the socket, and he pressed the button a few times to make sure it was working. The next thing he did was put a big plastic sheet on the floor. If anyone had looked closely, they would have seen speckles of blood on it. Les was desperate, shaking from head to toe. He was around thirty years of age and had thinning blonde hair. His teeth left a lot to be desired, black stumps, old crowns. Whatever money he was earning from driving for them, he certainly wasn't giving it to his dentist.

'Jacob pal, I swear to you on my mother's grave that I knew fuck all about this. Like I've already told you, I was opening the gates and I was attacked, didn't see fuck all. Whoever it was must have been watching me because I'd just pulled up.'

Jacob sat forward in his seat, cracking his knuckles. 'Les, we are now down one hundred and fifty grand. It's not pennies we are talking about here, pal, it's proper money. See, you have to be careful what you tell me, because I'm like a fucking elephant, I never forget.'

Tommy pressed the drill button again but this time he placed it next to Les's ear.

Peter chirped in. 'Jacob forgets fuck all, let me tell you. If it's your round in the pub then he's the first to let you know,' he giggled.

Les wasn't smiling, he was white as a sheet. He swallowed hard and sat with both arms wrapped around his body. 'Please, honest, I'm nothing to do with this. I do a few drops to earn extra money. I didn't even know what I was carrying. I only drive the motor and wait for you guys to come and pick it up, don't I?' He held his hand out. 'Look at the state of me, I'm shaking like a shitting dog. Do you think I would ever, ever, do anything to have you over?'

Jacob shot a look at Tommy, the one that told him it was time to put the pressure on. Peter grabbed hold of Les's hand and squashed it down on the table. The drill was hovering over his knuckles and there was nothing he could do to move. 'So, I'm going to ask you again. Who took the money? All I want is the names. I know you are bottom of the list in all this and, once I get a name, then I'll deal with you accordingly. Don't make me hurt you, Les, when you can walk away from here. Names. Tell me their fucking names!' he screamed.

Les was trying to move but he was fighting a losing battle. Jacob nodded at Tommy. The drill pierced the skin and bright red blood splurted from the hole that appeared. Les screamed and his eyes bulged from their sockets. The sound of bones grinding as flesh flayed from his hand. He looked like he was going to pass out. But the drill had done its job and made contact with the table. Tommy dragged it out and wiped the drill bit with an old tea towel that he had hanging over his shoulder, like some sadistic waiter.

'I will drill every fucking finger, mate, if you don't start talking, Les. You know I will, so do yourself a favour and give me a name.'

Les was falling in and out of consciousness now, his head flopping to the side, his voice low. 'I know nothing, I swear down, nothing.'

Tommy shrgged his shoulders at Jacob. Usually, one go of the drill and their victims were telling them everything they wanted to know. They had to rethink this. Perhaps he really was telling the truth?

Peter let go of Les's hand and Tommy dropped the towel on his lap. 'Wrap it up for now. If you get any claret on the sofa, you'll be paying for it.'

Les slowly wrapped the blood-stained towel around his hand. His body seemed to be melting into his seat, no fight left in him. His voice was low, and he kept repeating the same words under his breath. 'I know nothing, I know nothing.'

Chapter Ten

Rico stood at his mother's bedroom door and held his hand on the door frame as he spoke. 'Just tell Ty I've cleared off for a few days. I'm going to get a bit of sun, so I won't be answering the phone. He needs to back off and let me do my thing, the guy is a control freak.' He pulled an iPhone from his pocket and walked further into the bedroom. His mother kept her space spotless, proper girlie, fluffy pillows, a furry bedspread.

Rico flung the iPhone on the bed. 'You can man the phone while I'm away, just keep it safe. Brian is here so I'll tell him the score. He knows what needs doing, it's time he stepped up a bit. He's old enough to graft, so you won't have to do anything, only speak with Tyler.'

Zara opened her mouth wide as she fanned her eyelashes out with the black mascara. 'Where have you got the money from to be jetting off into the sun, anyway? I thought you were potless – not even a spare few notes for your mam?'

Rico gave no eye contact. 'I won a few quid on the roulette in the bookies. Nearly a grand I put in my back pocket.'

Zara stared at him through the mirror. 'Since when have you been a gambler?'

'I'm not, just fancied a flutter, test my luck and all that. And you know me, Mam, I was born lucky.' He grinned.

'Who are you going away with?' Zara could sense something was off.

'Clara. She's been moaning all the time, saying we don't do anything, so this holiday should shut her up for a bit.'

Zara couldn't hold her tongue. 'Why does that not surprise me? Just make sure she puts her hand in her pocket too. She seems like a bit of a gold-digger to me. What's she hanging about for?'

Rico screwed his face up, annoyed that his mam was disrespecting his woman. She'd only met her a handful of times and who was she to judge anyone, with her track record? 'Mam, Clara is not just after money, she loves me. Are you saying she's only after me for my cash? She wants my time, not money. Why do you always see the worst in any girl I get with? It's like you're jealous of anyone in love.'

Zara smashed her hairbrush down on the dressing table. 'What are you saying that for? I wish all of you luck in finding nice girls, it's just sometimes when I get a gut feeling I'm usually right. Look when I told our Brian about that Gemma girl. I told him she was trouble and did he listen? No. Then he caught her seeing two other guys at the same time. I'm older and wiser, remember, and can smell a rat a mile away.'

'Shame you don't use this magic power you have when you start dating the men you do, then, eh? Most of them have been arseholes and you know it.'

Zara stood up and placed her hand on her hip. 'Don't you dare compare me to any of them girls you date. I'm the real deal, not just out for what I can get like some of them slappers you have on your arm.'

Rico knew she was off on one. He backed out of the room before he got the hairbrush launched at his head. But Zara was right behind him, dressing gown tied tightly, brandishing her eyebrow pencil. 'While we are on the subject of money, Tyler said you need to give me fifty pound a week starting now. Don't give me any sob story, because Tyler said it's his money, not yours, and you should hand it over without me having to ask for it. I feel like a right scrounger having to ask – but if you've got enough for a holiday, you've got enough to pay a bit of rent.'

Rico marched out of the room and came back with fifty quid in his hand. The last thing he wanted was his mam on his back when he was heading for the sun. 'Here, moaning Minnie, sort your mush out now. I never said you couldn't have it, just that I didn't have the money on me last time you asked. So, stop running back to Tyler chatting shit about me, because it's me who gets it in the neck, not you.'

Zara snatched the cash out of his hand and rammed it in the side of her bra. She walked back to the mirror and shouted, 'Thank you, and a kiss would be nice if you are going away for a week, or don't you do that anymore?'

Rico stomped back into the bedroom and bent to kiss her cheek.

She softened now and hated the thought of him being anywhere she couldn't watch out for him. 'Enjoy your holiday and keep out of trouble.' Her middle son was always the one she worried about the most. The other two had their heads screwed on, but Rico? Well, there was no guessing what his next move would be.

'As always, Mother. Eh, if you're not busy, will you give my bedroom a deep clean while I'm away? I'll bung you twenty quid for it, if you want?'

Zara scoffed. Rico was a lazy get and she knew without even looking in his bedroom that it would be a shit tip, food left on plates, rubbish all over, dirty clothes scattered about. But she'd rather it be clean than wait for him to do something about it. So she nodded as she watched him leave.

Zara popped her head in her son's bedroom to see the size of the problem and her eyes popped. There was no way she was cleaning it now: she had to be ready in half an hour for her date. But she couldn't help herself at least making a start on it. Her OCD kicked in, she walked into the bedroom and started to pick up the dirty washing: socks, jumpers, wet towels. She bent down to look under the bed. She would always find mountains of washing there, like he was still a teenager. Her eyes opened wide as she lay flat on the floor, scooping her arm under the bed. She crawled underneath and pulled the box out to have a quick butcher's what was inside it. Rico was always putting dodgy stuff in his bedroom and Tyler was sick to death of telling him that, if they got raided, he was getting nicked for whatever he had in his possession. It wasn't that long ago that Zara had found a silver pistol in his bedroom, wrapped tightly in a blanket. Yes, a bleeding firearm. If brains were dynamite, then her son couldn't blow his bloody nose. An idiot he was, never thinking of the consequences of his actions. Always leaving himself open – and the whole family. Zara sat on her bum and hesitated before she pulled the cardboard lid from the box. There could be things in here that he wanted to keep private: mucky mags, condoms, dirty photographs of the girls he'd dated. Her hand hovered over the box for a few seconds. Oh, what the 'eck, she was having a look. Her fingers slowly lifted the lid. Money. Bundles of twenty-pound notes, lots of money. Her hands were trembling, and she rammed the lid back onto the box, trying to unsee what she had just seen, but she couldn't pretend now, could she? Zara sat thinking for a few seconds and lifted the lid again. She started to pull single twenty-pound notes out of different bundles. He'd never miss it, as if he was going to sit and count each and every bleeding bundle out. She stashed the cash in her dressing gown pocket. This was money for a new dress, a few treats that she had been missing out on since Tyler had been away. Yes, she would get her nails done, even have her toenails painted. She shoved the box back under the bed, stood up and dusted herself down. Life was good again and she had something else to look forward to now. She checked her wristwatch and rushed into her bedroom. Shit, she was running late already.

Mike Patterson stood outside the boozer, waiting patiently for his date to turn up. It had been a while since he'd had a woman on his arm, since he'd even kissed a woman, he told his mates down the boozer.

As Zara approached Mike, she could see him checking himself out in the nearby window. In all fairness he looked alright, good dress sense. He'd made an effort, but not too much. He was wearing a nice pair of jeans, straight-legged, and a light blue shirt with tan brogues. Zara picked up speed and marched towards him. After Max had first left, she used to get so nervous on a first date, but now meeting a new man didn't faze her anymore, because she was always looking for love. She'd exhausted the dating websites, dated all friends of friends and yet was still riding solo. The last time she'd had sex was a few months ago and that was nothing to write home about, just a quick knee-trembler at the back of the pub one Saturday night with a guy she'd met that night. She didn't even know his name. She promised herself that was not happening again. She needed to save herself for the real deal, she told herself. Also, she'd had an itch down there for days after it, a burning sensation every time she weed. It was a good job it had passed, and she wasn't down the clinic, or else she would have found her lover and named and shamed him, just like Mona Jones had done with her husband when he was playing away from home. Everybody still talked about that moment even today. Mona had walked into the pub and clocked that her husband was in having a few scoops with his pals. Once she knew where he was seated, she went out and came back in with black bags filled with his clothes. She had launched them at him one by one, then stood staring at him for a few seconds before she delivered her killer blow. She shouted at the top of her voice and made sure anybody sitting there could hear what she had to say. Hands on her hips, she yelled, 'Josh, you are a dirty horrible bastard with no shame. How can you deny sleeping with someone when my results have come back from the doctors today and I have got chlamydia? Here was me, thinking it was a water infection. I hope your pecker falls off, you dirty scumbag. Don't ever darken my door again. Go back to your scrubber and see if she will have you, you disrespectful bastard.' And she wasn't finished there: oh no. 'And, to all the men here, if any of you are looking for a good, *clean*, fun-loving, loyal woman, give me a shout because I am back on the market. Josh,' she hissed as she picked up his pint, 'don't ever come crying to me, because I'll have you put ten feet under. Wanker.' She had meant every word as she swilled him with his pint of lager. Mona walked out of the pub, and you could have heard a pin drop. The busty blonde barmaid went beetroot and ran straight to the toilet. All the men knew it was her Mona's husband was having sex with and her who'd given him the STD. A few of the other punters looked concerned and could be seen scratching their crotches. Maybe the barmaid had a few of them on the go. Some lessons were learned the hard way.

'Have you been waiting long?' Zara asked as she reached Mike's side.

Mike smiled. 'Long enough, I thought you had stood me up.'

Zara kissed him on his cheek. This was the way she always greeted her men on the first date. 'I'm worth the wait, Mike,' she chuckled as they walked inside the pub only to be hit by a wall of sound. It was busy in here tonight and maybe she had not thought through bringing a new man here on a first date. It was heaving and there was a disco on too. Some of the people looked like they had been on it all day. Mike headed to the bar with Zara following close behind him.

'What are you drinking, sweetheart?'

Zara flicked her hair over her shoulder and replied, 'Pink gin and lemonade, please.' There was no way she was having half a lager on a first date. No, she was determined to show him she was a classy chick, like the ones you saw in all the wine bars in the city centre. The music was deafening, and she could hardly hear herself think. Mike got the drinks and held them up high over his head as he scanned the area for somewhere to sit. He placed the drinks on a table and watched as Zara squeezed past him to get to her seat. He was checking her out for sure, checking her backside in her black skinny leather trousers. At last, they were seated and, even though they were speaking loudly, they were struggling to hear each other. Zara looked over at the bar and swallowed hard as she spotted someone. Mike was still talking, and he never noticed she was looking somewhere else. Max's brother Ben had just walked into the boozer. She'd been in here lots of times and she'd never seen him here. Why was he back on her patch now after all these years? Zara took in every inch of him: he was too close for comfort to Max in his looks.

But Mike was good company and, once Zara had got over the shock of seeing Ben, she told herself she was not going to let him ruin her night. After all, this new guy was ticking all her boxes up to now and she didn't want to spoil it.

'So, Mike, why choose to work in the prisons?' she asked.

Mike took a large mouthful of his pint and moved in closer so she could hear him, his hand resting on her lap. 'I just fancied a change. I used to work the doors on the clubs in town and I was sick of getting spat at and verbally abused every week. Plus, I got a brick launched at my head a few months before I quit.'

Zara winced. 'Bloody hell, that's not a job I would be doing. I couldn't imagine anything worse than dealing with pissed-up people day in day out. Some of them are proper violent when they've had a bevvy.'

'Tell me about it, that's why I had a career change. I've been working in the nicks now for over ten years. I like it.'

'How can you like working with prisoners? Half of them don't deserve to be sent down and the other half, well, some of them give me the jitters just looking at them.'

'It's down to the way you treat them, love. I always respect them and tell them if they respect me then I will give it back. Don't get me wrong, there are some right cranks locked up and I would never turn my back on them, evil fuckers some of them. But most of them? They're just people who took a few wrong turns. I'm not always on the visitor centre desk. I work on the wings every week and I have some great laughs with the inmates. Honest, I would be a rich man if I was dodgy, the backhanders I could get.'

Zara tried not to look too inquisitive. 'What do you mean?'

Mike checked around him, made sure nobody was listening and let Zara into the secret world behind bars. 'Some of my pals bring mobile phones in. You can earn anything between eight hundred quid and a grand from supplying one phone. I'm not going to lie, I've been tempted a few times because, if I'm honest, being a prison warden is not the best paid job in the world. You can get anything in the jail when you know how.'

Zara banked the information he'd just given her. She nudged him in the waist. 'Come on, don't tell me you've never taken anything in for a few extra quid?'

He smirked at her and gave her a cheeky wink. He didn't say yes and he didn't say no, but he saw his chance and moved in for a kiss. Zara placed her warm lips on his and for a moment stopped thinking about anything else. The first kiss always said a lot about a person and, if the first snog wasn't up to much, Zara usually walked away without offering another date. But Mike gave her flutters for sure.

***

Before she knew it, the night was over, and she'd been dancing with Mike and non-stop laughing. It was just what the doctor ordered, even though his mobile phone had been ringing constantly and he had to put it on silent. But even that made her happy, made her think he was into her more than he was letting on – too many guys these days were surgically attached to their phones. Zara didn't want to play second-fiddle to a lousy mobile.

She linked arms with Mike as they were leaving the pub, and she clocked Ben looking right at her. 'Mike, wait outside for me? I'm just going to the loo for a quick wee. If I don't go now, I'll burst.'

He patted his palm on her backside and left the pub. Zara headed towards the toilets. On her way, she locked eyes with Ben. She reminded herself to be nice as she approached him.

It was Ben who spoke first. 'Hello stranger, how are you?'

She had to think before she put her mouth into gear. If this had come out of the blue, she would have given him a mouthful, told him to fuck off and not to talk to her, but since her boys had told her he'd been watching out for them, saying his brother should have never done what he'd done, she'd had time to realise she should give him a chance to explain himself. She reminded herself of that now. 'I'm good, Ben, how are you?' See, there you go, she could be nice when she wanted to be.

'Yeah, ducking and diving as always. It's been too long, Zara. I spoke with your lads, and they were telling me about Tyler. Gutted I am for him. If you ever need anything – a chat, money – just give me a shout.'

Zara lifted a gentle smile and replied, 'Thanks Ben, nice to know. I better go I've got someone waiting for me. Nice seeing you, take care.'

'You too,' he replied.

Zara stood behind the door in the toilet cubicle and inhaled deeply. She'd done herself proud and never snapped at him. She hadn't taken the bait and asked why he was back, hadn't shown him how much it ruffled her feathers to see him, bringing back all those thoughts of Max. She sat on the toilet and breathed. After only a few words, Ben was imprinted on her mind and, even though she should have hated him with a passion, he seemed to have stirred some kind of softer emotion in her.

Mike pulled up outside Zara's house in his black Merc. A nice whip he was proud of. The inside of the car was tip-top, not a bit of dirt anywhere. He'd had a few beers and Zara knew he shouldn't have been driving, but he'd told her he always did it, and a little voice in her head told her it might be useful to squirrel away this bit of info: the fact than even Officer Mike Patterson broke the law. And now here they were – back at hers. Her friends had always told her about not showing guys where she lived until after a few dates, but it was cold tonight and there was no way she was walking home. Her friends were just over the top sometimes and worried for no reason – you didn't marry a Makin and not learn how to look after yourself, she thought.

Mike sensed the opportunity and smiled over at Zara. 'Is it alright if I come in with you? I've enjoyed our night so much and it would be a shame to end it here.'

She paused, then remembered Rico was on holiday and Brian would be out until the early hours. Why shouldn't she have some company?

———

Zara kicked her shoes off and called over at Alexa to play her playlist. She liked this part of her dating better than any other: a few kisses, a few more drinks and probably sex. A feeling that this could be a fresh start – no history, no judgements.

Adele started to play. Zara loved her voice and the stories she told within her music. *Easy on me* was playing and she knew the words off by heart. She poured them both a drink and sat on his lap singing the song. When Zara let herself, she was a good singer, confident. These words meant something to her: you could see it in her expression, and how she connected with the song. Maybe this was her story too. She was telling him that she'd been hurt, and she was damaged goods. The song was coming to an end, and this time it was her who moved in for the kiss. She was no prude and she wanted to show this man she was confident in her own body, a good catch. The kiss was intense, and they were both lying on the sofa. As his hand slipped down the front of her black leather pants, her expression changed. Noises outside the living room door, keys jingling. Fuck, fuck, fuck! She jumped up quickly and tried her best to straighten her clothes and hair. She shot a look at the clock. Hell, it was only half past twelve. She turned the music down and sat in the armchair, trying to look relaxed.

The door opened and in walked Brian. He nodded at Mike then jerked his head over at his mam. 'Who's this muppet, then?'

Zara readied herself for a fight. As if she needed this now. Brian was a right mouth when he'd had a few drinks and she knew he hated that she brought fellas home sometimes. Zara normally told her son straight that it was her life and she would live it as she deemed fit. If the people on the street gossiped about her, well then, the neighbours were jealous, maybe because she'd been out with a fair few of them in her time. But tonight she didn't want a battle. She replied to her son. 'Don't be so bloody rude, Brian. This is Mike and he's a good friend of mine, so watch your mouth, will you. Have some respect. I haven't brought you up to be so bleeding rude. You were brought up, not dragged up.'

Brian burst out laughing. 'What, another "good friend"? How many *friends* do you have?'

Zara went bright red. What on earth was he saying that for? He was going to make Mike run a thousand miles. She spoke in a calm voice and changed the subject quickly. 'What are you doing in early, anyway? I don't usually see you until the early hours?'

'I'm not staying in. I'm going back out. I just come in to get changed. I'm going into town, and they won't let me in any clubs if I'm wearing trainers.'

Zara let out a sigh of relief.

Mike saw his chance to break the ice and jumped into the conversation. He spoke to men like this every day, blokes who had attitude, inmates who held no respect for anyone. He handled them, he could handle this one. 'If you mention my name on the doors, most places will let you in for nothing. Just say your Mike Patterson's family and you should be alright. If not, phone your mam's phone and I'll have a word with whoever is on the door.'

Brian stared at Mike, a look that told him he thought he was big and daft enough to get in any club he wanted to and didn't need this old-timer sticking his beak in. Brian wasn't fazed. He held the look even while Zara was chewing her fingernails, wanting the ground to open and swallow her. She held her breath and was ready to jump up if Brian thought he could start a fight with her new fella. Then he turned on his heel, wobbled out of the living room and headed up the stairs. What a nightmare.

'I'm so sorry about him, Mike. He's an idiot when he's drunk. Honest, the times I've had to bail him out because of his mouth is unreal. He's going back out soon anyway, thank God.'

Mike seemed relaxed and there was no way he was getting off now when he'd had a taste of what was on offer. They both sat chatting, listening, waiting for Zara's son to go back out, waiting for privacy.

'See you later, Mam! Don't lock the front door, I've got no key,' Brian shouted as he slammed the main door shut.

Once Brian had left, Zara had already decided she'd be dragging this guy right upstairs and getting him in her bed and locking the door behind her. She was ready to pounce.

She jumped up from her seat and went straight to the window. Brian was gone. It was back to business.

———

Zara was having the time of her life. She'd underestimated Mike and he turned out to be a fun lover. He talked all the way through sex, making jokes and making her laugh. For Zara, that's how sex should be, fun. Not straight-faced and by the book. She felt glad her Pilates videos were paying off. Before she learned the art of stretching, her eagle position looked more like a dead pigeon. Now she was in the zone, she was bang on the money tonight. The reverse cowgirl was her favourite position, and she quickly took Mike over the edge with it. He was out of breath. Clearly he'd not had a session like this in a long time. Zara collapsed next to him and lay on his hot sweaty chest. He was still catching his breath and she knew she had worked her magic on him. Whatever happened next, she'd enjoyed herself – and she had no doubts he had too.

Mike tickled the back of her neck and whispered down to her, his hot breath turning her skin to goosebumps, 'That was amazing, honest. I haven't had sex like that before, not even when I was married.'

'Don't lie,' Zara giggled.

'No, honest. Me and the Mrs were young when we got married, and she was a big Catholic, and having sex was something she struggled with. Thought it was dirty, thought she would be judged by the big man in the sky when she went to meet her maker.'

'I just like to let loose. Well, that and to look after my man. Relationships are hard enough without sex being awkward too. I always make an effort. You have to, don't you? If I'm getting looked after, I like to return the favour. Don't get me wrong: when I was married, I threw the odd headache in and faked lots of orgasms but that's what us women do when we can't be arsed.'

Mike chuckled and his belly moved. 'What, women fake orgasms? I thought that was just a myth?'

'Is it 'eck. When us girls are tired and want to watch the TV, we know faking an orgasm is the fastest way forward. Watch this.' Zara lay on her back. Her back arched in the air and her toes curled as she pretended she was reaching climax. 'Oh Mike, you're so good, I'm so wet, give it me, oh give it me, don't stop, I'm going to come.'

Mike gave her a round of applause. She gave a performance that any leading lady would have been proud of.

'Bloody hell, that was mint. Eh, was the one I just give you fake or what?' He was watching her expressions, feeling that he could have been a flop in the bedroom.

'Oh, relax, Mike. You made me orgasm. I made sure of that! I'm just letting you know that women fake them, that's all.'

He let out a laboured breath and you could see he was proud of himself. He might not have had the biggest penis in the world, but he made up for that by making the effort.

'Light a fag up?' she asked him.

He reached down on the floor and pulled out his cigarettes and his lighter. 'Do you smoke in bed, then?'

Zara should have lied and told him no, but she nodded her head and told him the truth. 'Yes, I do. I know I shouldn't but sometimes, when I'm lay awake in the early hours, I can't be bothered going outside in the garden to have a quick puff. Plus, when you're on your own, you set the standards. My room, my rules.'

Mike lit two fags and passed her one. He couldn't take his eyes from her as he blew the grey cloud of smoke from his mouth. 'I would love to do all sorts to you, you know. I'm a bit kinky like that.'

Zara never flinched. She'd tried all sorts and knew that everyone had a 'thing' they liked. She smiled over at him and spoke openly. 'Tell me what you like in the bedroom, I mean what you really, really like, and maybe I can help make sex even better the next time.'

Mike hesitated. 'Maybe, when we know each other a bit better, darling. I like to keep some things about me under wraps for now. It makes me a bit mysterious if I don't tell you everything about me in one night.'

Zara smiled. Nothing he could tell her would make her blush. She had gone out with a guy once who liked to wear her underwear while they were having sex. At first, she thought it was funny but when he started turning up for dates wearing his own knickers and bra it was just too much. He had better underwear than her! She'd had guys with feet fetish, guys who liked to have sex in public places and men who made animal sounds when they were having sex. But, whatever they'd got up to, she never told a soul. That was her business, nobody else's. Keeping secrets was Zara's speciality.

Mike stubbed his cigarette out and rolled on his side, looking directly in her eyes. He used his fingers to move the strands of hair that had fallen on her cheekbone. 'I've had an amazing night, Zara. On my life, I can't stop smiling. I have a great feeling about you. When they say you know when you have met the one, I know what they are talking about now.'

Zara blushed slightly. This was heavy stuff for the first date and not something she expected to hear so soon. He was staring at her, waiting on her reply, so she stuttered, 'Fingers crossed then. And I'm glad you feel that way, it's a good sign.' Mike looked at her a lot longer than he should have, and she didn't know where to look. She had to talk, break the silence. 'So, I hope now we know each other a lot better my son will get some VIP treatment in the jail,' she chuckled.

Mike looked awkward – as if he'd been able to push aside the forbidden nature of their relationship until now. 'Tell you what, I will go and see him when I'm next in work. And don't you worry, I'm not going to be saying *Oi, I just slept with your mam* and shake his hand. I will take my time with him and get to know him before I tell him anything. The last thing I need in my job is an inmate having something over me. That's why we need to keep us a secret. I'd get the sack if the prison service got wind of us being in a relationship. They have rules and all that stuff we can't do because of our jobs. A ball-ache really, but it is what it is. You do understand, don't you?'

Zara was smiling. Did she really just hear him say they were in a relationship or what? This was music to her ears.

She snuggled deep into his chest and started to close her eyes. Having a man in her bed made her feel safe, took the pressure from her fears of someone booming her front door in.

Mike could see she was tired and moved her from his chest with a gentle movement. His voice was low. 'Babe, I have to go. I'll ring you in the morning and perhaps we can arrange something nice for us both.'

But Zara was already dead to the world and never replied. Mike slipped his jeans on and tied his shoelaces before dragging his shirt over his head. He stood over Zara and licked his lips. Mission completed.

Chapter Eleven

Jacob Watts walked down the garden path and kept his head low. He clocked the "Ring" doorbell straight away and knew this could be used in evidence against him. His hairy fingers pressed the large black button. A voice answered, 'Hello, can I help you?'

Jacob swallowed hard and put on his most respectable accent. 'Hiya love, yes you might be able to. I had my car stolen the other night and I noticed you have a "Ring" doorbell. I'm just wondering, can I have a peep at it and see if I can see anything on the evening it happened?'

The voice stopped and a young girl around eighteen years of age opened the door. Pretty thing she was, someone he would have been interested in if she'd have been a bit older. Long honey-blonde hair, big baby blue eyes. Jacob started to relax. He could tell by the way this girl spoke that she was from the streets.

'Yes, sorted. Just tell me when it was and I'll have a gander for you. Thieving pricks around here will take anything that moves. That's why my dad got the doorbell. Twice they've tried nicking our car. Scrotes they are, pricks who need to get a job and buy their own whips.'

Jacob smiled at the girl. He didn't want to stand at the door for long. Too many eyes around here for his liking. 'Do you want to jump in my car and show me? I'll leave the doors open, I'm not a sex pest or anything.'

The girl chuckled and patted her tracksuit bottoms. 'I'd stab you up if you laid a finger on me, bro. I always carry these days after being chased by some lads the other week from the tram stop. It's a good job I can run fast.'

Jacob started to walk down the garden path and she was following him – this was easier than he'd hoped. The young girl pulled out her mobile phone and sat in the passenger side. 'What night was it, how long ago?'

'Friday night, it was – but I think they've been hanging around before that. Just show me everything over the past weeks and I should be able to see something.'

The girl started to flick through the events from the last few days. She started laughing out loud and turned the screen towards Jacob. 'Ah, look at me steaming there. I only went out for a few drinks and ended up getting on it. Look, I can hardly stand up.'

Jacob was losing patience. He stuck his hand in his pocket and pulled out forty quid. 'Here, that's for helping me. Can I look through your phone myself? I know what I'm looking for.'

She took the money from his hand and secured it in her back pocket. 'Yeah, crack on.'

Jacob scrolled through the events from the day he was looking for. He made the screen larger as he clocked the first sign of the men who'd had him and his driver over. He reached into the glove compartment and opened his glasses case. He hated to let on, but he was blind as a bat without them and had recently been to the opticians to get his mincers sorted out. He studied the images. When he was sure, he stopped the video at just the right place where he could see a man's face full on. 'Bingo,' he whispered under his breath. 'Can you send me the footage from that time where I've stopped it?'

He passed the phone back to the girl and she scanned the screen before she started scrolling through the settings. 'I need your phone number if you want me to send it.'

Jacob hesitated, but needs must, and he needed to get this footage. He smiled at the girl and put her on the level. 'Right, you tell nobody about this, and I'll give you an extra ton. I will give you my number. Send the footage then delete my number and everything you have sent me. How does that sound to you?'

The girl was buzzing. All she could think about was the money he was giving her, nothing more, nothing less. The deed was done. She left the car and Jacob flicked the engine over and sped off. He had got what he needed, and he was smiling from cheek to cheek. Like candy from a baby. Heads were going to roll for sure. No one messed with Jacob Watts.

Later, Jacob sat with Tommy and Peter, and all three of them watched the footage. Tommy pointed at the screen, shouting at the top of his voice, 'I know who that prick is, it's fucking Rico Makin! His brother is a name in the Collyhurst area, but as far as I know he's just been banged up.'

Jacob narrowed his eyes. 'I want him fucked up. I want my money back and I don't care if I have to go through his front door to get it. I'll cut his dad, threaten his mam. Whatever it takes. Who the fuck does this guy think he is when he must know the money was something to do with me? Is he thick or what?'

Peter was still watching the screen. 'I can't make out who the other two are, bro. Big bastard this one is too. No wonder Les was traumatised. Fuck me, he proper lays into Les too, knockout blows, no messing about.'

Tommy punched Peter in the arm. 'We need to grip Rico. I'm sure once he meets us, he'll start talking. They always do when the drill comes out.'

Jacob sucked on his gums. 'I'm not arsed if he tells us everything he knows. I just want my cash back, then we can send a wake-up call. We need to send out a serious message to all these cronies in the area that we don't fuck about. So I want him in a body bag, made an example of. You know the script, Tommy lad. Take him where nobody can find him and leave him there to fucking rot.'

Tommy inhaled deeply, nostrils flaring. He had done this before. Peter stood up and jerked his head forward. 'So, when do you want this sorting?'

Jacob looked down at his shoes and cleaned a scuff mark from his new white trainers. 'I want this chancer found sooner rather than later. Find out where his yard is, who his family is and who his crew are. Not that I think he's got anyone in his corner we need to be worried about. I like to know who I'm dealing with, that's all.'

'Rico Makin, you're a marked man,' Tommy replied.

Chapter Twelve

Rico was due home in a couple of days and Zara had visited his money stash under the bed more times than she would like to admit. There was a gorgeous Gucci handbag she'd had her eye on forever – but it had always been a wild dream. She had never had that kind of money and had always made do with knock-offs ever since Max left. But now she couldn't resist buying it. She still thought Rico wouldn't notice and, if she was asked about the missing money, she would deny it, tell her son: how dare he accuse her of robbing him?

Zara sat with both hands around her coffee cup as Brian wobbled into the living room. He looked like death warmed up, grey skin, eyes barely open. There was something strange about the way he was walking too, shuffling along like an old man. Zara waited for him to sit down, walked over, and sat facing him. 'What's up with your legs? Have you been fighting again? I know what you're like when you've had a skinful. I bet you have been ballooning again, haven't you?'

Brian turned to face her slowly. His words seemed stuck behind his front teeth. Zara was concerned now. This wasn't a hangover, this was something more. Had he been on something serious? Taken something to make him act like this? She jumped up and sat down beside him, gripping his cold hands in hers. 'Brian, you don't look right, son. Have you taken something? Ket, Magic, pills, come on, tell me?' She knew there was all sorts available on every street corner round here, even knew her boys sold most of the weed, but she thought they all had the good sense to stay off the hard stuff.

Again, no words came from his mouth. Panic in her eyes, she shook his body softly, tried to get him to talk. 'Brian, stop fucking about, tell me what's wrong. Tell me what you have taken.'

Zara reached over for her handbag and fumbled about in it for her mobile phone. She rang 999 and pressed the phone firmly against her ear. 'Hello, it's my son, you need to send an ambulance, something is wrong with him, he's not talking and he's just staring at me like I'm not even here.' She listened to the woman on the other end of the line and screamed down the line at her. 'How the bleeding hell do I know? I'm not a fucking doctor, that's why I'm ringing you. He needs help and fast.' She ragged her fingers through her hair, stressed, voice trembling. 'Oh, I'm so sorry, love. I'm all over the place, I don't know if I'm coming or going. I need help, please just send an ambulance. Please make it quick, please.' Zara eventually gave out where she lived and all the details she needed to give regarding her son and his health conditions.

Once the call had ended, she went back to look at her son again. She opened his eyes with her thumb and her index finger and spoke to him again. 'Brian, it's your mam. Speak to me son, just let me know you are alright.' Still nothing, silence. Zara rang her friend Molly who only lived a few doors down from her and she was always there when something went wrong. Molly normally came over for a brew at least twice a week, but she'd been on holiday the last couple of weeks.

'Hello, Molly, it's Zara. It's our Brian, something is wrong with him. Can you pop in? I'm all over, I can't focus and I'm going out of my nut waiting for the ambulance.' The call ended and Zara went back to sit with her son. She tackled him again. 'Brian, tell me what happened, have you taken something?'

Brian moved about slightly and this time he got his words out. 'Balloons.'

Zara screwed her face up, not sure of what he'd said. 'Did you say balloons?'

He nodded his head.

'Balloons can't do this to you. What else have you taken?'

Brian shook his head and a single fat bulky tear started to roll down the side of his face. Zara remembered watching a TV programme about this bloody laughing gas and all the information came flooding back to her. There was a knocking at the door. Zara jumped up and ran into the hallway to open the door. 'Molly, come and look at him, he's not right. I've rang an ambulance, it's on its way.'

Molly had bright ginger hair and a round figure. She belonged to the travelling community, and she had been married to Duncan for over twenty years. Duncan had been a good-looking man in his day and Zara had a drunken night of passion with him many years ago. She regretted what she'd done straight away, like she always did, and begged Duncan not to say a word to anyone. He kept to his word, and she had carried on with her life like nothing had happened, but it lay like a sliver of ice in her friendship with Molly. She tried to forget about it – after all Zara was good at blanking out the mistakes she'd made in the name of love. But she always hated herself that little bit more when Molly came round, being a good friend, no longer raising the question of betrayal. Still, today, she was glad she was here. Molly sat down next to Brian, and he seemed to be coming around, moving more, mumbling.

Molly turned back to Zara with a concerned look. 'What's he said happened?'

'He just said balloons. I know he's dabbled in them before but, come on, everybody's on them and they can't do this to you, can they? It said on the TV a twenty second high, I think.'

Molly raised her eyebrows and sighed. 'I don't know what they do to you, but I know a lot of the kids on the estate are on 'em. I've seen bloody loads of them silver canisters all over the street. Mary's lad at number twelve is always sat in his car with his friends doing them. I've seen him loads of times.'

Zara got on her phone and started to google the damage these balloons could do to a person. As she started reading, her face dropped, the colour draining from her cheeks. 'Nitroxide it is that's in them. They can cause brain damage, nerve damage. And I was right, the high only lasts for twenty seconds too. And they are not illegal, technically. The government should bleeding tell the kids this then. They think it's "laughing gas", something that causes them no harm. It even sounds funny.'

Molly let out a breath. 'Well, look at your lad. It's no joke now, is it?'

Brian was coming around a bit more and he tried to talk. 'Mam, I can't feel my legs. Have I had a stroke or something?'

Molly stood facing him and remembered the ads she'd seen on the TV. FAST was the word she associated with someone having a stroke. All she had to do now was remember what it stood for. 'Oh, bloody hell, Zara, let me think now,' she walked up and down the front room, then closed her eyes for a few seconds. 'Face!' she shrieked. 'Face, arms, speech, and time. I knew, I knew what it was.'

Zara bent her knees and looked her son in the eyes. 'Brian, can you move your face?' She watched him with eager eyes. He forced a smile, his cheeks growing into two balls on each side of his face. 'Move your arms. See if you can move your arms.' He rolled his fingers in response and lifted each arm up at the side of him. Zara let out a sigh of relief. 'I don't think he's had a stroke. It must be them balloons wearing off now. It said on the internet that it can freeze the back of your throat, stop blood supplies to your brain.'

Molly plonked down on the sofa, crossed her legs and folded her arms. 'Well, that makes sense then, doesn't it? Hopefully, it's temporary and he'll be himself again soon.'

Zara made the sign of the cross across her body. 'Please God, let him be alright.'

Molly made the sign too. She attended church each Sunday with her family. In her home you could always spot a statue of the Virgin Mary and rosary beads placed in different areas of the house, and if now wasn't a time to ask a favour of Our Lady, she didn't know when was.

Zara heard a vehicle pulling up outside the house and ran to the front window, pulling the blinds back. 'Thank fuck for that, it seems like we've been waiting forever. Molly, you open the door and I'll stay here with Brian.' Zara sat next to her boy and held his hand. 'Brian, the medics are here now. They will sort you out. Don't worry, son, you are going to be alright.'

Molly stood behind the two paramedics and waited until they approached Brian before she moved forward too. Zara still held tight to her son's hand as she started to tell them what had happened. 'He came downstairs, and I noticed something was wrong with him straight away. He wasn't speaking before, but he's started to communicate bits in the last fifteen minutes. Is he going to be alright? He said he's had balloons, no other drugs, just balloons?'

The medics looked at each other and started doing a few tests, blood pressure, heart monitor. Molly placed a comforting arm around Zara. 'Let them do what they are doing. He's in the best hands now.'

Zara burst out crying, her emotions getting the best of her. She was a tough cookie to crack but when her boys were involved, she just crumbled. Her boys were her heart. If they hurt, so did she. She'd fight anyone to protect them – but how did you fight something as impossible as a drug addiction? In the past, when they were children, if anyone came knocking on her door telling her her boys had been misbehaving, she would defend them to the hilt – even though she knew they were no angels. She wouldn't let anyone but her say a bad word against them. Since Max had left, she had been mother and father to them. Which for her, had meant more than keeping them fed and clothed, loved and looked after. It had meant being prepared to fight anybody. She'd have knocked anybody's block off if she'd had to, though it hadn't come to that as her boys had learned to protect themselves at a young age. It wasn't that she wouldn't read them the riot act herself – when the front door had closed, she'd give out to them and even boot them up their backsides for being in trouble, but she would never let anybody else see that. What happened behind her door was her business, nobody else's. Zara had always classed herself as a fair parent. She never went over the top when Rico was found smoking weed. She sat him down and explained to him what the drug did and how it affected his mental health. Rico took this information on board and from that day he'd kicked that habit on the head. Well, that's what he told her, anyway. She'd wanted each one of her boys to follow their dreams – whatever they might be – but she knew that when they dreamt of money, selling weed was going to cash them faster than a zero-hours gig in some warehouse or cash-in-hand gigs. It wasn't the life she pictured for them, but it was the life they'd chosen, and she only wanted them to stay out of the heavy side of that world. And now, here was her baby getting wrecked on drugs – it was any mother's nightmare.

The medics spoke to each other in technical terms. Zara was chewing on her fingernails, and she kept looking over at Molly for any indications of what they were talking about.

'We are going to take Brian to the hospital for further checks, Mrs Makin,' they finally decided.

Zara folded in two, falling to her knees.

Molly was right behind her, comforting her. 'Come on, lovey, it's only a few more checks to make sure he's alright. Better safe than sorry, eh? They'd have blue-lighted him straight away if it was more serious.'

One of the medics went outside to get a wheelchair and the other stayed with Brian, telling him what was happening. Brian seemed to understand what was going on, but he was still not his usual self, fear in his eyes.

Zara grabbed her bag and her keys as they pushed Brian out through the front door. 'Molly, thanks as always, you're a life saver. Hopefully I'll be home soon, and we can have a drink and I'll tell you how it's all gone. I'll definitely be needing one, without a shadow of doubt.'

Molly gave a gentle smile. 'Go and do what you have to. Phone me if you need me. Now follow your boy – it doesn't matter how old they get, every child wants their mum in a crisis.'

Chapter Thirteen

Tyler lay on his bed and smiled at his new pad mate. He'd spoken with the screws on the landing and practically begged for them to move Smidge into his pad with him. He knew that behind prison walls you never got anything for free, and a deal had been struck. The screw he'd made the bargain with was an alright kind of guy in his eyes, as far as prison officers go. Paddy Thompson was not much older than Tyler and they seemed to get on. Tyler made him laugh, told him about a few of his antics on the outside, and even told him when he was a free man they would hook up for a few beers and a night out on the tiles. Paddy was as hench as Tyler, dark blue tattoos down both heavily muscled arms. Sleeves of memories of his life. Tyler had always wanted a sleeve but up to now he'd only had a Manchester United badge tattooed on his back. It had faded now, and he always hid it away. It was a dodgy tattoo he'd had done when he was away with the boys in Blackpool on one of his pals' stag nights. He'd wanted more body art, but he'd been too busy grafting to spend hours in the tattooist's chair.

Smidge twisted his body on his bed and folded the pillow under his head. 'Sorted, this pad is, mate. I swear you should have seen the one I was in across the landing. A right shithole it was, fucking stunk.'

Tyler chuckled and started to roll a cigarette. He wasn't a big smoker on the out but being locked behind his door for hours on end each day had driven him back to being a full-time smoker. He licked the Rizla and rolled the fag about in his fingers. 'I need to ring my mam later. All night I was belling her phone out and she never answered. I bet she was out on another fucking date. The woman will never learn, honest, I don't know why she doesn't stay single and have done with this dating lark.' He lit his roll-up and plonked down flat on his bed. 'It worries me you know, Smidge, I mean really worries me. Don't think I don't know what they say behind her back, because I do. And, between us, they're right. Every month it's a new guy, "the one", she tells me. Growing up wasn't much different, either. Once my dad had done one, she went off the rails, well, when she wasn't crying. I often wonder how it would have turned out if my dad had stayed with her. Would he still have been cheating? Would she still have been sleeping with men to get revenge? Some couples – it doesn't matter, love, kids, whatever – they're just not destined to go the distance. They say things happen for a reason, and I think the best thing my old man could have done was to leave because, in my eyes, it would have only got worse.'

Smidge stretched his arms over his head and yawned. 'Yes, I think the same too about my mam and dad. They are so different; I don't even know how they hooked up together. They are like chalk and cheese. My dad left when I was a bin-lid, and I wasn't arsed, to tell you the truth. He was a bad pisshead, and he wasn't shy of giving my old queen a few slaps when he was beered-up. I was only a nipper, but I still remember hearing her screaming through the bedroom walls. Our kid was older than me and he's told me stories that made me feel sick in the pit of my stomach, the way he battered him, whacked him with the belt, spat at him and all that shit. I think that's why our Neil is a bit of a loner. I think he has the PTS, you know, that post-traumatic thingy. If that useless waste of space of a dad had tried any of that shit when I was older, if he'd even threatened to lay a finger on me mam or brother, I'd have knocked him into next week. He used to think he was hard, but battering a woman or a kid? That makes you the ultimate coward in my eyes.'

Tyler sucked hard on his bifter and nodded his head slowly as he blew the smoke from his mouth. 'Too right, mate. Growing up, I didn't know a lot of kids who had dads living with them. I suppose it was the norm. I remember when I was in school and the class were supposed to be making Father's Day cards, and the teacher came over to me and could see I was sat there doing nothing, along with most of the class. I told her I didn't have a dad, and she looked at me as if I was a weirdo or something, and I can always remember what she said to me, even to this day. 'What, you have no dad? Everybody has a dad, Tyler. So make a card for him and stop messing about.' He closed his eyes as he continued telling his story, a hint of pain in his expression. 'A few other kids joined the conversation, and the teacher was horrified, especially when Donna Jones told her she was a bastard and she would never know her dad because her mam didn't even know his name. Honest, about two kids in our class had dads living with them, and that's when the teacher had to admit defeat and tell us all to make grandad or uncle cards, or anyone in the family we looked up to.'

Smidge burst out laughing. 'Jesus Christ, it's a messed up life sometimes, isn't it? Do you see your old man now or what?'

Tyler reached over, stubbed his cigarette out and spoke through gritted teeth. 'Nah, not seen him for years. I see his brother Ben and he told me my dad is out of the area still grafting. He's always been a grafter and my mam has told me stories about him and some of the things he used to get up to. He's ruthless, tapped in the head, my mam said. His game is armed robberies, big jobs, big cash. But he's a bad gambler. In one hand, out the other.'

Smidge was engrossed, wanted to know more. 'What, guns and all that?'

'Yep, big dough too. Ben said his last job was meant to set him up for life but, when you like to gamble, there's no such thing as money in the bank. It's all just another stake. Casinos, bookies, slots: Ben tells me he's addicted to them, and he always blows his money once he gets a good till.'

Smidge licked at his lips. 'Fool's game, gambling. You remember I had a bit of a thing for the roulette machines in the bookies' years ago, and I'd blow a grand in fucking seconds. I used to boot the machines, threaten to fucking smash the gaff up. It got a grip of me, mate, I'm not going to lie, but eh, I've not done it for a long time now. Sure I play cards for money with the lads, poker nights and all that, but I only take a set amount of money with me because I know I'd blow the fucking lot given half the chance.'

'I've never missed my old man – you can't miss what you've never really had, I guess. But being in here, it's made me think. I might go and see my dad when I get out, see what he's about and all that. I wonder if I'm like him. My mam said it's Rico who has his ways, a shady beggar and all that, and she tells me that I'm the better half of my dad's personality. She said I've got his charm too, because he loved the ladies, just like I do.'

Smidge squeezed his crotch. 'Fuck me, mate, no sex for years in this gaff. I just hope, when Becks comes on a visit, she lets me have a feel. A few of the lads have told me the best table to sit at for all that stuff on the visits. A couple of seats where the guards can't see what's happening. If I'm lucky, I might even get myself a hand job from her too, because, at the moment, all I'm thinking about is what I'm missing.'

Tyler burst out laughing. 'When I'm on the phone tonight, I'll be on Instagram and might hook myself up with a few girls. I've seen how it works on visit days – women coming in to see men they've clearly never met before.'

Keys jangled outside the cell door. Tyler shot a look over at Smidge. 'Eh up, what do these little Hitlers want now?'

All eyes were on the door when it opened. It was Paddy Thompson. He stepped inside the cell and kept looking over his shoulder, spooked. 'Guys, giving you the heads up. Patterson is on the wing and he's a right twat. Get your ships in order. He'll be spinning a few pads today so make sure he's not going to find anything in here.'

'Message received and understood, Paddy lad. And thanks for looking after us. We'll make sure you're taken care of on the outside for this.'

Paddy was already on his way out before Tyler hissed over to him back. 'Yo, Paddy lad, any chance you can stash a few bits for us if this fucking Patterson fella is on the prowl? As always, remember the favour…'

Paddy swallowed hard, knowing he could lose his job if he got caught, not sure what to say until Tyler spoke again. 'A couple of ton should see you right, is that alright?'

Paddy smirked. How could he say no to an offer like that? It was easy money. And it would only be for an hour or so. 'Yeah, give me ten minutes to see where the geezer is and I'll be back to grab whatever.'

'No worries, Paddy. You take your time.'

The door closed and the inmates shot a look at each other.

Smidge whispered, 'We need to make sure we keep on our toes. No room for mistakes. I don't want dragging down to the block and getting extra time flung on my back. It would finish me off.'

Tyler jumped up from his bed, went to the door and pressed his ear against it. Not a peep: there was an eerie silence on the landing. He stood with his back against the door and inhaled deeply. 'I've heard stories about this Patterson guy. A few of the lads have told me that he's the one to watch. He's stitched some of them up, had them shipped out and all that, so let's keep our heads down when he's about. Anyway, we have Paddy on our books now, so he can give us the heads up. We've got a big parcel coming in later today too. One of the smackheads has arranged a visit to have some sniff brought in. I've told him it's a good wage for him if he gets it in, so he'll do his best.'

'Nice one, that's what we need while we're locked up in this shithole, mate, a good wage. Becks is already on the blower telling me she needs this and needs that. It's times like this that I wish I had stashed more money away. I've got a few quid behind me, but nowhere enough to keep her in the life she was accustomed to when I was on the out. Fuck me, mate, she's got handbags there worth five grand and all that. I told her the other day she might have to sell a few of them, and you should have heard the abuse she fucking threw at me, telling me she'd never sell her handbags, no way in this world. It goes to show when you get a bird, a lot of them are only after your money. The next woman I get with, I'm telling them nothing about what I earn. Gonna tell them I work on a building site and get a shit salary. That should sort the gold-diggers out from the ones that actually care, shouldn't it?'

Tyler went and sat back on the edge of his bed. 'And that's why I'm single, mate. I don't mind paying for girls when we are out and that, but I'm not kitting them out with handbags and new tits and teeth. Our Rico is like that. I've told him time and time again about flashing his cash about, but he never listens, the muppet. That's why he'll always be skint.'

Smidge was silent, knowing he was in the same boat as Rico and he didn't have a leg to stand on.

'Rico is still away, my mam said,' Tyler continued. 'The kid is still not answering his phone. He better get his arse straight up here when he lands. He's getting told too, thinking he's living some kind of rap star life on my cash.'

His pad mate agreed. 'I said it before, and I'll say it again: I think you've dropped a bollock letting your kid manage our shit. The guy is a liability. I'm not slagging him off, but he's let you down so many times in the past. Look at all the trouble he's brought to our doors with the shady things he's done. The guy doesn't think before he does anything. Look at that time when Sully from Harpurhey came to your gaff ready to blow his knees off. It was lucky we smoothed him over, otherwise Rico would have been in a body bag. Sully is a fucking head-the-ball and he doesn't mess around. Rico doesn't respect the rules of the street, doesn't care whose patch he's on. It's a recipe for trouble, Ty.'

'Yeah, not going to argue with that, pal. Our kid was bang out of order and he knows it. Like you said, he doesn't think sometimes and leaves himself wide open. Hopefully, though, he learned from his mistakes and does us proud while we are behind bars. And he's family. I don't care what they say, blood is blood, and I'd rather a Makin be keeping things going than trusting some random to caretake our business. This could be just what he needs to prove himself.'

'Don't hold your breath, Tyler. I don't want to put the mockers on it, but I'm just waiting on the call telling us he's fucked up.'

Tyler was getting angry: this was his fam they were talking about. He could slag Rico off all day long, but there was no way in this world anyone else could. He snarled at Smidge, reminding him who he was and what he was capable of doing. He'd had a few squabbles with Smidge in the past and had put him on his arse a good few times to remind him he was the boss.

'Rico will do what I tell him to do. Up to now he's collected the money, and everything is spinning over nicely so, until he fucks up, keep your mouth shut and let him do his thing. Rico won't let me down. He pleaded with me to run our shit, to show us how much he's changed, and there is no way he would let us lose everything we have grafted our balls off for with silly fucking mistakes.'

Smidge held his two palms up in the air. He knew Tyler's back was up and changed the subject. 'Fuck me, what time are we getting out of here today? It's half twelve. We should have been out half an hour ago.'

Tyler shook his head and picked up the newspaper, trying to calm down. Once his temper got the better of him, it took him ages to slow his heartbeat down and become normal again. 'Just chill ya beans. Relax bro, they'll let us out when they are ready. You have to remember these pricks owe us nothing. Some of them buzz from seeing us locked behind our doors. It's a them and us game in this nick and, for now, when they say jump, we say how high.'

Smidge sneered over at his pad mate and scratched the top of his head. He hated bang-up and, if he was being honest with himself, he wasn't coping well. Of course, he never told anyone that. He wasn't letting anyone see his weakness, not this big hard man he made out to be.

———

When they were finally let out, Tyler clocked Patterson on the landing and gave him a wide berth. He headed straight down the stairs, no eye contact. Smidge was tucked behind him and they could hear Rhino shouting from the bottom of the stairs. It was dinner time and most of the inmates were out of their pads to get some scran. Paddy was stood with his back to the wall as Tyler slipped him the contraband. Nobody saw a thing, Smidge making sure he'd covered anyone's view. A quick wink and Tyler was walking to the canteen to get some scran too. Simple pleasures.

Already his name meant something in the jail. News travels fast in places like Strangeways. Big Sam and his boys had been shipped out to a different wing and a few big names from other landings were intrigued as to who this new name was. Tyler was aware he was being watched as he walked into the canteen area. He could sense the air had changed. Rhino and Smidge at either side of him, protecting him, making sure nobody got a cheeky blow at him when he wasn't looking. That's how it worked on the outside and this was how it was working inside. Smidge covered his mouth with open fingers and kept his voice low. 'Eyes to the left, Philip Guy from Blackley, sat with Brendan Sykes. Double fucking trouble if you ask me, mate.'

Tyler never flinched, his ears pinned back, and his nostrils flared slightly as he carried on walking to the queue. Rhino twisted his head back and caught Brendan's eye. The two of them had had run-ins on the outside and he stared back letting him know he'd clocked him.

'He's a cocky bastard, that one is,' Rhino hissed. 'On my life, one word to me and he'll be on his arse. Nil by mouth.'

Tyler never looked back, cool as a cucumber. 'Wind your neck in and keep your eyes and ears open. If them two think they can play games, then so can we. You're right though – if anyone is going to make a move now we've put Big Sam out of the game, it'll be them two. But I've got it covered. Smidge, get Wade Perkins over there in for a chat as soon as. He's from down our ways and it would be good to team up with him. He's a top lad, met him a few times before and had a few drinks with him, so he shouldn't be a problem. He'll have our backs over Brendan and his lot.'

Smidge was all over the show, eyes one way then eyes the other. 'Yeah, soon as I spot him, I'll sort it.' He knew everyone in here needed a network of men to rely on – reputation alone was never enough, you had to back it up.

The lads got their food from the hatch and sat down. The noise was deafening: laughing, shouting, pots and pans clashing together. Rhino looked down at his food and screwed his face up. 'I wouldn't feed this to my dog. Look at it, mush it is, sloppy potatoes, and veg that has had the life boiled out of it.'

'Get it down ya grid, man, and stop moaning,' chuckled Tyler.

'Nah, I can't eat this shit. What I wouldn't give now for a big fat kebab on a naan bread and hot sauce.'

Smidge joined in the conversation. 'A big cheese and tomato deep pan pizza and chips and garlic bread would go down a treat too, I'm not going to lie.'

Tyler looked at them both and rolled his eyes. 'Wow, will you two turn it in? The food in here is something we are going to have to get used to. Give it a few more months and, if we play our cards right, we might get some decent food brought in.'

Rhino was like a small child and gripped Tyler's arm. 'Promise me, please tell me you can get me a kebab?' Rhino had always been a foodie and loved eating. He said his palate was second to none and if food was crap, he would say it was crap. Even when he was in a restaurant, he would shout the manager over and tell them about the food. He was always complaining about his grub if it wasn't up to much. But, in his defence, he went to the top places to eat in Manchester, knew his stuff. No wonder he didn't want to eat this mess they served up in here.

Wade Perkins entered the canteen and Smidge was straight on him, pulled him to the side and whispered a few words down his lughole. But he was being watched. Eager eyes were all over him, so he had to keep it short and sweet. He bounced back to his seat and the corner of his mouth started to rise. 'Sorted, he'll be over soon, he said. Oi, I didn't know he had half his ear missing? I just clocked it when I was speaking to him. He needs that sorting out, nearly made me sick.'

Rhino filled Smidge in. He knew the story, had heard it a few times when he was with the lads down the boozer. 'It was a kid from out of town. He'd come down with a few of his boys and tried to tax Wade. He macheted him on the sly and took his ear off.'

Smidge's eyes were wide open, always up for a new bit of gangland gossip.

'Wade destroyed the kid in the end and cut both of his ears off. Forget an eye for an eye! He was showing them off in the boozer in a small box. One even had the lad's earring still in it. He's not a force to be messed with. He's off the map when his cage is rattled.'

Tyler seemed to be getting the green-eyed monster. He was a name too: were they forgetting that? What about the time he macheted four men in a boozer? Ran in and swung the blade about, making sure each of them was sliced at the same time? He slammed his flat palm on the table and eyeballed his wingmen. 'Shut up waffling about this and that, bigging every bastard up. We can manage whatever comes our way in this jail. It's just nice to know, if I need heads, I can call some favours in. I'm aware, as you lot are, what Brendan and Philip are like. I do my homework and I know what I'm up against. Does this face look one bit bothered?' He never gave them chance to answer. 'Does it fuck, so go about your business and let me do what I do and earn us all some money.'

Enough said. Rhino dropped his head low and poked his fork into his food, eating unidentifiable bits of this and bits of that. Smidge, on the other hand, was sulking, a look that told you he didn't like the way he'd been spoken to. Resentment grew easily in a place like this.

Tyler shoved his tray forward and sat back in his seat. He had clocked every person sat in the room and made a mental note of who he could count on and who he had to watch. He stood up and headed to have a game of pool. Something to take his mind off everything. As he walked through the door, he found himself slap bang in front of Patterson and their eyes met.

'So, you're the big man on the wing now, I hear?'

Tyler screwed his face up and stepped back. If this prick wanted beef, then so be it, there was no backing off. 'You've heard wrong. I keep myself to myself, me. I just want to do my time and go home.'

Patterson's voice changed, friendly. 'I've read your file and I know you won't give us any trouble. If you don't spin out, I hope we can be friends. After all, you're going to be here for a few years yet, aren't you?'

Tyler was confused. He'd been ready to square up to this guy and now he was being all nicey-nicey. Friends? Nah, no screw was ever, ever going to be on his friends list. The inmates would have disowned him, called him a sell-out. Tyler never replied, just dodged where the screw was and headed towards the pool table. He was telling nobody about it, embarrassed that a screw would even say that to him. Tyler nodded his head at the two inmates playing pool and that was enough to let them know their game was over. There were a few balls left on the table and Tyler let them finish the game. If he would have been in a bad mood, he would have pushed each remaining ball into the pockets and snatched the cue from them, just like when he was in the pub back home. He never waited for his turn usually: he was number one. But it wasn't like he was short of time in here, so he sat down and shot a look back over at Patterson. He was a strange one, he was, and he gave Tyler an uneasy feeling in the pit of his stomach, the way he looked at him. Tyler passed the other cue to Wade Perkins who'd wandered over, and the two of them set the balls up. They didn't need any big meeting room to talk, they could do it here. Rhino and Smidge moved inmates from the area and made sure nobody could hear what these two men were discussing.

Wade shook Tyler's hand, and the game began. 'So, Tyler, I guess you need a bit of back-up? I guess that it's Brendan and Philip you're watching?'

Tyler nodded his head. 'How did you know?'

'Pricks tried the same thing on me last month. Come to my wing, boomed my door in and tried fucking launching boiling sugar and water on me. I was two steps in front though and had my boys all over them in seconds. Check Brendan's face when you next see him. I sliced the twat up. He couldn't get away fast enough. They think they can take the piss when they should do what they are doing on their wings and keep away from our end. It's all about greed, pal. We're all in the same boat in here and there is enough graft to go around. Greedy pricks, that's all they are. Fucking muppets.'

It was Tyler's turn to take his shot. He lined the cue up and the ball slowly rolled into the pocket just like he'd planned. He lifted his head up and smirked at Wade. 'So, do

I wait for them to come to me or fucking Shanghai surprise them when they least expect it?'

'Your fight, your choice, mate. But, for me, it's strike while the iron is hot. I'll come with you. We can take them both down that way and throw our lads on their landing, earning us a crust. It's a dog-eat-dog world in here. Only the strongest survive. I'm game as fuck, mate.'

Tyler licked his lips and looked over at Rhino and Smidge. Was it too soon to strike? After all, Brendan and Philip had never said a word to him yet, though anyone could see they had eyes on his turf. But there was a chance to do more than defend it - the pound signs were already flashing in his eyes: more cash, more money to be sent home for his stash. And he didn't fancy waiting around until they gave him the boiling sugar and water treatment. Wade was right, it was all about greed, about lining your pockets. But only fools rush in and Tyler knew that more than anyone. If he was taking these two men down, then it needed careful planning. He jerked his head over at Wade. 'Nice to know you have my back and I'll remember this if you ever need a bit of man-power. I'll give you a shout if I need you.'

And that was how simple it was. No paperwork, no long telephone conversations in the boardroom. In this world, a handshake was all that it took to strike a deal. Wade finished the game of pool and walked back to his own crew. It was up to Tyler now to set the wheels in motion.

Chapter Fourteen

Zara had been at the hospital for hours and she was waiting for a taxi to pick her up and take her home. Brian had been kept in for more tests, but the doctor had spoken to her and told her he suspected it was nerve damage caused by the nitrous oxide he'd been inhaling. It could take months for her son to walk again, he'd told her. And, until the brain scan came back, he didn't know how much damage had been caused to his brain cells. Her head was all over the place. Her eyes were red and puffy, like she'd peeled ten onions.

She sucked hard on her cigarette and fumbled about in her handbag for her mobile phone. She'd had it on silent and hadn't had time to look at it once while she'd been in the hospital. Text alerts started to come through, one, two, three, four, five, one after the other. Her eyes squinted as she read through the messages. They were all from Mike. Nice messages about how much he'd enjoyed their date, messages asking her if she was free tonight for another date. Zara wasn't in the right head space to reply. Instead she rammed her phone back into her bag and carried on smoking.

———

Hours later, Zara finally sat drinking a glass of wine back at home. The music was on low, and Molly sat with her, listening to her problems. 'What if he can never walk again? What will he do? He'll never cope with that. He's already told me, if he can't walk again, he will end it all.'

Molly swallowed hard and her eyes clouded over. She'd known Brian since a small child. He'd even played with her children when they were all growing up; he was like one of her own. 'You have to wait for the tests to come back. Nothing is set in stone until the results are right there in front of you. I'm a positive person and I believe the outcome will be good. I just hope, if he recovers, he will never, ever put one of them bleeding balloons in his mouth again. This should be enough for anyone else who's sucking on them to bin them off. I've already told my lads about Bri, and they can't believe it. I could tell by their faces that they've had a go of them too. I wanted to scare the life out of them telling them it causes brain damage and all that.'

'You're right, Molly, I need to keep a positive mindset. Honest, I feel so drained, my heart has been in my mouth all bleeding day. I thought things couldn't get any tougher than watching Tyler get sent down, and now this? I tell you it's testing me. I left Brian sleeping. He needs lots of rest, the doctor said, because if it's the worst outcome, he's going to need all his strength to learn to walk again.'

'Have you told Tyler and Rico yet?'

'No, I've had a few missed calls from Tyler, but I'll speak to him later when I'm more settled. You never know when Ty is going to get chance to use his phone without being seen, but I swear to you he's easier to get hold of now than he was when he was walking free.'

Molly raised her eyebrows. 'And Rico, have you spoke with him?'

'No, he's too busy soaking up the sun and enjoying himself to even think about us lot at home. All he cares about is that Clara and what he can buy her. On my life, why can't he see through her and see she's only out for what she can get from him? Between us two, she used to have a thing with our Tyler. He said she's only with Rico to be near him. It makes sense, doesn't it.'

Molly had covered her mouth with her hand and her eyes widened. 'Shut the front door,' she shrieked. 'Bloody hell, if Rico got wind of that, he would go ballistic. He idolises that bloody girl. You can see he is smitten by her.' She made the sign of the cross. 'When it rains in this house, it bloody pours.' There was a silence before Molly spoke again. 'Are you letting his dad know what's happened? I know you don't have any results yet but if it's bad news he will need to know. After all, he is his son too.'

Zara nearly choked on her drink, her cheeks beetroot. 'He can fuck right off. Since when have I ever needed that twat to help me with the boys? That prick is dead in my eyes, might as well be six feet under.'

Molly knew when to keep her mouth shut and this was one of those moments.

Zara kept looking at the clock and sighed. 'Bloody hell, I better get a bit of slap on before Mike comes. He'd run a mile if he saw me like this.'

Molly stood up and pulled her cardigan tighter around her: she could take a hint. 'Right, I will get going and let you get ready. I'm here if you need me.'

Zara stood up and gave Molly a great big hug. 'You're always here for me, Moll, I'll never forget that.' Zara walked her neighbour to the front door and said goodbye. The second the door was closed she ran upstairs and into the bathroom. Mike had been really supportive when she told him what had happened with Brian – not judgemental or cold. He'd seemed genuinely concerned. And when he'd offered to keep her company and try to cheer her up while Brian recovered, she knew it was just what she needed. Trying to be the strong one all the time was wearing – sometimes, Zara wanted someone to lean on too.

Chapter Fifteen

Mike walked into the living room and smiled. He was holding a bottle of red wine in one hand and a bunch of flowers in the other. What a guy, Zara thought. She blushed slightly, walked over to him and pecked him on the cheek with her warm red lips. 'I'll get a couple of glasses. On my life, I've had the worst day.'

Mike sat down and looked about the front room. He'd been here before, but he'd not really noticed how nice this place was. The last time he was there, he'd only had one thing on his mind. But, taking in the place properly, he saw that the living room was cosy: grey velvet sofa, thick silver carpet, and hints of pink in the wallpaper. It was clear Zara was a woman who took care over her home. It was nothing like his gaff which needed a woman's touch, a good cleaning, a bit of warmth.

Zara was back, glasses clinking in her hands. She sat down next to him, eager to crack open the wine. She needed something to help her relax, get her mind off her stress. She was in the mood for romance. She reached over for the TV remote and turned it down. 'So our Brian got rushed into hospital this morning. He's my youngest and he was out last night, on them balloons.'

Mike was listening, concerned. 'I hope he's alright? Have you had any more news from the ward?'

Zara dropped her head as she poured two large glasses of wine. 'The doctor is running some tests. They don't know if he will be able to walk again, or if there is any brain damage.' Her voice broke with emotion as she got through the full details.

Mike placed his warm hand on her shoulder. 'He'll be fine. These doctors are amazing at what they do. They wouldn't have sent you home if they thought it was touch and go.'

Zara lifted her drink and took a large mouthful. 'I hope so, I bloody hope so.' Her mobile phone started ringing and she glanced at the screen before she clutched it in her hand. 'One minute, it's Tyler. I need to speak with him.'

Mike clocked that it was a mobile number flashing on the screen – not an approved prison call. Zara went into the kitchen and Mike held his ear to the door, making sure he heard everything.

'Hiya son, sorry I've not been answering. I've been at the hospital with Brian all morning. He's had some kind of an attack after sucking on them balloons.' Zara held the mobile away from her ear as Tyler shouted down the phone. 'Calm down, I know you warned him about them just like we all have. The doctors don't know if he will have any lasting damage or if he will be able to walk again. You said it was harmless fun, we thought they were safe.' There was a silence on the call and Zara had to ask Tyler if he was still there. 'It's early days, Tyler. And the doctors are doing all they can. Just say a prayer that he will be alright.' Tyler was doing all the talking now and Zara was the one who was listening. 'Rico? No. He's home tomorrow night, I think. He's not called home, ignoring my texts, so I've not even told him about Brian yet.' Tyler's voice was raised again, and she closed her eyes as his voice drilled her ears. 'Just give me a few days to get my head around everything and I'll be up to see you again. Just relax and don't be getting stressed out. The last thing I need is you getting in more trouble.'

After a few more minutes, the phone call ended, and Zara stood with her back resting against the door. Three deep breaths and she made her way back into the living room, her happy face on. She smiled over at Mike. Yes, he was doing all the right things, but she couldn't let her guard down fully yet. 'I thought these lads of mine would have all been settled down by now and married, but they are more trouble now than when they were bloody children.'

Mike patted the seat next to him. He could see she was in need of a hug. He waited for her to sit down and kissed the top of her head. 'Everything will be fine, and I'm here now to support you.'

'Our Tyler is going off his head. He hates it when he has no control over things. He sees himself as the protector of us all. Since his dad pissed off, he felt he had to step up, I think. He'd never admit it, but he did. Even with me, he thinks he can solve everything. There was a time when he was only sixteen and I got myself into a bit of a mess with the loan sharks who used to come around the estate. When I was a bit short one week they were putting pressure on me at the front door, telling me they would be coming in the house next time and taking my telly and all that.' She hung her head in shame, remembering how hard times were back then. 'Our Tyler must have heard them and came sprinting down the stairs. He gripped the man by the scruff of his neck and flung him right down the garden path. Honest, the strength in that lad is unbelievable. He shouted me to go back in the house. Whatever he said to the loan man, he never came back to my door again.'

Mike was engrossed in the story. 'Yeah, he looks like he can handle himself. I met him on the landing today and introduced myself. Before you start going wild, I never told him who I was or that I was seeing you – if that's what we're calling this.'

Zara gasped, afraid Mike was going to let the cat out of the bag before she'd had chance to tell her son all about her new man. Of course, he knew she had her eye on one of the staff there at the prison but, as far as he knew, it was all on the backburner.

They were two glasses of wine in, and Mike had kicked his shoes off and started to make himself comfortable. They were both swapping life stories. It was Zara's turn now to find out a bit more about her new lover. 'So, I know you were married. Tell me a bit more about your ex and how your marriage ended? I mean, you know enough of my secrets already.'

Mike swallowed hard, fidgeted, making no eye contact. 'It's not something I like talking about, to be honest. The woman turned out to be a right piece of work in the end and, if I never see her again in my life, it wouldn't bother me. I thought when I married her we were soul mates, you know. We liked the same kind of stuff, wanted the same things and all that, but she had me over. One minute she was all over me and the next it was like she'd turned into a nun. Sex was every six months if I was lucky and, even then, it was only a quick leg-over. I'm a man and I had urges, but every time I touched her, she cringed and told me she had a headache. I kept asking her what was wrong, if there was something on her mind, but she shut me out.'

Zara fluttered her eyelashes and fanned her red-glossed nails out in front of her. 'Sex is a big part of any relationship and once that goes down the Swanee it's often game over. I've always enjoyed sex. I mean with the right guy sex can be amazing.'

Mike blushed. 'I thought it was all over for me. I'd never find that spark again. But the moment I clocked you in the prison I was instantly attracted to you and that's why I had to get your number. Honest, I saw you and knew right then you were special.'

Zara was impressed that she still had that pulling power with the men. At the age of fifty-two, she was starting to think that maybe she was going to be alone for the rest of her life, without a man who loved her, but looking at Mike the game wasn't over yet.

Mike coughed. 'So, tell me about the lads' dad. Were they all with your ex-husband?'

Zara needed more wine and a fag if she was going to talk about her ex. She sat up, reached over for her cigarettes and passed Mike one. With a quick flick of the lighter she was ready to talk. 'Max was my world, my happy ever after, or so I thought. We met when we were young, and he was the Yin to my Yang, so to speak. When they used to say love at first sight, I never believed it but, if I close my eyes, I can still remember the first time I ever saw Max. He took my breath away, made my heart beat faster.'

Mike sucked hard on his fag

'I never made the first move though, Mike.' Her eyes were alive with the memory. 'No, I played it cool and never approached him. I knew when I was on the dance floor he was watching me and within minutes he gripped me by the waist and started spinning me around. I think once our eyes met for the first time, we both knew this was special. And I suppose the rest is history. We were inseparable from that moment on. He virtually moved into my mam's house and all my family loved him. Max was a big character, and you always felt his presence when he was in the room. He oozed confidence.'

Mike was fed up already hearing about this bloody Prince Charming and looked sorry that he asked. 'So, how did the fairy tale go wrong?' He needed to get her to remember the hurt, the pain this man had caused her instead of remembering all the good things.

'He hurt me so bad, Mike. My world fell apart when I found him in bed with my best friend.' Zara rubbed her hand up her windpipe and licked her lips frantically. 'It was sad that he would risk everything we had for a woman who'd had more nob ends than weekends. I wished he would have begged me to have him back, tried harder to beg for forgiveness, but he never did. I wasn't worth fighting for in his eyes.'

Mike was straight in with a reply. This was his time to shine, a chance to put his name on the map. 'His loss is my gain.'

Zara was still in her memories of Max and didn't respond. 'I often wonder what he looks like now, how I would react if I ever saw him. For years I told myself that I would spit in his eye and say nothing, but there is a lot of things that were left unsaid, answers I never got.'

Mike held his head to one side. 'But the guy is a cheat. Shagging your best friend is the ultimate sin. He never deserved you, otherwise why did he stray?'

Zara was back in the moment now and she bit down hard on her bottom lip. Mike was right, Max was a wanker, and the more she told herself that, the less she would still crave his touch, miss his voice when she was alone in bed each night. She was sure seeing Ben had stirred it all up.

Mike took his chance and went in for a hot steamy kiss, his hands in her hair, his touch firm. He whispered into her ear, 'Get up the stairs. I want to feel myself inside you.'

Zara smiled. He said it how it was, just like her Max had. And, in a way, that was one of the main reasons she was attracted to him: his confidence and his directness. She came alive when she felt wanted, felt she could let her own desires rise to the surface.

Mike ravished every inch of Zara's body. This time, she let him be the one in control. He whispered sweet nothings into her ear, then let out his real desires. 'Where are those handcuffs you told me about?'

Zara rolled over on her side and reached into her bedside cabinet. This was where she kept all her private stuff. She had all sorts in this drawer, vibrators and an array of sex toys. Mike went straight for the handcuffs and his eyes seemed like they were dancing with madness from the second the cold metal touched his hands. Zara had a moment's doubt – was this the real reason he was a prison guard? Was control his thing? She realised they hadn't agreed a safe word.

He clipped them open and placed them around her slim wrist. Within seconds, he had her handcuffed to the bed. Now he had to secure her legs, make sure she couldn't move a muscle. Zara reminded herself that they were two consenting adults. She'd done all this before and enjoyed testing her boundaries.

'Close your eyes, enjoy,' he whispered. Zara was gagged now, and Mike stood over her. From the drawer, he pulled out the long leather whip. Zara flinched as she saw his eyes held anger now and he let the leather leash connect in a way that felt like he wanted more. Zara was wriggling about on the bed, her eyes wide open, shaking her head, trying to move her body. Starting at the bottom of her legs Mike started to lick her body, biting hard, biting soft, all the way until he got to her mouth.

'You like that, don't you?'

Zara froze, surely, he must know this wasn't pleasurable anymore. He inserted his member inside her and held her hands as she lay there motionless. He didn't take long; he reached climax in seconds. Zara remained still, waiting on him to release her. He stroked a single finger down her cheek and pulled the gag out of her mouth.

'Get them bleeding handcuffs off me and untie my legs. What the hell are you playing at? I thought you meant a bit of gentle fun. I'm not into shit like that. You're a bloody idiot, freak. What happened to a safe word? My body is burning everywhere. Untie me now.'

Zara was untied and ran straight into the bathroom. She was upset and tears rolled down her cheeks. Standing in front of the bathroom mirror, she examined her body. No, no way she was into anything like this and, if he was, it was never going to work. She picked up a tissue and dried her eyes. This dickhead was getting told: who on earth did he think he was? Christian bleeding Grey?

Mike was laying on the bed and smiled at Zara when she came back into the bedroom. She went straight to the drawers and pulled a cigarette from the packet. Her hands were shaking, and her heart racing.

She sat down next to Mike and looked him straight in the eyes. 'I'll tell you now, don't ever, ever do that to me again. What you just did was on another level. I'm open-minded during sex, but I'm not into getting punished like that. Because that's what it felt like, like you were punishing me. It wasn't one bit sexy. It was sick and twisted.'

Mike pulled a fag out of the packet too and lit it. 'I'm sorry if it was a bit much. I thought you loved it when you let me put the cuffs on. I thought you were turned on by it?'

'Well, think again, Mike. I'm covered in marks all over my body.'

He shot a look over at her body and pulled her back onto the bed. 'You're so gorgeous, I got carried away.'

Zara didn't know what to make of this situation. She'd been handcuffed before and it was nothing like this. It had been enjoyable, sexy, even kinky, not painful. It had been about trust not about power. But she'd told him she was up for anything; told him she enjoyed sex. Had she misjudged things? Did other people think this was normal? Mike didn't seem bothered by it all. He lay on the bed, enjoying his cigarette. She started to doubt herself.

Mike watched her stub her cigarette out and pulled her nearer. Her skin was touching his and he stroked his hand along her forehead. 'If it's something you don't like, then I will never do it again. I thought you were open to anything, that's all?'

She opened her eyes wide and replied, 'I am, but that hurt. It was like you were in a world of your own and I was just a piece of meat to you. I like to be seduced, caressed, to feel loved.' She knew she could either tell him to leave forever, or give him one more chance to earn her trust, and if she needed eyes on the inside of Strangeways, maybe she would have to find a way through this. 'Mike, I would hate for us to lose what we could have over a misunderstanding. We need a safe word before we do anything like this again. And now I know what you like, maybe next time you can be the one who gets handcuffed and I can be the one whipping you?'

Mike sat up with speed. 'No, I have to be the one in control, otherwise it's not a turn-on.'

She sat back and watched him from the corner of her eye. 'What's with the control? Why do you need control of me? Am I that dangerous?'

He fidgeted. 'Zara, stop trying to be my bleeding therapist. It's sex, everyone's got a different turn-on. But if you're not into it like that, then no problem. It won't happen again.'

Zara stood up. She didn't know what to make of this guy – was he the caring, bring-you-flowers guy who'd shown up to support her earlier, or was he getting off on power games? She was determined to find out, but one thing was for certain: she was never letting him dominate her again. She was Zara Makin, she told herself, and no one was going to hold her down.

Chapter Sixteen

Jacob Watts stared over at Eastford Square in Collyhurst. It was busy today and the shoppers were out in full force. Despite it being near his patch, he'd only been a few times. He turned to Peter and jerked his head. 'So, tell me more about this Rico guy.'

Peter wound the window down and let some fresh air inside the car. Over an hour they had been waiting here and up to now they'd not moved. He kept his eyes on the square and started to speak. 'Tyler Makin's younger brother, I'm told. Bit of a hot-head and fancies himself as a bit of a fighter.'

'Tyler Makin,' Jacob mused. 'That name rings a bell.'

Tommy jumped into the conversation and leaned in from the back seat of the car. 'I've done business with him a few times. Tyler is a sorted guy. He works his patch well, respects the lines. He's just been banged up with a few of his boys for class A stuff, though, so I guess there's a vacancy at the top.'

'So, what's the crack with this chancer, then? Surely, he must have known it was our stuff. Come on, you don't piss on your own doorstep, do you?'

Peter nodded his head. 'Exactly. This muppet is getting chopped up. Does he think he can just go around taxing people without doing his fucking homework? Nobody works like that unless they want beef.'

Jacob played with his fingers. 'So, once we see one of his boys on here, we'll be all over it. Rico's back from his jollies today, I hear, but before we get a grip of him, I want to know what his boys know. Once we hold a gun to their head, they will start singing like a fucking budgie. I like to know what's what before I make my move. No one has me over and, when we get our hands on this Rico prick, we'll make an example of him so all these clowns around here know what will happen if they step on our toes.'

Tommy agreed. 'Maybe, we should have a chat with Tyler first. Give him chance to try and get our cash back because, let's fucking face it, there is still missing money here, our fucking wages.'

Peter agreed. 'Tommy is right, what are we going to get out of twisting this prick up without thinking of payday? I want the cash back. Let's at least speak to the older brother and see if he can sort it out. If he can't then the fucking full family will get it. On my life, the lot of them will be wiped out.'

Jacob smashed his flat palm onto the dashboard, fuming, frustrated that this Rico kid had not showed his ugly face yet. He was ready to rumble and since his money had been taken, he'd not slept properly. He didn't like the feeling that someone was coming for his territory, and he wouldn't get any peace until he'd hit back.

Peter pulled his mobile phone out of his pocket and scrolled through his contact names. He stopped at the name Pike. 'This kid is in the same nick as Tyler and his lads. I'll give him the heads up on it all and get word to Tyler to get in touch with us.'

It was all a waiting game now. Tick tock, tick tock. But Jacob and his boys knew well enough: most countdowns ended in an explosion.

Chapter Seventeen

Rico left his suitcase in the hallway and shouted into the front room, 'Mam, I'm home, where are you?'

Zara heard her son's voice and jumped up from the sofa, excited that he'd made it home safe and in one piece. 'I'm in here.'

Rico opened the door and stood smiling from cheek to cheek. Bloody hell, he looked like he'd been living his best life – tanned, toned and happy as Larry.

He held his arms out towards her and she ran into them. 'Rico, why on earth have you not been phoning me? I've tried for days to get in touch with you, but nothing. Tyler is going ballistic too. He's been trying you around the clock. We needed to get in touch with you.'

Rico stepped back and looked at his mother. Two minutes he'd been home and already she was stressing him out. 'Mam, I've been on my jollies with Clara. I wanted a nice break without any mither. What is so important that you needed to speak to me?'

Zara plonked down on the sofa and curled her legs up beneath her, fed up. 'It's Brian. He's in hospital. He had a funny turn on them daft balloons and now the doctors are saying he might not be able to walk again. He could even have brain damage. Which you'd have known if you'd answered a single call or text.'

Rico went white, colour draining from his skin. His words seemed stuck behind his teeth. 'Whoa, what, just from balloons? They can't do nothing to you like that. It's just a quick buzz you get from them, that's all. He must have been on some serious other shit as well.'

Zara was right back at him. 'No. That's what your kid brother thought and look where he is now? This is serious, Rico. If he can't walk again, what then? Go on, tell me that?'

'Which hospital is he in? I'm going up to see him.'

'North Manchester General. He's meant to have been sent home by now but there's always another test they want to run, it seems. And you wouldn't know because you don't answer your bleeding phone.'

'Do me a favour, Mam, and stop moaning. I've only just walked through the front door and you're down my neck.'

'What do you expect? Your big brother is banged up and your little brother is in the hospital in a bad way, and I can't get hold of you, and you call that moaning? Get a grip, lad, and see where I am coming from.'

'Just let me think for a minute, woman. Where did all this happen? Who was he with? I'll go around to each of his muppet mates' houses and snap their jaws for letting him get in states like he does.'

Zara's jaw dropped. 'How's that going to solve anything? Use your head, not your fists, for once, Rico. Why on earth are you blaming his mates? It's his choice what he puts into his mouth so don't be going around to see them – it was his bloody choice, nobody else's.'

'Nah, they're all on 'em. You should see how many they have when they are on it. They have them all night long, one after the other, no wonder our kid has had a reaction.'

Zara was trying to talk some sense into her boy, but she knew he would never listen to anything she had to say, it was always somebody else's fault.

'Do me a favour, Mam, sort that washing out of my suitcase while I run and get in the shower. I'm sweating my back out here and I've been up early this morning to catch my flight. If I'm off to see Bri, or his idiot mates, I'm not going like this.'

Rico stood in front of the mirror in his bedroom with a white towel hanging around his waist. The sun had done him good. As had a week of ignoring his phone in case anyone was belling him about the van job. He'd needed the head space, needed the time to give Clara some attention, show her she was onto a good thing with him. He flexed his muscles in the mirror and smiled at himself. Then, quickly checking behind him, he bent and dipped his head under the bed. With a full beam on his face, he brought out the box where he'd stashed his money. Maybe he would go on another holiday with Clara before long because she had already told him that travelling with him just made her love him more. This time he would go somewhere romantic, though. Ibiza was a brilliant holiday, but it was partying every single day. Rico reckoned he needed rehab after this holiday. Sniff, balloons, weed, magic, ket had all been on the menu over there. Rico opened the box, and froze. The cash was in nice, neat bundles when he left, but no more. Somebody had been at it. He clenched his teeth together tightly and licked the end of his finger as he started the count. 'Fucking thieving bastards,' he mumbled under his breath. At least three thousand had gone missing. He shoved the money back into the box and kicked it under the bed before he stormed out of the bedroom. He stood at the top of the stairs and screamed, 'Mam, get your arse up here as soon as. Money has gone missing, and there's only you in the house.'

Zara appeared at the bottom of the stairs with her hands on her hips. She doubled-checked what he said and growled up the stairs, 'I hope you are not blaming me, because I'll run up there and bleeding swing for you. Since when have I ever been a thief? You know what you're like with money and, when you sit down and think about it, it will come back to you where you have spent it.' She sucked in a large mouthful of air before she continued, 'You've probably spent it on that dolly bird. She just takes, takes and takes, and never gives anything back. Don't try and defend her because I've never seen her put her hand in her bleeding pocket.'

Rico stormed down the stairs, barging passed his mother. 'Oh, how did I know you would bring her name into this?

You've never liked her. It's always the same with you, Mam, you always find something you don't like about any girl I start seeing. Go on, what was wrong with Katie before her? She was a nice chick. Worked, drove and she was always buying me gifts. And even then you had something to say. I should be like that with all the losers you date. Yeah, sod it, I'll be having a voice with the next waste of space you bring home from now on. You just watch, I'll scare off any fucker who steps over the doorstep.'

Zara squared up to her son. He didn't scare her, he never had. 'You won't do Jack shit. There's the front door if you don't like what I have to say in my own house. How dare you even put me in the same sentence as Clara. You mark my words, that girl is trouble. You wait until you're skint and you won't see that girl for dust.'

'Blah de fucking blah, Mother. Change the record. I'm saying my money is short. So, shoot me for asking a question about where it's gone.'

Zara backed off and headed into the living room. Rico followed her. 'I'm thinking about moving out, anyway. This holiday proved to me that Clara is the one, so get used to it. She's here for the long haul.'

Zara let out a sarcastic laugh and rolled her eyes. Knowing what she knew was tough and it took all her self control not to blurt it out.

Rico walked into the side ward the nurse had pointed him to. He hated hospitals and the smell of them made his stomach churn. He walked slowly over to the hospital bed and looked down at his brother who was asleep. The sound of Rico scraping a chair across the floor didn't stir Brian. Rico tried to make sense of it all. This was his baby brother, the one he should have been protecting. He'd let him down. He'd let Tyler down too. They both knew Brian wasn't as tough as them. He was just a normal kid who generally kept himself out of trouble. Brian had always lived in the shadow of his brothers and, although he was there if they needed him, he would much rather have gone to work and kept on the right side of the law. He was the only one of the Makin boys who'd stood half a chance of living a normal life. Tyler often said he'd gone into the gang life because he had no other option – but also to give his brothers the choice he never had. Rico had chosen to follow, but Brian – it wasn't too late for him to pick a different path. But only if the balloons hadn't written him off.

Rico's voice was low. 'Yo bro, it's me, Rico, wake up.' He wasn't sure what else to say.

But it worked. Brian's eyes opened slowly, taking a few minutes to focus, the bright lights clearly hurting him. He twisted his head and squeezed his eyelids together. Rico raised a smile and patted his brother's arm. 'Fuck me, mate, what the hell has gone on?'

Brian licked his dry cracked lips and dragged himself a little more upright in the bed. 'Pass us a drink of water. My mouth is like Ghandhi's flip-flop.'

Rico chuckled. If Brian could crack a joke, he must be doing OK. 'Mam just filled me in. I was away on holiday, you know that. But as soon as I found out I come straight here to see you. What's the doc saying? My mam said your legs might be done in?'

Brian swallowed hard, emotion bubbling in the back of his throat. 'Waiting on the test to come back. I still can't feel my legs, numb they are.'

Rico sat back in his chair and folded his arms tightly across his chest. 'You'll be sorted, our kid. I know a few lads who've had problems after balloons, but it's only temporary. Ignore these fuckers in here, they are just scaring you. They know fuck all.'

Brian sighed and shook his head. 'Rico, they told me I might never walk again, they're talking about wheelchairs.'

'Get a grip, our kid. I'll make sure you walk again, trust me. I'll have a word with the doc and see what he is really saying. I'll bung him a few quid - see if that doesn't magically speed up your recovery. I bet if I give him a few notes we'll find it's hours not days before we get these test results back. Mam was going on about brain damage too – but I told her, you'd need a brain to damage first before they diagnosed that.' Rico laughed at his own joke.

Brian tried to smile but the corner of his mouth seemed weighed down. 'I'll tell you something for nothing. I'll never ever touch them balloons again. I know I was bad on them, but that's because I thought they were just harmless fun. More fool me, eh?'

Rico changed the subject, aware his brother was ready to break down. 'I need to speak to Tyler after I'm done with you. Mam said he's been stressing out. He's getting told too, I have a life and it doesn't revolve around him. I'm not his puppet – I'm running the show now.'

'You know what he's like though,' said Brian. 'And you did promise him you would look after his shit while he was in the big house, not go swanning off on holiday.'

'I kept my promise. I have kept a close eye on the grafters and it's all running like clockwork. You see the thing with Tyler is he's a control freak. Thinks no one else can do what he does, and that everyone's out to get him. He's always been like that. Go on, tell me he's not a paranoid fucker.'

Brian shuffled about in the bed, not wanting to join Rico in slagging off their older brother. Tyler had always been there for him for as long as he could remember and there was no way he was willing to get into this conversation. He stared at the wall in front of him and spoke. 'Ben come to see me last night. I'm dreading telling Mam, you know what she's like. She'll hit the roof.'

Rico started to play with his fingers, aware this was a touchy subject with his mother. 'It is what it is, Brian. Ben is pretty much our flesh and blood, and so what if our dad pissed off and left us? That's not Ben's fault. Our mam needs to take that up with my dad, not Ben.'

'He's an alright guy, you know. He stayed for a few hours with me, telling me lots of stories about Dad when he was younger. He asked me if I wanted him to let Dad know I was in hossy.'

Rico let out a laboured breath. 'That's a hard one, mate. Mam will kick off if our old man comes back into our lives. You know what she's like when she hears his name, she goes on a mad one.'

'Exactly, but does that warrant me not having a relationship with my dad just because my mam can't get over the past? Ben told me my dad has always loved us. It was my mam who cut all the ties with him and told him not to darken our door again. What was he supposed to do? He'd hurt her enough, shagging around.'

Rico sat thinking before he replied. 'There are three sides to every story, Bri, his side, her side, and the truth. At the end of the day, he's our dad and, if we choose to have a relationship with him now, Mam should take a back seat. I'm not being funny, but Mam has tried hard enough to move on from him. We've had to see endless men in and out of her life for as long as I can remember. And, just for the record, none of them have ever stayed around for longer than a few months, so that tells you something, doesn't it? She's not the easiest woman in the world. I mean I love her, but she's made of tough stuff.'

'Yeah, I know what you mean. But she's got to be to raise us three, I guess. Anyway, Ben's coming again later and I'm going to tell him to give Dad my number. Let's face it, I'm going to need all the help and support I can get if my legs won't work anymore, aren't I?'

Rico patted his brother's arm again. A touch that told his younger brother he had his back, would always be there if he needed him.

Rico's mobile phone started ringing and he smiled as he saw his girlfriend's name flashing across the screen. 'Hi babes, what's happening?' Rico slumped back in his seat and started laughing.

Brian raised his eyebrows at his brother. What the hell had happened to his voice: he sounded more lovey-dovey than he'd ever heard him.

'I will bell you when I get back in the car. Get ya glad rags on and I'll pick you up. We can go out somewhere nice and show our tans off.'

The call ended a few seconds later and Brian grinned. 'Wow, since when have you been acting like that? *Love you babe, yes babe, no babe.* Our Tyler would go ape if he heard you under the thumb. Proper loved up, aren't ya?'

'Tyler is just jealous that he's never hooked up with a proper classy beauty like Clara.' Rico checked his wristwatch and stood up. Now he'd seen his brother with his own two eyes he felt better. His mother was going over the top worrying. Even Brian sounded hopeful. His brother would walk again, he only needed rest and a few more days in hospital. Lot of fuss about nothing, he thought as he left the ward.

———

Brian was alone again. You could see the strain in his face as he tried to move his legs up. Nothing. A tear ran down his cheek. 'Please God, let me walk again. Please,' he whispered.

Chapter Eighteen

Zara walked down the street to meet Mike. She was dressed to the nines, having been promised a nice meal in a top restaurant and cocktails as well. Her strong floral perfume filled the air. She had taken more money from Rico's box to get it, figuring she deserved it for all the cooking and cleaning she did for him without a word of thanks. She clocked Mike as she turned a corner. She felt a flutter of butterflies in her core – was this anticipation, or fear? She still couldn't make him out and she knew her track record showed she didn't always have the best judgement in men. But she had to find out which was the real Mike – the caring, decent guy, or the dangerous, dark personality he'd shown the other night. Leaving wasn't an option – not now – she needed to know who he really was, for her sake, and for Tyler's.

Mike walked up the street to meet her. 'Come on, our table is booked for eight. They're funny bleeders here and, if we are not on time, they'll cart us.'

Zara smiled and gripped hold of his hand. 'Relax, we're only a few minutes late.'

Mike rolled his eyes. 'Women, eh? Never on time.'

Zara sat eating her rump steak and watching Mike. He seemed edgy tonight, never took his gaze from her but rarely looked her in the eye. His phone kept vibrating and he was constantly looking at the screen. 'Is everything alright, Mike, you seem a bit stressed?'

'Yes, course it is, just a bit of mither from work. An inmate was shoved down the block earlier today and my line manager wanted a full statement writing. I've told him I will do it when I'm back in work tomorrow, but he's pecking my head about it.'

Zara saw a chance to ask more about her boy and if Mike could keep an eye out for him, keep him from harm. 'Sounds messy. I worry for my Ty being in a place like that. But I hope he's safer than most with you watching over him.'

Mike nodded and, after slowing finishing his mouthful, he said, 'Of course, I will. I've met him now and soon I will tell him who I am. You have to remember that this is my job on the line here, though, and I have to make sure nobody gets onto me. I don't mind Tyler knowing, but I need to trust him not to mouth off. I have a bit of a reputation in the jail for being a hard nut so I can't be seen to be giving inmates favours.'

Zara refilled her glass with red wine and stared over at Mike. 'Honest to God, if I'm not worrying about Tyler locked up in prison, I'm stressing about Rico not answering his phone. And, if it's not Rico, it's our Bri. I keep thinking about my baby laying in that hospital. When Tyler was at home, he took a lot of the stress from me, and I felt like I had some support. Since he's been banged up, it feels like my world is falling apart.'

Mike snapped, leaned over the table. 'Oi, I'm here with you now. If you need anything, ask me. I'm on your side.'

'I know you are, Mike, but it's early days for us and I'm so used to fending for myself. I hate asking anyone for anything, I always have. I've never really had anyone I felt was in my corner since Max.'

'Those other men have not been me. I knew from the moment I saw you that you were wife material. Look, I know it's only been a few dates, and I don't know if you feel the same, but I've already got feelings for you.'

Zara blushed but knew she couldn't let her defences down too easily. 'Mike, if I had a pound for every man that gave me the smooth talk, I would be a rich woman. A rich, single woman.'

Mike reached over and squeezed at her hand. 'I'm your man now and I'm not planning on going anywhere anytime soon.'

Zara was stuck for words. For years she'd wanted a man to say all these things to her and, now a man had, she wasn't sure if that's what she really wanted to hear.

Mike's mobile vibrated again, and he rammed it into his coat pocket. 'How about we treat ourselves? Get a hotel room tonight and have a proper night of it. We can relax then, no bother from your boys coming home early and finding us, and all that?'

Zara knew Mike was trying, but did she really want to be in some hotel room when her lad was in hospital? What if he needed her during the night? What if Rico started ringing her to see where she was? No, she needed to be at home.

———

Mike stopped his car outside Zara's house.

'Are you coming in for a coffee?'

Mike checked his wristwatch. 'No, I'm going to leave it tonight. I've got the early shift in the morning, and I'm knackered, if I'm being honest.'

Zara wasn't surprised that he'd blown her out. He'd been quiet ever since she said no to the hotel plan. She acted cool and leaned in for a kiss. 'Tonight has been lovely. Thank you for all the nice things you said. It means a lot and I know I don't show a lot of my feelings. I think in time I could open up to you.'

'That's nice to hear. I'll ring you tomorrow. I'll see what I can do for Tyler too. Like I said, I'm here to help.' His voice softened a little.

They shared a kiss and Zara doubled-checked with him that he wanted to leave the night here. 'Are you sure you don't want to come in for a nightcap?' She could see he was tempted.

'Honest, babes, I'm dead on my feet. I'll ring you tomorrow and we can arrange a weekend away or something, if you are up for it?'

A weekend away! Her friends were always going away for a few days with their loved ones and, up to now, Zara had never had the chance. She hardly ever left Manchester. 'That would be lovely, Mike. Yes, I'd be up for that. Just give me some notice of when you want to go, and I'll sort it out.'

Zara opened the car door and shot a look back at him. He was on his phone again. 'Night,' she said as she closed the car door.

'Erm, yes, night,' he replied, more interested in reading his text messages.

Zara walked down the garden path after she had waved Mike off. A voice to the left of her from a parked car. She froze on the spot and turned back to where the voice was coming from. 'Hi Zara, can I have a quick chat if you're not busy? I've been here for over an hour waiting to catch you.'

Zara swallowed hard, what the hell was he doing here, what did he want with her? 'Bloody hell, Ben. I don't see you for years and suddenly you're popping up everywhere. What's it about? Is it not something that could have kept until the morning?'

'Not really. I've been to see Brian and there are a few things I need to fill you in on. I'd never go behind your back or without speaking to you first.'

Zara dug her hand into her handbag and pulled her keys out. 'Do you want me to sit in the car or do you want to come inside? I don't really want to sit in the car at this time of the night. Nosey neighbours and all that.'

Ben got out and followed her down the garden path. 'Bloody freezing tonight, isn't it?'

Zara already had the key in the front door and was eager to get inside. Ben walked into the front room and looked about. 'Nice gaff you have here, Zara. Mind you, you always liked the finer things in life, didn't you?'

Zara sat down on the sofa and pulled her red platform heels from her feet. 'I don't know why I wear shoes like this when all they do is chew my feet up. Look at the marks from them.' She held her feet out and examined them.

Ben sat down on the sofa, and she could see he was awkward, not like how she remembered him. 'Do you want a beer or a glass of wine?'

'Yeah, I'll have a beer if you have one.' Ben seemed relieved not to have to dive straight into the reason why he was here.

Zara went into the kitchen and came back with the drinks. Then she reached down to her handbag and lit a fag. 'So, come on then, what's up?' She sat back and folded her arms tightly in front of her.

Ben swigged a mouthful of his beer. 'I went to see Brian tonight and he told me he's spoken with our kid. He said he's coming to see him.'

Zara gulped, had to make sure she'd heard him right. 'What? Max is going to hospital to see Brian?' Ben nodded and sat back in his seat. 'Why is he getting involved in his life now after all these years when he's clearly not given a fuck about any of his kids since the moment he left?'

'Zara, listen to what I have to say first before you start kicking off. Our Max has had loads of shit going on lately, and maybe he's got regrets, sat down and thought about the days gone by.'

'Like this face gives a fuck. He's a twat. He's never been a father since the day he left, so why start now?'

'It's Brian who wants to see him, and Max asked me to come and see you to ask if that's alright?'

'What, Max gives a shit what I have to say? Well, that's a first. He's never given a flying fuck about anything but himself. What's changed?'

Ben raised his eyes to the ceiling and sighed. 'Zara, after the breakup, you cut us all off, not just Max. You had nothing to do with any of us.'

She was right back at him. 'If I cut you off then you must have passed me the scissors. As far as I remember, when we split up not one of you came around here to see if the boys were alright, if I was alright. My world was turned upside down. The man I thought I'd grow old with I found in bed with another woman. My best bleeding friend. Come on, Ben, how do you ever forgive that?'

'You met when you were young. Too young to know how to say no to dangerous things, maybe. And, as far as our kid said, your mate was the one doing all the running. And you were busy with the boys. Max said at the time you were always tired, and you never showed him any affection anymore.'

Zara stubbed her cigarette out. 'Don't make me laugh, Ben. Max was my everything. I loved him with all my heart. And, so what if I was tired on a few nights – raising *our* kids – it doesn't give him the right to shag my best friend. Even to this day, I still go over it and ask myself why?'

'Shit happens, Zara. People make mistakes – a moment's weakness. I know for a fact you were the best thing ever in my brother's life. He's told me when he's pissed, told me he fucked up, told me you were the love of his life.'

Zara took a few seconds to digest what he'd just told her, and her eyes flooded with tears. 'It was always me and Max. Yes, we had our problems like every other couple, but we could have worked them out, spoke about them. When he left, that was it. Why didn't he fight to get me back, camp outside the front door, send me a letter, tell me how sorry he was?'

Ben dropped his head low. 'I can't answer that, Zara, only Max can. I'm not here for you or Max, I'm here for the lads. You know I've kept in touch with them over the years, and I've always been there in the background. I know more than anybody my brother was a dickhead, but time has passed now, water under the bridge and all that. The lads need as much support as they can get over the next few months, and I'm here for them, Zara.'

'Bit late to start playing the loving uncle, isn't it? Where were you when they were crying for their bloody dad at night? Where were you when we were skint and didn't have a pot to piss in? In fact, where were all your family? An elephant never forgets, and neither do I.'

Ben knew when to keep quiet, and this was one of those times. He needed to let her calm down. 'Do you want me to get us another drink? I know how upsetting this must be for you.'

She didn't reply, only held her glass up to him. Ben poured her a large wine. He placed his arms around her and gave her a gentle squeeze. 'Time's a good healer, Zara. I'm sure now you and Max are older and wiser you can hold a civil conversation. I get he owes you some answers, but sometimes things are best left unsaid, aren't they?'

Her mouth was moving but no words were coming out, probably for the best. Ben sat looking around the house. He stood up, walked to a small silver table and picked up a photograph of his three nephews. He smiled and turned to Zara with the photo in his hands. 'Good-looking boys, aren't they?'

Zara smiled. 'Bloody womanisers, they are, all three of them. Like father like son, I suppose.'

Ben shook his head and placed the photo frame back on the table. 'Hats off to you, Zara. You've raised three strong kids there. Max always says that too, not just me.'

Zara looked puzzled. 'So, have you kept in touch with Max all these years?'

'Not at first, no, but more and more over the last five years or so. My mam was ill, and Max came to see her. That's the first any of us had seen of him in a long time. My mam got the odd phone call from him but apart from that he'd been like the Scarlet Pimpernel. *They seek him here, they seek him there, they seek him everywhere,*' he chuckled. 'He spent a lot of time with my mam before she died. Hours and hours at her bedside, talking and talking. And she told him alright, never held anything back, told him he was an idiot for walking away from his kids for all these years. It was a bitter pill for him to swallow at first, but it made him think about it. Once my mam passed, he was in bits, and I thought he would stay around Manchester, but after the funeral he packed his bags and got on his toes again. That's the thing with our Max, he's never been able to face things. He runs away. He's always been like that, even from being a kid.'

Zara had calmed down. She went to the cupboard and pulled out an old cardboard box. One by one, she pulled out the photo albums. 'Have a look at these of the kids growing up, though you won't find any of Max. I cut up all his photographs when he left.'

Ben opened the gold photo album and started to turn the pages. 'Oh my God, look how young the lads are here. Bleeding hell, Tyler is the double of his dad, he's the spit from his mouth.'

'I know, I always say it. Ty is a carbon copy of Max, Rico has his snidey ways and our Brian is a bit of both of us.'

Ben looked at every photo and then placed them down next to him. 'So, I know a bit about the kids over the years, but tell me about you and how you've been. Any men in your life? Are you working?'

'I've not worked for years. Looking after the lads is still a full-time job and our Tyler has always provided for me. He's a good lad and made sure I never went short.'

'That's nice. I was like that with my old queen too. You only get one mother in this life, and you have to look after her while she is still on this earth. I would give everything I owned to have my mam back. Honest, when she died, part of me died with her. Losing your mother is the worst pain anyone can ever feel. It never leaves you, a dull ache that's there every bloody day. You hear a song on the radio, you cry. You watch a film, you cry. I have never been so emotional in my whole life, let me tell you.'

Zara gulped as she could see he was getting upset. She knew Max and Ben had worshipped their mother. She felt a stab of envy that she'd never had a mum like theirs, never had someone to show her how to be a parent, in fact. She'd had to work everything out as she went along. Trial and error – with plenty of both. 'I've not bothered with my mam since I left home and moved in with Max. I never really knew my dad, and when my mam hit the bottle, I knew I had to get away from her. I know she's in Bolton somewhere living with some pisshead, but she never bothers with me, and I never bother with her. I'm a lone ranger, always have been.'

Ben agreed. 'You've always been a tough cookie , and that's one of the things that's so attractive about you. You fall down and you always get back up and carry on. Takes balls that.'

Zara flicked her hair back and her cheeks blushed slightly. 'Yep, I always dust myself down and carry on. No other choice. Don't get me wrong, when I split up with Max I could have easily curled up in a small ball and locked myself away from the world. I lost so much weight and, when I looked in the mirror, I didn't even recognise myself anymore. Those were my dark days, Ben, days when I didn't know if I was coming or going. I'm sure I had some sort of mental breakdown.'

'But look at you now, gorgeous as ever, and tough as nails,' Ben said.

Zara looked at him in more detail, aware he was saying so many nice things to her tonight. It stirred up an old excitement inside her.

Ben got up as he heard a car pulling up on the road outside. He stood back from the window and spoke in a low voice. 'Two dodgy-looking guys clocking your house, Zara. Both sat staring over here.'

'Oh, it's the norm around here, Ben. Lots of cars come onto the street all night long. Honest, I've seen some proper dodgy dealings going on from my bedroom window. One night I went to check on a car that had been parked out there for at least ten minutes, and saw a woman and man going for gold in the back seat, dirty bleeders.'

Ben was still stood by the window with a concerned look. 'I don't like the look of these two, though. Go up to the bedroom window and see if you can get a better look at them.'

Zara stood up and left the room, shouting behind her. 'Come up then. I don't want to be caught gawping out of the window, you can do it.'

It was pitch black outside, a few yellow sprays of light coming from one lamppost by her fence. She crept up to the window and hid away in the shadows. Her expression was serious now as she clocked the strangers. 'Who the hell are they? I've not seen them around here before. Why do they keep looking at my house?'

Ben was at her side now. Slowly he peeled one of the blinds back from the window. 'Big fuckers too. Try and get the registration of the car. Keep it for future reference. They look as iffy as fuck. Quick – move back, they're looking up at the window.'

They both froze, breathing doubled. The car started its engine, and she could see the passenger on his mobile phone as they drove away. The moment they were gone, Zara was back at the window, clocking the reg and make and model of the vehicle. She placed a hand on her neck and rubbed it as a cold chill passed over her body.

Sitting on the edge of her bed, she dropped her head into her hands. 'It's always been like this with the lads. Every night I lie awake until they are in bed. Never knowing who's going to come through my door. And that's happened before, Ben, on my life, team-handed they were when they come looking for our Tyler and Rico. It's a good job they weren't in when they came because they would have both been six feet under, let me tell you. I hate the world my lads live in, hate everything that goes with it. Tyler told me time and time again he would get a job, live a respectable life, but up to now it's never happened. Tyler wanted me to move up the hill, away from it all, but why should I move from my home because of the world my lads live in? I have been here for years, have friends, know the community.'

Ben sat down next to her and placed his warm hand on her leg. 'I never knew, Zara, never thought this was how you were all living – in fear of who's going to come knocking. I feel like I've let the lads down now, let you down too.'

Zara lifted her head slowly and looked into his chestnut brown eyes. Eyes just like her ex-husband's, eyes that held so much love for her and her boys. With a single finger, she stroked his cheek. 'You never let us down, Ben, it was Max.

And I blame myself too for being so bleeding stubborn. I was so caught up with my own drama that I forgot the lads needed a dad, or at least a father figure, to look up to. I'm so selfish, so messed up.'

He gripped her, pressed her head against his firm chest and kissed the top of her head. 'Don't be silly, you've been an incredible mother, strong, independent, a survivor.'

'I've not. I've been so wrapped up in my own personal battle against Max that I've let things slip. I should have got help for the boys when they stepped into this world, should have phoned their dad and told him what was going on. Max always said he never wanted his boys to do what he had to do to survive. Honest, many a night when he'd had a few beers he would pour his heart out to me and tell me what he wanted for his boys. They were his pride and joy, the apples of his eye, and I took that away from him because I couldn't admit that he just didn't love me anymore.'

Ben held her face in his hands and looked her directly in the eyes. 'Stop saying things like that. We are all to blame somewhere along the line. Max has to own his shit too and he knows he's played a part in all this. When Brian spoke to his dad on the phone, our Max broke down crying, telling him how much he loves him and how he will make it up to him. You need to let Max do that, Zara, give him a chance to right his wrongs.'

Zara snivelled, her nose running. 'I know I do. And thanks, Ben, for helping me see that. You're such a lovely person. I'm so sorry for the way I've treated you and your family. I got so caught up in my own misery and felt that I had a personal battle with you all, when I should have been thinking about my boys.'

Ben went nose to nose with Zara, looking straight in her eyes. 'Please don't get upset, dry your eyes.' They held this look for a few seconds. Before she knew it, she was kissing him.

Zara lay staring out of the bedroom window at the silver moon. She turned her head slowly and looked at Ben lying next to her. This should have never happened. Ben was wide awake, and he looked back at her.

'Now this wasn't something I was expecting.'

Zara tried to force a smile. She'd made mistakes before, slept with people she shouldn't have because it made her feel safe or needed. But this was a whole other level. She folded her pillows behind her and said, 'So, that's me and Max equal then, isn't it? He slept with my best friend, and I slept with his brother.'

Ben looked away. 'So that's all I was, a score you needed to settle with our kid?'

'No, you're taking this the wrong way. I didn't know what to say and it just come out. It was a dig at me really. I mean, I've spent years hating Max for what he did and now I'm just as bad.'

'So, answer me straight, did you have sex with me because you wanted to or only to settle the score with Max? Because if you did, I'm gone. It's cards on the table time – we're too old for pretending. I always thought our Max didn't deserve you. You were too good for him, and I watched that from afar for years. You always had a place in my heart, always will.'

Zara reached over and took his hand in hers. She was shocked for sure, thought perhaps he'd had a few too many and wasn't speaking the truth. 'Ben, you were a young guy when I was with Max. The years have gone by, and you have never been near me. If you felt that way, why didn't you do something about it?'

Ben sat up straight. 'Because you are my brother's wife. I always asked the lads how you were, and it sounded like you'd moved on – they told me you were hooked up, in a relationship with somebody or other all the time, so what was the point?'

Zara didn't know what to say, then decided that enough lies had been told, enough things left unsaid. She may as well as be open with Ben. Her voice was low. 'Why is my life never straightforward? Men are like buses: none come along for ages, then two turn up at once. I have just started seeing a lovely man. I think he could be the one, and then you come along and put a spanner in the works.'

Ben was agitated. 'This is our secret for now. I'm not promising you the world, but I know the way I feel about you goes deeper than the few dates you have had with that other guy. Why don't we play this by ear and see where it goes? If we are the real deal, then we can tell everyone. If this works, I'm not arsed who knows, even Max. Abuse it and lose it. He had his chance and messed up.'

Zara lay in the dark feeling torn. She knew both these men who had walked into her life had something to offer – but a part of her rebelled. She'd waited years for a good man to come along. She'd kissed a lot of frogs. But right now, she'd give up every chance of a happy ever after if she could just get her boys all home safe. A mother's heart was never going to belong to anyone as truly as it did to her children. She only hoped heartbreak wasn't coming her way.

Chapter Nineteen

Tyler sat in the visiting centre waiting for his brother Rico to come through the doors. Already he was raging inside. The kid had not answered his phone to him since he'd been home and once he was sat in front of him he was getting told.

Finally, the doors opened. Rico oozed confidence as he walked into the room. The girls on the visit clocked him too, their boyfriends growling over at the eye candy, threatened by his presence.

'Yo, it's a shithole in here – at least half an hour I've been waiting downstairs and it's rough as.'

Tyler found it hard to hold his tongue and looked over at the canteen. 'Do us a favour. Go and queue up for a butty and a drink for me, some chocolate too. Starving, I am.'

Rico shot a look behind him at the line of people at the canteen and huffed. 'Yeah, just let that queue die down. I'm not standing there for ages.'

Tyler gritted his teeth. His brother had always been a selfish prick but he'd hoped he might have grown out of that since stepping up. But he didn't have time to teach him some manners – not while there was business to sort. 'Right, I'm going to say this once and once only, so you better listen. You need to start answering your phone when I ring you. Fuck me, Rhino and Smidge are all over me about you, and I've vouched for you, told them not to worry, told them you were the man for the job. And all you're doing at the moment is swanning off on holiday.'

'Chill the fuck out, will you, and tell them two idiots I am looking after everything. Fuck me, I've only been on a week's holiday and didn't want any mither. Now I'm back you will get a full report of everything that's going on. Come on, Tyler, I've been stressed out of my arse lately what with you getting slammed and our kid being in hospital.'

Tyler eyeballed his brother, not buying his shit. 'We're all stressed out. Mam's had no money and you're jetting off to the sun with your bird. Sort out your priorities. Family comes first, before any woman, before anyone else. Are you understanding that?'

Rico sized his brother up, a cocky look in his eye. Was Tyler forgetting he was the one banged up? He didn't have to listen to this shit, he was getting told. 'Listen, I'm doing you a favour. Your business would have been gone if it wasn't for me still running it. Don't forget that. So, when you get on your high horse chatting shit to me, remember I'm the one calling the shots now.'

Tyler checked no screws were about and leaned further over the table that separated the two of them. 'Listen, you daft prick, carry on and I'll have a few lads on you and take the fucking lot back. Don't ever think you can double-cross me and take what I've worked my balls off for. If you want to go down that road, then bring it on and I'll show you what I'm about. Trust me, Rico, test me and see what happens.'

Rico moved back in his seat, aware his brother was ready to punch his lights out. There was fear in his eyes now, fear of his older brother and what he could do to him. Rico loved to talk the talk, but he knew Tyler walked the walk. There was only so far he could push his brother and even Rico recognised when Tyler was on the edge. Even though Tyler was locked up, Rico knew he could still call shots on the out. A couple of texts, a call or two and he could give the order for Rico to get his kneecaps shot through, have him put in the boot of a car and taken to a lock-up somewhere and tortured. Rico wasn't about to apologise, but he knew he needed a peace offering. He looked behind him and saw that the queue had gone down. He stood up and pulled the twenty-pound note out of his pocket. They both needed a breather for sure. 'I'll go and grab some scran.'

Rico piled the food in front of his brother, the closest he'd get to saying sorry. 'I got you some mint chocolate biscuits there, our kid, like my mam used to get us. Get your mouth round one of them, peng they are.'

Tyler seemed to have lost his appetite. He picked at the food, still raging. 'You sort this shit out, I mean it, Rico, no more chances.' His words were firm, eyes never flinching.

Rico wouldn't hold eye contact. He spoke as he looked around the room everywhere but at Tyler. 'OK, I get you.

Like I said, just had some heavy shit on my shoulders lately. Hopefully our Brian will be alright. And I'll hook my mam up with some money when I get home from here.'

Tyler wasn't letting it drop. 'Where did you get the money from to go on holiday?'

Rico looked down, cracking his knuckles. 'I had a bit of work I sorted out and got a good treat.'

'What kind of work?'

Rico was on the spot, and he knew his brother would drill him until he told him the truth. He kept his voice low. 'Good till it was, thirty grand. Found out someone was dropping off and had him over the minute he pulled up.' Rico rubbed his hands together as he continued. 'I've told you before, I'm a big boy and I can look after myself. I've not been taxing your stuff, in case you think I've been nicking from you or bollocks like that. I wouldn't do that to you, Ty. This was new money, a little extra venture on the side.'

Tyler looked suspicious and delved deeper. Money like that came at a cost and he wanted to know who, when, where, what. 'Where was it and who was involved?'

Rico sat back and folded his arms. 'I hired in a couple of kids from out of town to help. Nutters they are, but they get the job done. Like I said, no comebacks, straight in and out.'

Tyler jerked his head forward, still unsure.

Rico took his chance to change the subject. 'Brian said Dad wants to come and see him. Ben's already been up to the hossy and, well, the ball's in his court if he wants the old man to come and see him.'

Tyler sat tall, chest expanded. 'Brian needs nobody to look after him except me. I've had his back all my life and he's never wanted for anything.'

'I know that. Bri knows it too. But Dad was just saying he wanted to come and see him. Tyler, the years have passed by, don't you think we should all try and get to know him?'

'He's a shady sod. All the stories my mam has told me about him, he must be after something.'

'For fuck's sake, our kid, he's our dad. Shit happened years ago and it wasn't our shit, it was his and my mam's. Come on, let's face it, it's not like my mam sat about crying all these years, is it?' Rico opened his eyes wide, a look to remind his brother about all the men she'd dated.

But Tyler had loyalty to his mother, and he stood by any decisions she made. He was the man of the house from an early age and there was no room in his world for a man who'd been out of the picture for years and wanted to come back now playing daddy. He could do one. 'Brian can do what he wants to do with him. I'll respect any decisions he makes. But I wouldn't trust him as far as I could throw him, so I'm staying on the fence. Anyway, it's not like he'll be coming here to see me, is it?'

Rico hunched his shoulders. 'Maybe he will, if that's what you want?'

Tyler scoffed. 'What, sit facing me for an hour, and talk about what? I don't know him, and he doesn't know me. He's like a stranger.'

Rico was still fighting his father's corner. 'So, *get* to know him. Maybe when you both sit down together and talk, he might be able to explain a few things to you, tell you why he never came back to see us.'

'Nah, a man who leaves his family behind for a piece of tail is no man in my eyes. Just make sure you don't make the same mistake with Clara.'

'So, what you saying? I have to choose between you and Clara? What's your problem with her? You've never had a good word to say about the girl when you don't even know her. I'm in love with her, Tyler, she makes me feel good about myself and I've never felt like this when I've been with any other woman.'

It was Tyler's turn to look away now. He could have wounded him with what he knew about his girlfriend, could have made his world crumble down. 'I have no problems with Clara. Just remember where your loyalties lie, that's all. Women are ten a penny.'

Rico knew this bollocking from his older brother had been well overdue, and maybe he had let things slip, not answering the phone. He had to keep the peace. 'My family come before anything, bro. And from now on I'll be on the blower to you all the time, but please remember I do have a life too, and if I don't answer the phone straight away it might mean I'm busy.'

Tyler nodded, relieved his message was clear and understood. That's what Rico had always needed every now and then. A quick reminder of his rank in the family and that Tyler was the top man, in jail or not.

The visit was nearly over and, by the end of the session, Tyler had filled Rico in about the beef behind bars. Rico had lapped up the story, excitement in his eyes when Tyler told him he was going to be running most of the jail before the month was out. More cash, more of a reputation for his family name. The two brothers shook hands and even gave each other a quick hug at the end of the visit.

Tyler sat back down in his seat and watched Rico leave the visiting room. An ache formed in the pit of his stomach: he was missing home and missing being able to protect the ones he loved.

Chapter Twenty

Brian lay in bed and strained his face as he concentrated on moving his toes. There was some feeling there, he was sure. He tried again. He swore he'd been able to wiggle them, just a little. It was like all his birthdays had come at once – here it was, some hope that he would walk again. His eyes were wide open, excited, wanting the doctor to come in so he could tell him his news. The door opened but it wasn't a medic. Instead, Ben walked in with another man. Ben walked towards the bed and blocked Brian's view of the other visitor. 'Alright lad, how we feeling today?'

Brian straightened the white sheet on top of him and smiled. 'I think I can feel my feet today, you know. I've been trying to move them all morning and I have some feeling, I really do.'

The other man sat down in the chair not far from the bed, his head dipped low. Brian shot a look over at him and even the quickest of glances gave it away. Anyone could see how close this man looked to Tyler. The Makin genes were shouting out loud. But what would he say to a man he didn't know anymore, had no connection with? This guy was his father in name alone.

Ben sat down next to Max and patted his brother's leg. 'And here's your old man to cheer you up, Bri.'

Max Makin lifted his head and threw an anxious smile over at his boy, his head heavy with the shame he felt inside. 'Hiya son, long time, eh?'

Brian bit his bottom lip, emotions bubbling in the back of his throat. 'Yeah, a really long time.'

There was a silence and Ben could see he had to step in. 'Your dad's back in Manchester now to live. He's got a pad in the town centre, smart place too, all the mod cons.'

Brian looked at his father again, still shellshocked from seeing him. 'Be nice to have you back down these ends. Is it a long-time stay or a short one?' He felt like he was speaking to some long-lost cousin at a wedding – not his own dad.

Max pulled his shoulders back and smirked. 'In the words of Take That, son, I'm back for good.'

Brian nodded but didn't smile. 'Have you got work sorted out and all that?'

'Nah, not yet. Got a few mates who can hook me up with work when I'm ready, but for now I'm going to chill out.'

Ben took his chance to leave them together and stood up. 'Anyone want anything from the canteen? I'm going to grab a coffee.'

Max dug his hand in his pocket and pulled out a twenty-pound note. 'Here, get me and my lad a few treats.'

Brian chuckled without meaning to when he heard his dad call him 'my lad'. He'd waited years to hear someone call him his lad and now it had come he didn't know how to act. 'Ben, can I have a Twix, a packet of cheese and onion crisps and a can of Fanta. I've not eaten today, the food was crap earlier. Some soggy broccoli pasta they brought for dinner, and it looked hanging.'

Max chirped in. 'Hossy food is the worst. I've never been one for eating my greens. Just give me peas and carrots and I'll be fine, not all this butternut squash crap and all that.'

Ben took the money from his brother and left the room. Max looked over at Brian and his confidence had grown. 'You look like your mam, lad, do you know that?'

'Yeah, she is always telling me I'm the best-looking one. Our Tyler is your double, honest. I've seen some photographs of you and never really thought he did look like you, but now, seeing you in the flesh, he's a ringer of you.'

Max sat playing with his fingers, his chest rising faster. 'Son, I'm sorry, you know. Sorry I never came back to see you all. It's a mistake I made that I will never forgive myself for. Shit happens and you think you will sort it out the next day and then the next day becomes the next week and before you know it, it's another year that has gone past then another year and then you just lose the bottle to come back.'

'I suppose because I was young and never had a dad from an early age I never missed one. Don't get me wrong: when I was at school and I was asked about my dad, I always closed up and didn't know what to say, but apart from that you can't miss what you never had, can you?' Brian's words were sharp, but honest.

Max could see he'd have to try harder to win him over. 'I fucked up son, but your mam played her part too. Don't ever let her tell you any different. I was trying to come back, trying to sort it all out but she wouldn't give me the time of the day. She made it so hard.'

'Dad, you slept with her best mate, didn't you? What did you expect?'

'It was a daft mistake, not something that should have ended our marriage. I would have jumped through hoops, done anything to get back with her, but she blocked me out of her life, *your* lives, and that was it. She threw everything I owned on the streets, and she didn't give me any other option except to do one. I couldn't have stayed in Manchester. She would have hunted me down and told everyone what I'd done.' Max knew Rome wasn't built in a day and changed the subject. 'So, tell me about you, about ending up in here. I'm not going to start preaching to you because I know I wouldn't have a leg to stand on. But I care, I've always cared about you, and I want to help, help you all.'

Brian looked out of the window, gathering his thoughts; did he really need to explain himself to this man he barely knew? 'It is what it is. I was out with my mates, and we were just having a buzz. Everyone does it, but I've probably been tanning the balloons a lot more than I should have. Shit happens – like you said. I woke up one morning and I was frozen – slurring, could barely move. Honest, I thought I was going to die, couldn't speak and all that.'

'Scary shit, son. See in my day, it was only weed and pills. Nowadays they are coming up with all new drugs that nobody knows nothing about.'

Brian wiggled his toes again and showed Max. 'I'm buzzing my feet are getting some feelings back. I know it might be a long road, but I'll do everything they say and get myself back to normal. Clean my act up properly.'

Max reached over and patted Brian's legs. 'I've said a few prayers for you over the last few weeks, son. The big man in the sky will sort you out.'

Brian smirked, 'You a bible basher now or what? Plenty of stuff you've got to confess, I bet.'

Ben walked back into the room carrying all the goodies. He spread them out on the bed, and everyone grabbed something to eat.

Ben said, 'Rico said he will meet up with your dad in the boozer later on, Bri. And, after that, there is only Tyler left for him to go see.'

Brian cringed and shot a look over at Max. 'Tough cookie to break, our kid. Good luck with that, just saying. Plus the nick probably isn't your happy place, is it?'

Max didn't take the bait. 'I'll go on the visit and see what the script is with him. If he's having none of it, so be it. I'm not begging, sack that.'

Ben jumped in. 'What he means is he can't force Tyler to have a relationship with him, can he? It should be baby steps for now with all of you.'

Max looked sour. 'Nah, fuck baby steps. These are my boys, and I know I didn't fight for them when I was younger, but I will now. They're my boys, my flesh and blood. If Zara wants beef over it, then so be it. My plan is to go and see her too. See if we can put the past behind us. I've grown up a lot and hopefully she has as well. Ben tells me she has a fella now anyway, so why would it bother her if you lot are back in touch with me?'

'Because she's the one who's worked her arse to the bone for us, Dad. She's the one who's always been there when we needed her. My mam might be a lot of things in your eyes, but she's been a good mother, stood by us all even though we're no angels.'

Max could see he was upsetting his son and backpedalled. 'And for that I will always be thankful. I owe her a lot and I'll be telling her how sorry I am when I go and see her.'

Brian raised his eyebrows. Did his dad know what he was up against?

Chapter Twenty-One

Z ara sat in her kitchen with Molly, on a phone call with
Mike.

She rolled her eyes and looked over at her friend. 'I'm
just tired tonight, Mike. What with our Brian still in hospital
and Tyler in the nick, it's all taken its toll on me. Can we
reschedule for Friday night instead?' Zara held her head
away from her phone and ran her fingers through her hair
as she smiled over at Molly. 'Right, yes that's fine. I'll call
you tonight.'

The call ended and Zara sighed. 'Wow, eager beaver or
what. Molly, on my life, you have to be careful what you
wish for sometimes. I always thought I wanted a man to
ring and text me all the time and always want to see me, but
Mike is giving me the ick. Honest to God, too bloody needy.'

Molly popped a fag from the packet on the table and slid
it over to Zara. 'Get a cig and calm down. I can't understand
you sometimes. One minute you're telling me this man is
the best thing since sliced bread, and the next you're hating

on him. Make your mind up, woman, it's not like you have men queuing up at the front door, is it?'

Zara blushed. 'Well... I might have another man on the go too.'

Molly looked astounded. 'Well, you dirty cow, when did this happen? You never said a word.'

Zara lit her cigarette and blew a straight line of grey smoke from her mouth. 'Only since last night. You're not going to believe who, either. It's going to shock you, for sure.'

Molly sat thinking. 'Oh, don't tell me it's that pervy Paul from the Vine estate? He's always had his eye on you.'

Zara couldn't stop herself smiling from cheek to cheek. 'Nope, you'll never guess, so I'm going to tell you. And before you start going on about him, remember I'm a grown woman and can make my mind up myself. Mike and I aren't what the kids call "exclusive" anyway, so who's to say I can't try someone else on for size?'

Molly was chomping at the bit, chewing on her finger-nails. 'Spit it out then. I think I've seen it all but then you always go and surprise me. You're a one-woman soap opera, Zara Makin!'

'OK, so last night, after a date with Mike, he dropped me home and, when I was walking down the garden path, I heard someone shouting my name. I turned around and Ben was stood there.'

Molly stopped her dead in her tracks. 'Ben who?'

'Max's brother.'

Molly made the sign of the cross over her body and shook her head. 'Zara, you're playing with fire, my girl. Ben is your

207

brother-in-law. I know what has gone on between you and Max, but his brother should be forbidden fruit. They're a dangerous family – like a grenade waiting to go off – and if anyone finds out, this will pull the pin, mark my words. Do yourself a favour and cart him before it gets any deeper.'

Zara looked defiant. 'How can the past dictate to me who I see now? I owe that dickhead Max nothing. Karma, I call it.'

'I still don't get how he ended up in your bed, though? What was he there for in the first place?' Molly folded her arms tightly in front, waiting on a reply.

Zara stubbed her fag out. 'We were chatting about Bri when Ben spotted some iffy characters sat outside in a car, clocking my house. Did you see them last night? I know you're always at that bloody window, watching everything?'

Molly went beetroot. Bloody hell, did everyone know she was the local plant-pot. She thought she was hidden away. In future she would look out of the bedroom window and keep a fair distance from it so nobody could see her. 'No, I never seen a thing. I don't sit at the window all night, love. I do have a life.'

'Well, like I was saying, Ben clocked these two men sat in a car and we went upstairs to the bedroom window to get a better look and, I'm not going to lie, I ended up getting upset with one thing and another and he comforted me.'

'Is having sex what you call comforting these days or what, because in my eyes comforting is a cuddle, a bleeding pat on the shoulder.' Molly was laughing now. 'You're so bloody vulnerable, Zara. They must see you coming. How many times have we had this conversation about men and not sleeping with them before you know what they're really like?' Molly tapped a single finger against her temple. 'For a smart woman, you don't half make some daft decisions. These men are just after a quick leg-over. Go on, tell me he's taking you out next, wants to make a go of it with you. He's probably got some grudge with his brother and, by sticking one up you, he feels empowered. Brothers are like that, always in competition with each other. You should know that, as the mother of sons.'

Zara was bright red. 'Why does it bother you who I sleep with?. It's never bothered you before. I'm having fun, you know – that stuff that makes you smile? You should try it some time.'

Molly realised she might have overstepped the mark and raised a gentle smile, backtracking. 'Love, I care about you. It's me who sees you heartbroken when it all falls apart. I want something better for you. Mike seems nice, and, until Ben showed up, you were happy with him. Ben will be bad news for you, so think twice before you go and get involved with him any further. You know I've got second sight – I can't ignore it when I get one of my bad feelings.' Molly was serious now.

Zara chuckled. 'Oh, you and your Romany blood, Moll. How many generations back is that? Because I don't think you've ever been right in any of your predictions since I've known you. Remember that guy Gary? You told me he was the one, happily ever after, you said. Then he turned out to be a right shower of shite, a proper sponger.'

Molly sat up with her shoulders pulled back. 'OK, so sometimes it's hard to interpret the feelings – but I have to tell it like I find. My mother had the same gift as me and you can ask any of my family, they will tell you too. I can feel the future. You mark my words, lady, keep clear of Ben, he's your yesterday, not your tomorrow.'

Zara was sick to death of arguing with her friend but before she could change the subject in rushed Rico.

'Mam, have you seen my black Armani top? It was in the washing the other day and I'm praying you *have* washed it?'

Zara sat thinking. 'Yep, it's on top of the dryer, washed it yesterday. Oi, while you're here, there were two men sat in a car outside here last night. They never took their eyes from the house. I might be being paranoid, but they were definitely looking at our gaff.'

Rico was more interested in getting ready. 'Nothing to do with me, Mother. Stop flapping, why would anyone be looking for me? If anyone wants to find me, they come direct.'

'I'm not saying they were looking for you, I just said two shady geezers were parked up outside. I'm being vigilant, that's all.'

'Well, stop and chill out, woman. Anyway, got to rush. I'm going out for the day with Clara. Might drive up to Blackpool and have a scout around there for a few hours.' Rico left the room as Molly gathered her things to head off too.

———

Night fell and Zara was lying in bed. She'd been on the phone for half an hour, talking to Ben. When she called, she'd been half expecting him to say it had all been a mistake, half preparing to say the same herself. But somehow, she heard his voice and, before she knew it, they were planning a second date. If you could call the other night a first date – rather than a twist of fate or a night of passion. But they'd spoken about other things, too. He told her about Max being back in Manchester and that he'd been to see Brian in hospital, and that unsettled her, she couldn't deny it, She wanted to be happy for her youngest son. After all these years he'd finally met up with his father. He must be buzzing, but there was an anger in the deep pit of her stomach that wouldn't leave her, a rage that rose from her toes and wound its way through her until it was wrapped around her windpipe, strangling her words. After she ended the call, she tossed and turned in bed and couldn't settle. Her mobile phone started to ring, and she reached over to answer it, thinking it was Ben again.

Zara sat up when she heard Mike's voice on the other end. Shit, shit, shit: she had promised him she would call him back tonight.

'I'm so sorry Mike, I must have drifted off to sleep,' she lied. She gazed at the silver moon outside as she listened to him speak. Compared to the feeling she got when she spoke to Ben, this felt tame, a duty call. 'Yes Mike … Don't be thinking that, I've just had a lot on my plate.' She looked over at the clock at her bedside. Bloody hell, it was half one in the morning. Why on earth was he belling her at this time of the night? She yawned and stretched her hand over her head, aware she should be asleep at this time. She was going to see Tyler tomorrow and she had to get up early to wash her hair and put the laundry on. 'Right Mike, I'm at the jail tomorrow, so I'll see you then and we can sort out where we are going and all that. Honest, I'm dead on my feet lately and I'm normally full of beans. But,' she stressed, 'nothing seems normal right now. Not with my boys, not with me. But let's talk tomorrow, it's late.' Zara listened to Mike for a few more seconds and ended the call.

What was she going to do? She still didn't understand Mike – was he angel or devil? But either way, keeping him close was her best way of looking out for Tyler. But Ben, he never pretended to be a saint. He was a ducker and a diver, lived life on the edge. In anyone else's eyes, he'd have been a bad boy. But compared to Max, Ben had always been the safer bet. Her mother had warned her about bad lads until she was blue in the face. Maybe Zara would have to learn the hard way. Or maybe she never would.

Chapter Twenty-Two

Zara walked into the visiting centre and sat down. She was glad to see Jane over the other side of the room. They could have a catch-up and put the world to rights after. She'd not seen her here for a few weeks and she was looking forward to a chat. Zara had been glad to find a friend here, someone who didn't judge, who understood what it was like to have a loved one locked up.

Zara booked in then walked towards Jane, but Jane looked away and headed to the toilets: not a hello, goodbye, nothing. What the hell was wrong with her today? Zara plonked down on a chair and looked around until she saw Jane return from the toilet and head to another seat. Lesson learned, Zara twisted her body to face the other way.

She was still apprehensive when she spotted Mike coming in via a side door. She looked at him behind the desk. He had his grumpy face on and no doubt he was going to have a go at her too, but she figured she had nothing to lose so put her shoulders back and strode over.

'Afternoon, Mrs Makin,' Mike said.

'Afternoon,' she replied, still tense.

Mike checked behind him and leaned in. 'So, are we on for tonight, or you going to blow me out again?'

Zara felt relieved he wasn't giving her the cold shoulder. 'Mike, I told you what was going on. I've been up to my neck in it all. You need to understand that if my boys are hurt or unhappy then so am I. I'm a mother before I'm a lover.'

Mike nodded his head and moved over to the other side of the desk to book in other visitors. He waited until they had left before he spoke to Zara again.

'I like you. I think we could be good together, but I'm not pissing about if you don't feel the same about it all. I've told you I'm not a time-waster.'

Jane walked past and completely blanked Zara again, pretended she'd not seen her. Mike saw the tension between them and kept his voice low. 'Bloomin' barm pot, that one is. I only told her to fill a form out and you should have heard the abuse she gave me. Definitely got out of the wrong side of bed today.'

Zara agreed. 'Yeah, she was like my best friend a few weeks back, never shut up nattering, but today it's like she doesn't even know me. I hate folk who blow hot and cold like that.'

Mike looked around shiftily. 'Well, you better not try that with me. I just want to touch you, kiss you, feel your warm body next to mine again. If you bin me off again, I don't know what I'll do.'

Zara didn't like the undertone in his voice. He was freaking her out. She was never ever any good at saying no to men and today was no different. 'Let's meet up later, then, and maybe go and get some nice food. I'm sorry if you think I've been swerving you. Like I said, I had shit going on.'

Mike rubbed his hands together. 'Lovely jubbly, pick you up at eight. You never know, we might not even make it to a restaurant if what's on the menu at home is even tastier.'

Zara tried to look enthusiastic, but she was failing miserably. She was glad that she got called through for her visit before she had to think of a convincing reply.

———

Zara placed the tray of food in front of Tyler. 'I got you a bit of everything. Chocolate, crisps, sweets, and a can of Fanta.'

'Smashing, I'm Hank Marvin today, I could eat a scabby horse. Mind you, that probably is what they serve in our canteen slop trays some days.'

Zara smiled over at her boy, happy to see him. 'So, Brian must have told you the doctors are letting him home next week. He can feel his toes again, and doctors said he's a good chance of getting all the feeling back in his legs.'

'Buzzing, Mam. I spoke with him, and it was nice to hear him in a better mood for a change. Honest, he had me worried for a while when we thought he wasn't going to walk again, I'm not going to lie. I know he's your baby, but he's my kid brother.'

Zara sucked on her chocolate. 'Yep, I totally agree. I only hope he's learned from it and never puts one of them silly bloody balloons in his mouth again. Because the doctor has already told him that, next time, it will definitely cause permanent damage. His mental health is not good either. He told me himself he's finding it hard to try and get his head back in gear. I can't cope with all that suffering, Tyler. I watched my own mam struggle with it for years and it drove her to drink – I can't see one of my boys go through it.'

Tyler frowned. 'I'll have another chat with him and tell Rico to keep a closer eye on him. They've asked me if I want to sign up to some sort of "men and their mental health" programme in here, so I'll tell him if Tyler Makin can man up and talk about stuff, he can too. You can't make someone open up, but tell him we are all here if he needs us.' He sighed and rolled his eyes as he continued, 'Did he tell you my dad went to see him in the hossy?'

Zara tried to keep a neutral face, but her bitterness was shining through. 'Yes, he did. I'm not going to lie, I hate that that prick can walk back into his life after all these years and be bloody father of the year. Brian was like, oh my dad this, oh my dad that. Honestly, all I wanted to do was tell him to shut his bloody gob and stop going on about him. It was winding me up. But I kept my cool and played the part well.'

'We need to watch him, Mam, keep him at arm's length. I don't want him coming back into our lives, thinking we need him and all that. Plus, he's a dodgy fucker. I don't trust him not to try and come in and take over what I've grafted so hard to run. Doesn't make sense him coming back just because our Bri is in hossy. We've all been ill before and he's not been arsed showing his face, so why now?'

'I'm glad we're singing from the same hymn sheet, son. I agree, strange him coming to Manchester.'

Tyler clocked Mike over the other side of the room staring at his mother. 'Fucking Patterson is all over you like a rash. Honest, he's a nasty fucker with everyone else but he can't do enough for me. I think he's got the hots for you.'

Zara couldn't put it off any longer. She took a swig of her drink then told Tyler the full story. Or almost the full story – no son needed to hear what his mam got up to between the covers.

She was expecting Tyler to kick off – he'd never liked any of her boyfriends, and now telling him she was dating a screw? She tried to hint it was basically over already. She moved in closer, making sure nobody could hear her. 'I can't put my finger on it, but he's a bit strange. I don't think he'll be around long.'

Tyler gripped her hand and pulled her closer. 'Nah, Mother, for once you've worked out what side your bread is buttered. This could be nice, really nice for me. If you can him, he'll make my life a misery. Plus, he's good to have on side in here. It might be just what I need. You need eyes in the back of your head here, Mam. I'm working hard to make this prison mine, make sure I've got a cut of all the action, but it's not easy with just me, Smidge and Rhino. I've been making a play for power, but I know that earns you enemies, so I could do with a screw on the take to watch out for me. Just you keep him sweet for now, don't fuck things up for me.'

Zara knew she'd walk to the end of the earth for her boy. 'Alright, alright. I'll do it for you. But not for long, just until you're sure you've got this wing stitched up.'

'That won't take long. I'm getting a name. But while I'm making it in here, I'm worried Rico is trashing our family name on the outside. All I hear on the grapevine is people who've seen him and Clara out partying and flashing the cash. I'm sick to death of hearing about Rico with Clara, like they're *Love Island* stars or something. Sick of him telling everyone he's loved up. So I put Clara to the test and sent her a text message. Friendly, like. Just to see what she would say and all that.'

Zara didn't like the sound of this. 'And did she reply?'

Tyler nodded and smirked. 'Dead right she did, straight away. She's coming to see me. I've asked her to keep it on the low and she said she would. She's just what I need to keep me updated on whatever that clown of a brother is doing. I'll keep her sweet, tell her I still have feelings for her, and that should be enough to get her to spill the dirt on Rico.'

'You can't do that to her. Yes, she irritates the life out of me, but you can't go playing with her head like that. You'll break her heart, break Rico's heart.'

'I'd be doing him a favour. If she loved him the way she's been telling everyone, then why is she even entertaining coming to see me and not telling Rico. Go on, answer that?'

Zara thought about it, and knew he was right. If Clara was keeping Tyler a secret, what else could she be hiding? A storm was brewing. But Tyler had to do what he had to do. His empire was what he'd worked hard for. He had to do whatever he had to, to keep it safe, to keep them all safe.

Chapter Twenty-Three

Mike ordered a bottle of red wine and sat facing Zara in the Italian restaurant, never taking his eyes from her. 'You look gorgeous tonight, darling. You smell amazing too. What perfume is it?' Zara lifted her hand to smell her wrist. 'It's called "Aoud Violet" by Mancera.'

Mike closed his eyes slightly and inhaled deeply. 'It's amazing. As soon as you sat down, I could smell it. It's getting me in the mood already, if I'm being honest.' His eyes shot to his crotch.

Zara ignored his last comment and carried on chatting, in no mood for dirty talk. 'They say if you can't smell it on yourself then it's a good fragrance. Bloody potty, if you ask me. I want to smell whatever I have bought, not bloody everyone else,' she giggled. The waiter came back to the table with the bottle of wine he'd ordered, not the cheap one either, the dearest one they had. Mike was out to impress tonight. One hundred pounds he'd splashed out for it. The restaurant was gently lit and soft music played in the background. On any other day, she'd think it was the perfect place for romance. But tonight, she was on edge – she hated the way she felt carrying secrets. She waited until her glass was full and lifted it to her mouth for a sip.

'Come here,' Mike whispered into her ear, his hand fumbling for her knee under the table. Zara looked around the room, cheeks on fire. Back in her day, she would have sat back and enjoyed every second of this, met him in the toilets for a quick knee-trembler. But not now, not today. She squeezed her legs tightly together. There was no way he was getting inside her knickers. Her voice was low. 'There will be plenty of time for that later. Let's enjoy the food and talk for a bit.'

Mike pulled his hand from under the table and chuckled. 'I wanted to see if I could surprise you, keep you on your toes.'

'I like sex, as you know, but don't have me down as some kind of a slapper. I've been on a handful of dates with you, and let's just say I want wining and dining, not sixty-nining all the bloody time. I promised myself that this time I would take things slowly. I know we've already slept together, and that was my mistake, but I want you to respect me.'

He answered her quickly, aware she was upset. 'I respect you already, Zara. I think you've got me all wrong.'

'No Mike, listen to me. If we are going to work, then you need to ease up on the pressure. I know you're a bit kinky, and I don't mind that if it's just for fun, but it really unsettled me. I want to go back to dating – getting to know each other – without any expectation of anything more.'

Mike sat back and stared at her. 'Wow, I thought we were having a bit of fun. We're both grown adults – why wait if we fancy each other?'

Zara left an awkward silence broken only by a ping as her mobile phone received a text message. She shot her eyes to the screen. Quickly she picked it up, scanned the message and shoved her phone back into her bag. 'It's just our Brian. He always texts me at this time.'

'I wish my mother would have been like that with me – actually wanting to hear from me,' Mike said. His eyes changed: fear, anger held inside them. He picked up his glass and gulped a mouthful of wine. 'My mother used to lock me up in my room, tie me to the bed and piss off out until all hours. Why do you think as soon as I was old enough I cleared off and joined the army? I very rarely see her even now. There is no bond, no love lost between us. She's still an alky and, every now and then, I'll get a phone call from her begging for forgiveness, telling me how much she loves me. Her words are lost with me though. She chose her life and who she wanted in it, and neglected me because of it.'

Zara felt for the first time that she might understand something real about Mike, something that sounded worryingly like her own past. 'That's so sad, Mike. And what a terrible thing to do to you. She should have been arrested.'

'When the neighbours reported her and the police came knocking, I never said a word, denied it all, I did. I was a kid, scared, vulnerable.'

Zara reached over and squeezed his hand. 'Well, you made it through – that young boy you were would be proud to see what you've made of yourself.' She might not want to date the guy anymore, but she hated to see anyone damaged by the hurt in their past. She knew only too well what a long shadow it cast.

She realised now she might not only be hurting herself keeping two men on the go – but them too. She was burning the candle at both ends. It was Ben, not Brian, who had texted her minutes ago telling her he wanted to see her tonight. Some people lived for the thrill of juggling different lovers – but Zara realised now you could definitely have too much of a good thing.

The rest of the night passed in light conversation – no more fumbles or deep and meaningfuls. At the end of the evening, Mike pulled up outside Zara's house. He could tell she wasn't in the mood for him coming inside for a coffee. He played it cool though, played the part well. He twisted his body to face her. 'It's been lovely tonight, Zara, and I'm sorry for the way I made you feel in the bedroom. I promise you I will never make you feel that way again. My intentions have always been to make you happy . I'm gutted I've fucked it up already. You see, I try too hard, don't I? I should chill out and just be me. I've always been the same though, always feeling not good enough.'

Zara stroked the side of his face softly. Maybe she'd written him off without giving him a real try – everyone's issues came from somewhere, she supposed. 'All I'm saying is small steps.' Her phone buzzed again with a message alert. She didn't dare look at it, aware it was probably Ben again. 'So, thanks for a lovely evening and when we are both free again it would be nice to meet up.'

Mike agreed. 'What about a day out to the seaside or something? We can stay overnight in a hotel if you want?'

Zara was still not sure how to play things. 'Let's see. Our Brian is home from the hospital soon and he'll need me around until he's back on his feet.'

'Of course, of course. No pressure.'

He came in for a kiss. Zara made sure it was a peck rather than anything more, then opened the car door and dipped her head low as she got out. She turned to face him. 'Goodnight, Mike, thanks for a lovely evening. Speak soon.'

'Night, gorgeous,' he replied.

Zara watched as he flicked the engine over and drove out of the street. The moment he was out of sight, she dug her hand in her bag and searched for her phone. She dialled the number and held the mobile to her ear. 'Hi, sorry I've not replied. I've just got in.'

The conversation went on for a few minutes more and the call ended. Ben was on his way. She rushed down the garden path and opened the door. She would have just enough time to freshen up, brush her teeth, spray some more perfume and get changed. This was all too close for comfort.

Ben kept his head low as he walked down the garden path, his hood up so nobody could recognise him. Zara opened the door and quickly ushered him inside. 'Come in before anyone sees you,' she whispered.

She plonked down on the sofa and gestured for him to join her.

But Ben declined and sat opposite. 'Max wants to come and see you. He told me last night. I don't like his tone. He said something about coming to take back what was his.'

Colour drained from her face. 'What the hell does he want to come and see me for? Got nothing to say to the wanker.'

Ben stared at her and shook his head. 'Our kid has never been one to listen, though, has he? Be prepared, Zara, be very prepared because, the way he was talking last night, it's any time soon that he will turn up on your doorstep. What we did the other night was rash – I should have known, the past is never really dead and buried, is it? And you know what Max is like when he's on a mission. He won't let anything get in his way.'

A cold chill ran down the back of Zara's neck, goose-bumps appearing on her skin, the small hairs on her arms standing on end. She wasn't ready to face Max again, she'd never be ready. Love him or loathe him, or even both, she knew he was about to turn her world upside down all over again.

Chapter Twenty-Four

Tyler paced around his pad. He looked like he hadn't slept, eyes red with dark circles framing them. 'What the fuck am I going to do, Smidge? I'm locked up in here and can't protect Rico. You heard the phone call last night. Our kid will be in a body bag if the money is not back pronto. Of all people, why did Rico go on the take from Jacob fucking Watts! You know Jacob, he's a nutcase and, even if I can smooth this over and get the money back, some grudges don't die. Rico's still done what he's done. He's taken the piss, stepped onto turf that he knew he shouldn't have. Try our Rico's phone again and see if he answers. He needs to sort this, like fucking now. If he doesn't, they will be through my mam's front door and I dread to think what will happen then.'

His rage and frustration boiled over and he punched the wall, blood blooming on his hand where it connected with the rough surface. Smidge had been trying Rico's number for over an hour but still no reply. He shot a look at Tyler and shook his head. He ended the call and stashed the mobile phone back in its hiding place.

'We all knew Rico would fuck up, Tyler. He's always been a liability. If it wasn't for you, I would never work with him on anything. He doesn't think, fucking idiot. But I assumed he'd fuck up in a small way – not like this. This is even more stupid than I could have imagined.'

Tyler knew his mate was right and there was no way he could defend his brother this time. Tyler had got the message last night to ring Jacob Watts and he knew as soon as his name was mentioned there was trouble. The call was feisty at first, threats being made, reputations at stake. Tyler had remained calm and told Jacob that if his brother had taken his money then he clearly didn't know it belonged to Jacob. He told him it was a mistake, and he would get the money back once he'd spoken to his sibling. At least he'd bought a bit of time. Jacob was threatening to go through his mother's front door at first, smash the gaff up, kick fuck out of anyone who was there. Twenty-four hours Jacob had given him to sort this mess out and here was Rico not answering his phone. Tyler was going ape. He walked up and down the cell, he stopped at the window and stuck his forehead against the cold metal bars. He sucked in mouthfuls of the cold air and scanned the little bit of horizon he could see. He couldn't believe he was just fifteen minutes from home. But he was locked away, behind bars, helpless.

The cell door opened, and Mike stood at the door smirking. 'Heard a bit of commotion, lads. Is everything alright in here, or what?' He looked at Tyler's bloodied knuckles.

Tyler twisted his head slowly and looked Patterson right in the eyes. 'Sorted, pal, nothing for you to worry about.'

'That's fine, then. Anyway, doors are open now, breakfast is served. Bon Appetit!'

Smidge growled over at the screw and jerked his head slightly. 'Well, do one then, what are you still hanging about for?'

Mike stepped into the cell and stood tall. Tyler could see this escalating and stepped in just in time. 'Smidge is just having a bad day, boss. His Mrs is giving him a hard time.'

Mike took a step back, nostrils still flared. 'Just watch what you're saying next time, lad, because I don't stand for any shit on this wing, none whatsoever.'

Tyler walked over and patted Mike on his shoulder. 'Thanks for understanding.' Then Mike was gone.

Smidge stood up and confronted Tyler. 'What the fuck are you licking his arse for? I can't believe you of all people have sucked up to him. He's a fucking screw, a prick.'

Tyler sat down on the bed and come clean. 'You won't believe this, but he's been seeing my mam, and I need to keep on the right side of him because he can help us in here, get us stuff in, make our lives easier.'

Smidge looked shocked. 'What, your old lady is banging a screw? For fuck's sake, how have you allowed that to even happen? You should have told her to get rid. It's like shagging a copper.'

Tyler bolted up from the bed, didn't like the way his pal was speaking about his mother. 'Shut your mouth before I do it for you, Smidge. Like I said, she's doing it for me. He fancied her from the moment he saw her, and she told me she was going on a date with him. In fact, my mam said she wasn't really that into him. It was me who told her to keep seeing him.'

Smidge swallowed hard, and aware Tyler was ready for snapping, he backed down. 'OK then, if he can bring something to the table then so be it.'

There was silence for a few seconds, Tyler staring into the distance trying to work out how he could save his family this time. His brother was a dead man walking, and his family were in danger, and it felt like there was nothing he could do about it except sit and watch.

The cell door flung open suddenly and in rushed two men, their faces covered. They gripped Smidge first and slammed him to the floor, no time for him to fight back. In a flurry of arms and legs, he was kicked and punched, a short iron bar whacked over his head. Tyler tried to protect his friend, but more men rushed into his cell and held him down while the others beat him within an inch of his life. This was turf wars and although the goons hid their faces, two guys were very clearly showing their faces to prove a point.

Brendan Sykes stood over Tyler as he pummelled his fist into his face 'You think you can have me over, you prick, then think again. I've heard you were planning on taking my place, fucking snake.' Tyler's head was smashed into the side of the bed and a thick trickle of deep red blood started to gush from his head. This was a blood bath. Brendan stood over Tyler and gave him one last final punch to his nose. 'Next time, think before you go shouting your big mouth off.'

The men were gone, and Tyler and Smidge left out cold on the floor. Not a prison guard in sight. Tyler opened his eyes slowly, already feeling the swelling around his eyes making it hard to see. He tried to move but it was impossible: a burning deep in his stomach, a hot pounding pain, blood still flowing from a knife wound. Smidge crawled to the open door and tried his best to get help. A screw from the other side of the wing clocked him and immediately started to raise the alarm. Sirens were going off now, immediately matched by noise from the inmates, shouting, screaming, prisoners all gathering on the landing to see who had been attacked.

The screw ran into the cell and stopped. He'd seen some beatings before, but nothing like this. 'Tyler, it's Officer Hargreaves, it's Keith, can you hear me?'

Hargreaves had built a decent relationship with Tyler and to see him like this had knocked him. He knew plenty of old army colleagues who'd ended up on Tyler's side of the bars, and knew most of the prison wasn't filled with guys who were born bad, more ones who had few options. He always hoped he could get to men on their first stretch on the inside, help them turn their lives around, before they got too deep into prison culture. But he knew, once the lads were drawn into vendettas, there was no good outcome. He could see Tyler moving and knew he not only had to help him, but also to get the names of whoever had done this to him before they tried to finish what they'd started. 'Tyler,' he repeated, 'can you hear me?'

The cell was swarmed now with officers, Mike among them. Keith roared at the top of his voice. 'Get on the fucking CCTV and see who's done this. Somebody go now. I want these bastards hung, drawn and quartered. I'll do it myself once I've found them.'

The whole wing was put on lockdown. All the prisoners were flung behind their doors and, as Smidge and Tyler were stretchered out, the shouting was swapped for a brooding silence. Not a word was spoken as the men were carried past locked doors. But as they passed the whispers started. Prisoners stuck their heads to the hatches and muttered to each other behind the closed doors. Tyler Makin's brief stint at the top was over: he'd been taken down. There was a new gaffer in town. Brendan Sykes had let Tyler take Big Sam out, then stepped in and taken over. The gossip spread like wildfire. Almost before the stretchers had left the floor there were rumours Tyler wasn't going to make it. You live by the sword, you die by the sword.

Brendan and Philip meanwhile sat quietly in their pads, having cleaned up, hidden or flushed any evidence that would point the finger at them. Not that anyone would dare.

Tyler and Smidge were blue-lighted to North Manchester General for emergency treatment. Mike and Keith both offered to escort the two prisoners. They were aware it could mean long hours sat by their bedsides, but until they both knew what had happened, and what the men's chances of recovery were, it was the safest way.

Neither officer was allowed near the prisoners until the doctors had assessed the two men. Eventually, Mike was ushered through a blue paper curtain and sat by Tyler's bedside. Tyler had been stabbed in his stomach and his leg, and had lost a lot of blood, as well as carrying a slew of smaller injuries.

Mike knew Zara would be here anytime soon and already dreaded seeing her. He'd promised her he would look after her boy, told her his life would be good in the jail now he was looking after him. She'd hate him for sure, she'd never believe a word he told her again. But he thought of Smidge's family too – Smidge was in a far worse way. He was on a life support machine. The next twenty-four hours were crucial for him, and his relatives had been told to expect the worse. He had bleeds on the brain, had been stabbed countless times, and it wasn't looking good. Keith was sitting with him while Mike waited for Zara to arrive.

Zara was hysterical when she saw her son. Mike didn't recognise the man with her, but he said Tyler was his nephew as he introduced himself. There was a look of cold fury as he stared at Tyler's battered form lying there, his chest rising and falling gently, not stirring at the sound of Zara's cries.

Zara screamed over at Mike. 'Who the fuck has done this to him? I want them finding and hanging for this. Look at my poor boy, look at what they have done to him?'

Mike was aware he was on the clock and he had to act professionally. Plus the man by Zara's side didn't look like the kind of man you messed with. 'Mrs Makin, all investigations are being held and the men who have done this will be found. I was one of the first to your son's side and got him here as soon as I could. The doctors have told me any later and this would have been a murder enquiry, but they're optimistic he'll pull through.'

Ben came to Zara's side and hugged her tightly. 'He's in the best place now, Zara. The doctors are here, and he will make it through.'

She quivered as she walked closer to the bedside. She closed her eyes as she touched her son's hand. 'Son,' she snivelled. 'Please don't leave me. I know you're strong and you will pull through, please for me, don't leave me.' Tyler's eyes flickered, and his fingers moved. She wasn't sure if he had heard her, but it was a crumb of encouragement. 'Son, I'm here with you. I'm not going anywhere until I know you are alright.'

Mike was aware of the security risks in this room and the rules for inmates when they were in hospital. He shot a look over at Ben and paused before he spoke to him. 'I'm sorry, only one person is allowed in the room and that has to be his next of kin. I'm only doing my job so can I ask you to leave?'

Zara was sobbing her heart out. She dug her hand into her coat pocket and pulled out a bunch of keys. 'Here, take my keys and go and wait at my house. Brian is due home today, and he'll need looking after. Can you please go and make sure he has everything that he needs? I can't believe it – we should be celebrating my baby getting out of hospital today and here I am at another son's bedside. My head is in bits. If anything happens to Tyler, I don't know what I will do. Try Rico's phone again, Ben, and tell him to get over here.'

Ben took the bunch of keys from her hand. Mike closed the door and turned back to Zara. She was rocking to and fro, hugging her body tightly.

He rushed to her side. 'Zara, I promise you now, I will get these bastards for this. I'll get names, I'll make sure each and every one of them pays for this, mark my words. I won't let you down.'

She sniffed as she said, 'You have let me down already, Mike. Look at him, look at my son, my boy. I don't even recognise him. Look at his face, his beautiful, beautiful face.'

He was by her side, hand resting on her shoulder. 'Please don't say that, Zara. I feel bad enough. I know I said I would protect him, but I took my eye from the ball for a split second and I'm so sorry for that. Please don't hate me. Please.'

Zara lifted her head slowly and looked him directly in his eyes. She licked her dry cracked lips. 'I want my boy out of here as soon as he's well enough to move.'

Mike nodded. 'Yes, he will go back to the hospital wing in the jail. I'll make sure he is looked after there too.'

Her words were slow and meaningful. 'No, you don't understand me. I want my boy gone from that jail. Or any other jail. He can move to another country, start a new life. I won't ever rest knowing he is locked away somewhere, at risk of suffering at the hands of those bastards again. Mike, you said you would do anything for me, you said I was special. Get my boy out of here and we could all move abroad. Live a peaceful life.'

Mike's heartbeat doubled, mouth dry. 'Zara, this is my job, my livelihood. If I got found out, I would be flung into jail too. You're not thinking straight.'

'I am of sound mind and body, Mike. Help me, please. If you feel anything towards me then help me move Tyler away from all this shit.'

Mike flopped down on the black plastic chair next to the bed and dropped his head low, cracking his knuckles. 'Zara, let's get Tyler on the mend before we talk about anything else. I have heard what you are saying, and I need to digest it all.'

She reached over and stroked the side of his face, looking deep into his eyes, preying on his emotions. 'If you did this for me I would be forever thankful. It will show me that you do really care for me and want to protect me. Don't let my baby go back to prison, please, I'm begging you.'

Mike dropped his head onto her shoulder. His fingers tightened around her hand. He inhaled her perfume as he closed his eyes, imagining a life on the run, a new identity. 'I don't know, Zara. I need to think. But I know we'll work something out – you're a fighter, and I know no one fights harder than a mother for her child.'

Chapter Twenty-Five

Rico gripped Clara by the neck and pushed her up against the wall. He was nose to nose with her, eyes bulging from their sockets. 'Tell me why you have been texting my brother behind my back. I've just read all those messages to him, you fucking cheat. Here am I thinking you're a decent bird when all along you've been getting wet about my brother. Tell me the truth, because on my life, I'll—. Don't take me for some daft prick, don't ever think you can have me over.' His eyes were dancing with madness.

Clara knew this was serious. Her face was turning blue, her feet barely touching the ground, her windpipe restricting her breathing. She tapped his arm rapidly, her desperate voice barely a whisper. 'Let me go, Rico, I'll tell you everything. I can't breathe.'

Rico dropped her to the floor like a sack of spuds and watched as she scrambled to the other side of the hotel room. He stood over her again, waiting on an answer. 'Now, fucking tell me,' he roared.

She was petrified and knew any second now he would grip her again if she didn't spill. Why hadn't she deleted all the messages? She'd asked herself that a thousand times and she could have kicked herself for being so stupid. But she liked reading over them, feeling loved by Tyler, planning a future with him.

They'd had a lovely evening at the hotel until Rico had taken her phone when she was sleeping and started going through her messages. Hundreds of messages there was, and he'd scanned through them all, ignoring his own phone, until he got to the latest texts telling her to get Rico to ring him as soon as possible. But he wasn't calling anyone, least of all Tyler, until he'd got to the bottom of this, so he'd woken Clara and told her she'd been found out.

His temper raged wilder and wilder. 'So,' he sneered, 'start talking, I'm listening.'

His body slid down the wall and he sat near her with his head resting on his knees.

'I used to see Tyler before you. I've never mentioned it because it was past and I liked you, didn't want you running a thousand miles away just because I'd had a thing with Tyler.'

His face creased with pain, the thought of his older brother laughing at him behind his back, the thought of the two of them lay in bed together. 'Sick in the head, you are, Clara. If I'd known my brother'd had you, I would never have gone near you. Leftovers aren't my bag. It's wrong in so many different ways.'

Her voice was desperate. 'It was ages ago, Rico. A few months we spent together. It wasn't a relationship like we have. He used to ring me every now and then and we'd hook up.'

'So just a shag, then? Basically, Tyler would ring you for a quickie?'

Her eyes clouded over, and she started playing with her fingers. 'Yes, you could say that.'

'And did you love him? Because all those text messages I've read tell me there are feelings still involved?'

A big fat salty tear landed on her lip. She stuttered, lips trembling, aware he could strike at any second and hurt her. 'I got mixed up, Rico. Yes, at the time Tyler was someone who I felt a lot for, but it never worked out. He stopped ringing me, never answered my calls and just left me standing.'

'So, it was you who was into him, then. If Tyler never bothered with you, that tells me it was you who was doing all the running. You were just a notch on his bedpost, nothing more.'

Clara bit down on her bottom lip. The truth hurt.

But Rico wasn't done. 'So, why did he get back in touch? How did you get his new number for this prison phone? Go on, tell me that?'

Clara felt her own anger rising. 'He texted me, so there, wind your neck in and have this out with your brother, not me.' Yes, she'd been playing fast and loose texting Tyler, but he'd started it.

'Don't you worry about that. That prick will be getting told. I'll ruin him now, take everything he owns. I bet he's been laid on his bed laughing his bollocks off at me over this. I bet everyone has, and here's me taking you on holiday, buying you gifts, handbags, perfumes and everything else, and all the time you've been having me over.'

'No, I have not. You and me were real – *are* real. It was just that, back when Tyler sent me a message from Strangeways, I had to reply. I wanted to see what he had to say. It was him, not bleeding me.'

'Yeah, you would say that now I've caught you out. Honest, I thought you were the one, but my mam was right about you, you're just a gold-digger after what you can get for yourself. You were using me until Tyler got out then you were planning on moving onto him. Well, our Brian is single, and he's due out of the hossy soon, so why don't you fucking move onto him next? Then you will have the treble. We can all compare notes then when we are sat having our tea.'

Clara gritted her teeth, sick of listening to the abuse. 'Since when did your mother know me to even have an opinion about me? How dare she call me a gold-digger when she's the biggest bike around! Everyone talks about her. Everyone's had a go on her, so stick that in your pipe and smoke it. And you can tell her that too. Like I'm arsed what that tart has to say about me.'

Rico cracked his knuckles. 'Don't you ever even mention my mother's name again. You know fuck all about her. You're only saying that because she had you sussed out from the start, you daft bint.'

Clara got to her feet, always keeping her eyes on Rico. 'So, I guess this is it, then? I'll get my stuff together and go home. For the record, Rico, I never used you and I never touched another guy while we were together.'

'As if I believe a word you say. I could never touch you again knowing my brother has been all over you. Damaged goods, you are.'

She flicked her hair over her shoulder, went over to her handbag and started packing her make-up away. She could see him through the mirror. His head was dropped into his cupped hands, and he looked devastated. She turned around slowly, one hand on her hip. 'We could have been good together, Rico Makin – it's your own family that ruined this.'

He held his mobile towards her. 'Do you want to borrow this to tell someone who gives a fuck? Because I'm done. Sloppy seconds is not my style. Get your stuff and do one.'

Clara stood for a few seconds looking at him, then picked up her handbag and hooked it over her shoulder, ready to leave. He sprang to his feet, ran at her and ripped the bag from her shoulder. He emptied its contents on the bed. 'You can fuck off if you think you're having this. Six ton, it cost me. I'll sell it and get some of my money back. Go and ask our kid to get you one.' Clara picked up an empty plastic bag from the floor and scooped all her stuff from the bed into it. 'I didn't have you down as that type of man, Rico, but eh, I know now, don't I?'

He went to the door and opened it wide. 'Good riddance,' he sneered as he watched her walk past him. Once she was gone, he slammed the door shut and stood with his back to it.

Then he remembered the messages from Tyler saying to call him. His nostrils flared as he walked over to the mirror and looked at his reflection. He lifted his head slowly. 'And now for you, Tyler. Nobody laughs at me behind my back, fucking *nobody*. You watch, brother, watch this space. I'll take everything you have, that you love, and ruin you.'

Rico plonked down on the bed – he was done with his brother telling him to call him and expecting him to jump. Things were changing from this moment on. He needed to work out his next move.

Chapter Twenty-Six

Brian walked shakily about the living room. His legs were still not working properly, and they strained with each step he took. Ben sat facing him and yawned. He'd stayed the night with him and slept in Rico's bed, but he'd hardly slept a wink, worrying about his nephews.

Brian sat down and shot a look over at his uncle. 'I need to go and see Tyler. He was always on the end of the blower when I was in hospital – I can't get my head round the fact he's in there now. I feel helpless. What can I do to help? Where the bloody hell is Rico?'

Ben reached over to the table and popped a fag from the packet before he sparked it up. 'Dunno, kid. I've been trying him all night and it keeps going to voice mail. Not good is it, when we need to get hold of him. Clara's not answering her phone, either.'

'Have you spoken with my mam yet this morning? I feel sick thinking of our kid beaten like that. They must have set it up, surprised him, because there is no way in this world he would have fallen in a fair fight. Smidge too, he's a tough sod, he doesn't go down easily. I can't get my head around it.'

'Me neither. All we can do is pray he's going to be alright.'

Brian didn't look convinced. He had plenty of other things rather than prayer in mind.

'I'll bell your mam again now and see how he is.'

Ben reached for his phone and rang Zara. 'Zara, how are you? How's our Tyler?… Right let me have a wash, then I'll come up to sit with him. You can come home for a bit, have a sleep and get yourself together.'

Brian chirped in from the other side of the room. 'Mam, tell him I love him. Tell him we will get things sorted. Nobody fucks with my brother and takes liberties.'

Ben tried to listen to Zara on the other end of the phone. 'Right, give me ten minutes and I'll fly up there. Brian has had a good night's sleep, and he's tried to do a bit of walking around the house to find his feet. He'll be fine until you get home.'

The call ended and Ben looked over at Brian. 'What a mess. I never thought I'd see the day the Makins were in the crosshairs. I'll get a wash before I go to give your mam a break.'

'Yeah, sorted. If you need some clean clothes, go in Rico's wardrobe. He's the same size as you. Shove something of his on.'

Ben had been gone for over ten minutes when the front door banged shut. Rico came into the living room, raging. 'Did you know what our twat of a brother's been up to? Even in bloody prison he's ruining my life. Did you know he's been messaging Clara—?'

Brian cut him off. 'Rico, why the hell have you not been answering your phone? Everyone's been belling you out all night. Our Ty is in hospital. Some guys had him and Smidge over and both of them are in a bad way. Smidge is on a life support machine and my mam said it's not looking good for him. Mam thought we were going to lose Tyler too, but he's got through the night. You need to get your arse down there right away.'

Rico froze, processing the news. 'Not arsed, mate. He's a snake and he can rot in hell as far as I'm concerned. How dare he try and get onto my woman. Did you know he used to see her before me? Am I the only person who doesn't fucking know?'

Brian slammed his palm onto the arm of the chair. 'Can you forget about yourself for one sodding minute, Rico? This is not about you or Clara. I've just told you your brother is in a bad way. Sort your napper out and get up there to see him.'

Rico growled, 'Don't tell me what to do, you tool. I'm sick of everyone always dropping everything for Tyler in this fucking house. He was stupid enough to get caught and sent down, stupid enough to text my bird and think I wouldn't find out, and now he's been stupid enough to get jumped in jail. Stupid is as stupid does, I say. He's brought it all on himself. I'm doing my own thing from now on, you just watch.'

'Oh, stop trying to play the head case, bro. Family comes first. If Clara has been getting onto our kid, then she's the one in the wrong. Bin her and move on.'

'Nah, he should have told me he used to have a thing with her. I would have told him. But no, the shady bastard kept his trap shut. If he wasn't so busy messaging my Mrs, he probably wouldn't have turned his back long enough to get beaten up—'

Before he finished, Rico heard banging on the front door, loud banging like the door was going to go through if he didn't open up. He looked out of the front window. Two stocky men dressed in black stood there looking up at the windows. Rico was still pumped with fury and adrenaline so marched to the door and threw it open. As soon as it swung back, he was gripped by the neck and flung inside the house.

Jacob Watts meant business and he wasn't here to make friends. Pete was by his side and within seconds of the door opening Tommy was there too. Brian sat in the chair. His legs wouldn't let him move – he couldn't tell whether it was from fear or the nitrous damage.

Rico was on the floor and Jacob was laying into him with his boots. Just a look from Tommy over at Brian told him to stop his attempts to move and stay where he was. Jacob lifted Rico up by the scruff of the neck. 'That was my fucking money that you took. I want it back *now*. I told your brother twenty-four hours or bust, and now that time is up. I hope for your sake you have it, otherwise you'll be coming

with me, and I'll tell you now, you won't be coming back.'
He dropped him back to the floor.

Rico was dazed, blood dripping from his nose. For all his
talk, Tyler had always been the one who gave the beatings.
Rico was usually hanging back, keeping out of the action.

Jacob crouched down beside Rico and set out in no
uncertain terms who he was and what he'd come for.

Once he'd finished, Tommy took over to do the rest of
the dirty work. 'We're not waiting about you, fucking clown.
Do you have the money or what?'

Rico was shaking from head to toe. He'd wet himself. 'I
didn't know it was yours. I were given a tip-off about the
van. Thought it was out-of-towners.' He tried to pull himself
up against the wall.

'You thought fucking wrong then, didn't you,' hissed
Peter.

The gang was hungry for the money they were owed
and, if Rico didn't start talking soon, the shit was going to
hit the fan.

Jacob nodded over at Tommy. 'He's not talking, is he?
Give that other one a few belts and see if that loosens his
lips as to where my money is.'

Tommy rushed over to Brian and headbutted him. He
pulled his fist back ready to launch it into his face until
Brian screamed, 'Tell him Rico, tell him where the money is!'

Rico flinched as he saw his younger brother's panic. He
pulled himself onto all fours, every broken rib pulsing
with pain. 'Right, I'll get it. Honest, I never knew it belonged
to you. Give me a minute to get up and get my head
together.'

Jacob winked at Tommy and Peter. This was going to be easier than he first thought. He sat back and watched his victims tremble with fear. 'I spoke with Tyler last night and told him to sort it. I respected your brother, but it looks like you don't, otherwise the money would have already landed back on my lap, wouldn't it?'

Rico held his fingers to a cut on his cheek and then looked down at them: they were dripping blood. Brian was cradling his clearly broken nose, and Rico knew he would never get out of this alive if he didn't cough up the money.

'So, honest mistake. I'm holding my hands up here – I never wanted beef with you. Once you have the money back, we can shake hands and forget about this, do you hear what I'm saying?'

Jacob spat at Rico. Who the fuck did he think he was, calling the shots? He was lucky he wasn't ten feet under already. 'I said, fucking money, now. I've not decided what will happen with you two clowns yet, but the longer you keep me waiting here, the worse it will get for you both. So, stop time-wasting and go and get the fucking money before I lose my rag and end you right here, right now.'

Rico scrambled to his feet. 'It's upstairs, I'll go and get it.'

Jacob eyeballed Peter. 'Go with him. I don't want him getting any smart ideas about getting on his toes.'

Peter dragged Rico by his jacket and flung him out of the room. Tommy looked over at Brian and smirked. 'You need to word your brother up and tell him not to touch other people's work. We have a code where we come from, and he should abide by it too.'

Brian was coughing blood and he didn't even look up.

Footsteps could be heard walking about upstairs. Then shouting, screaming.

Tommy raised his eyebrows. 'Looks like we might have to get the drill out for this prick, Jake.'

Jacob held his ear to the door and snarled, 'If there is no money, the runt is coming with us.'

The door flung open, and Rico was thrown back on the floor with Peter stood behind him. 'You won't like this, boss. The smart-arse said the money has gone. He's playing fucking games with us, buying time or something. Let's take him to the lock-up and we'll do what we have to do with him.'

Jacob was aware he'd already been at the property longer than he'd planned. He didn't have to think twice. He jumped up to his feet and dragged Rico up. 'I don't like paying house calls normally, so I was hoping this was going to be cut and dried, but now you're going to see what happens when you mess with the big boys. Peter, get the twat in the boot of the car.'

Rico spat a tooth out and his head lolled to the side as they dragged him from the house.

Peter turned to Brian. 'No need to tell you to keep your mouth shut to the dibble, is there? Because if you so much as whisper a word, we'll be back, and next time I'll finish you off myself.'

Brian was in no fit state to speak. He was in a bad way, his chest rising slowly, his breathing wheezy. He heard the car screech off as he reached for his mobile, but as he tried to make a call, the blackness that had been threatening to engulf him swept over him and he slumped.

Chapter Twenty-Seven

Zara was grabbed by Molly before she got to the front door. 'Bloody hell you look like you've been through the mill, love. What's up?'

Zara gulped. The ball of emotion that had been stuck in her throat for the last few hours exploded and she broke down crying.

Molly held her in her arms. 'Oh, my lovely, what on earth has happened now? Come on, come to my house. I'll make you a nice cuppa and you can tell me all about it. Look at you, you're a mess.'

Zara's legs buckled and Molly had to support her all the way to her house. Once they were inside, she sat Zara down and passed her some tissues. 'Please don't tell me that Mike has pissed you off, because I could have bleeding wrote this. I never said anything to you before, but I had a feeling about that man. Some of the stuff you were saying about him didn't sit right with me. You're better off without him, if you ask me. Stay single and have peace of mind.'

Zara dabbed the tissue into the corner of her eyes. 'It's not Mike, Molly.'

Molly waited for her friend to explain, but when Zara dissolved into more tears she carried on talking. 'So, it's Ben then. I did tell you, you were playing with fire and we all know when you touch fire you get burnt, love, don't we? Go on, what's he done?'

Zara blew a long hard breath and sucked on her bottom lip. 'It's not Ben, either. It's our Tyler, he's in hospital. Some heavies in the nick got to him and beat him within an inch of his life. I've been at the hospital all night by his bedside and he's not good, Molly, not good at all.'

Molly's hand paused on the kettle. 'Stop it, no bloody way. How can he get battered in there? Surely, they have staff who stop all that happening? I'd be straight on the phone to the bloody governor if I was you. Bleeding disgrace, it is. But your Ty is a strong one, Zara – he'll come through it, I'm sure.'

Zara pulled her cigarettes from her coat pocket and slowly slid one from the packet. 'It's all getting too much for me, Molly. I've had all the shit with Brian, and now our Tyler. When will it all calm down? Honest I'm at the end of my tether. Ben stayed with Brian last night to make sure he was alright, but how the hell am I going to be at the hospital and at home to look after Brian too? It's impossible.'

Molly helped the best way she could – she made the tea and brought it over to the kitchen table. 'I've put an extra sugar in that for you, love, it will help calm you down.'

'My nerves are shattered. Valium would have been better than tea.' Zara blew the top of her drink and took a small sip. 'I feel so tired, like I could sleep for a week. Every time I close my eyes all I can see is our Tyler lay in that hospital bed and there is nothing I can do to help him.'

Molly shook her head. 'I'll tell you what. You can go and have a few hours' kip in my bed. Hubby's at work and he won't be home until late tonight. I'll nip over to yours and make sure Brian's got everything he needs. Has he got medication to take, or does he just need something making to eat? I'm going down to Eastford Square later. I can pop in the shop for a pie for his tea. Do you want me to make you something to eat before you go up, a bacon butty, cheese on toast?'

'No thanks, Mol, I couldn't stomach anything. I've been sick three times this morning already, even just trying a sip of hospital tea. I think I'm suffering from shock or something.'

'You probably are. Come on. You go and have a sleep and things will seem a bit better when you've rested. I don't know how you are still standing, love. The shit you've had to deal with lately, I'd be six feet under.'

'They are my boys, Molly. My life. I do what I must for them. They hurt, I hurt. You know how it works, you have kids of your own.'

'I know, love, but when is all this stress going to stop for you? They are grown men, not babies. This should be your time now. You should be kicking back having a stress-free life with the lads looking after you.'

Zara sounded defeated as she spoke. 'Our Tyler has always looked after me, Molly. Even from being a small child, he has always helped out. I remember having no milk and no money to buy it, and he went straight out and came back with some.' She smiled as she continued, 'He'd nicked it from some poor bugger's doorstep though. I only found out weeks later when Mrs Jackson came knocking at the door telling me she'd followed him home.' Zara's eyes changed and she shook her head. 'It's a shame Rico isn't like him. That tight git won't give a bleeding door a bang. I don't know why he's like that when he's been brought up the same as the others. I always made sure he shared growing up, so God knows what happened to him. Our Brian is like Tyler. He's never got any money, but when he has, he will always share, always asks me if I have cigs and that when he's going out.'

'You've tried your best by those boys, Zara, there is no denying that. I just hope and pray they all sort themselves out. There is only so much a woman can take, isn't there?'

Zara played with her fingers and looked into her empty cup. 'I suppose the big man in the sky thinks I can handle it,' she said softly.

Molly shot a look over to the Virgin Mary statue on the windowsill. 'I'll say a few Hail Marys tonight for Tyler and the family, Zara. I'll ring around my sisters too and tell them we need their prayers. Strength in numbers, I always say.'

Zara nodded and smiled. 'Thanks, Molly, you're an angel in disguise. You'll definitely be getting your wings when you reach them pearly gates.'

'I'm doing what any good friend would do,' said Molly. 'Now come on, go and get in bed.'

Zara lay on the bed and closed her eyes as memories of her children playing in the garden in the summer came back to her: laughter, tears, and lots of games and water fights. They were the happy times, days when all she had to worry about was getting her children ready for school each day. Was the way her boys turned out her fault? Had she let them down somehow? Was it because she was a single parent, and her boys had no real role model to look up to? She wasn't sure. It wasn't like Max would have been a shining example to her lads, even if he had stuck around. Her spirit felt crushed as she got up and pulled the grey curtains together across the window, blocking out any sunlight, any troubles from the outside world for a moment.

———

Molly was singing in the kitchen. Just a few jobs left, and she would head over to see Brian. She opened the fridge and popped her head inside. Yep, a nice ham butty she would make for him with a few cherry tomatoes on it. Everybody loved a bit of ham, didn't they? Molly made the sandwich and wrapped it in tinfoil. She looked for her chunky cardigan to shove on. then headed out and down the path towards Zara's house. If the place was untidy, she would give it a quick dusting, and hoover the front room, even wash a few pots. She knew a few of the neighbours called her a nosy bastard, but she wanted to do anything she could to help Zara in her hour of need.

She called out as she pushed the door handle. 'Brian, it's only me, Molly. I hope you're decent because I'm coming in.

Don't be giving me a heart attack being naked or something,' she giggled. Molly closed the door behind her and opened the living room door. It looked like a bombsite. From the corner of her eye, she spotted Brian on the floor behind the chair. She rushed to his side, panic flooding her as she saw the state of him. 'Jesus Christ Almighty, what has happened to you, Brian? Look at the state of you. Have you fell? Oh, bleeding hell, your nose looks bust to me. What on earth has happened? Speak to me, Brian, are you alright, lad?'

Brian's mouth was moving but no sound was coming out. She bent down and heard his whisper, 'Get Mam. I want my mam.'

Molly placed her hand on his shoulder. 'Brian, you need medical help. I'm going to ring 999 – you're fresh out of hospital and it looks like you need to go straight back in. Your mam is at my house, but let me get an ambulance first, then I'll run over and get her. Come on lad, let's help you up. Sit on the chair and let me have a proper look at you.' With all her might she yanked Brian up from the floor and made sure he was sat properly in the chair. She could see him clearer now, see his cuts, his open wounds. This wasn't a fall. His breathing was ragged and he was sweating from head to toe. She placed her hand over her mouth and her eyes said it all. With haste she rummaged in her pocket for her mobile phone and rang for an ambulance.

He stared deep into her eyes and his bottom lip trembled. 'They've taken him, they took Rico.'

'Who's taken him, Brian? What has happened?'

Brian swallowed hard. He gripped her hand and squeezed at it tightly. He stuttered, 'Rico, they've taken him, said they will do him in. We need help, I need my mam.' Brian dropped his head onto his chest. He was falling in and out of consciousness.

Molly was in a panic, listening to Brian in between giving the emergency services the details of the injured man. 'Please hurry, please be quick,' she pleaded with them.

She ended the call and told Brian help was on its way. Before she'd even got him as comfortable as she could, the ambulance arrived. One look was all it took for the paramedics to usher him into the back of their vehicle, and Molly knew she couldn't wait to hear their verdict. Instead she gripped the cross from her silver necklace and kissed the crucifix as she fled back over the road, dreading having to break the news to Zara. She said her prayers as she ran. She only hoped God was listening.

Chapter Twenty-Eight

Rico lay limp on the floor, his eyes twitching every few seconds the only sign of life. Voices outside the room, keys jangling, a cold air blowing in from underneath the door. The heavy door opened and Jacob Watts stood there like a man of steel. Pete and Tommy stood behind him. Tommy had the drill in his hand and a large transparent plastic sheet. Jacob walked over to Rico and dug his foot into his body, so he flipped over.

'Wakey wakey, dickhead.'

Tommy knew his role well and plugged the drill in. He pulled his gloves on and pressed the power on the drill. The sound was loud, ominous.

Pete nodded at Jacob. 'Let's get this twat sat up and listening. I swear to you if he's not talking he's going to meet his maker.'

Jacob smirked and shot a look over at Tommy who was more than ready for business. Peter dragged Rico up and launched him onto the leather sofa. The furniture was old and tattered and covered in stains already. Rico could barely open his eyes, but as soon as he heard Jacob's voice he was back in the moment, back in the nightmare that was his life.

'So, I want names. Who were you grafting with and who's got what money?'

Rico was struggling to lift his head up. Every now and then it flopped down on his chin. 'I know my cut was in the house. My mam must have moved it, stashed it away. Let me ring her and see. She'll tell me straight away then I can give it back to you.'

'Not as easy is that though, is it, Rico? That's just your cut. We want all the fucking money back, not just the part you say you have.' Pete was on a mission.

'Mate, all we want is the cash. You can walk away from this and lick your wounds once we know who else we need to go see, but if you start fucking us about, chatting shit, then we have no other option than to step up a gear.' Tommy pressed his finger on the black drill button, a piercing sound ringing out.

The message was understood loud and clear by the look on Rico's face. But to be labelled a grass, a Judas, was just as much of a nightmare as the thought of the drill. His name would be dirt when everyone had found out what he'd done. Bubbling his mates was a sin never to be forgiven. Rico swallowed hard, every bone in his body pounding in pain. His eyes nearly closed, purple and black bruises under them, dried blood stuck to his cheeks. 'I need a drink, ' he mumbled.

Pete scoffed. 'Fuck the drink, mate, you'll need a priest if you carry on wasting my time. Do you know I should have been on golden sands now with my Mrs and my kids. Yeah, should have been soaking up the sun and getting pissed. But, because of daft pricks like you, my family are sat at home in the bleeding cold weather, crying because I promised them a holiday. Now you tell me where the money is, prick, and who is involved, then it will be sweet. I'm only going to ask you once more, then my friend over there will take over if you're not telling me what I want to hear. Do you get me, pal?'

Rico swallowed hard: his life was at stake. 'Freddy and Wayne were with me. I don't know their second names, but Tex introduced them to me a few months ago. I think they are Salford lads.'

Jacob sat thinking for a few seconds. 'Yeah, I know fucking Freddy Watson and his cronies. I had a bit of beef with him a few years back. He labels himself as a bit of a nutter. Don't get me wrong, he can handle himself, but he's nobody who is going to give us a problem.'

Peter chirped in. 'And the money, how much have they got?'

Rico was singing like a canary now, telling them everything they wanted to know. He valued his life and, if there was any chance he was getting out of here alive, he was doing everything they wanted him to do. 'They took sixty grand each.'

Tommy coughed to clear his throat. 'I'm not a mathematician but one hundred and fifty grand split three ways comes to fifty grand each?'

Rico dropped his head, aware the numbers were not adding up. He had to think on his feet, lie. 'I told you I didn't hurt your guy. I didn't really do anything, so I was happy with my cut. It was Freddy and Wayne who battered the driver, more so Freddy I'd say, and Wayne drove the van to the lock-up and got rid of it. Like I said, I was just there for a quick earner.' No longer did he want to claim to be the big man. He'd have given anything for Ty to be there, like he'd always been before when trouble came knocking.

Jacob growled and shook his head. 'Cheeky twats, they are. It's all shared equally in our team. Nobody gets more than the next man in our game. It goes to show what greedy pricks they are. And you, Rico, what a fool you are for even agreeing to it. I thought you come from a decent background. Your kid Tyler has got his head screwed on. What are you, the runt of the litter or what?'

Rico had nothing to come back with. He knew they were talking the truth. If Tyler had been on the job with him, there was no way Freddy and Wayne would have tried to cut his money. They were right: he was the runt, the one with no voice, no power, no influence over anyone else.

Jacob pulled his mobile from his pocket and stared at it for a few seconds. 'Right, we need to get tooled up and get a few heads together for these two clowns. We will have a fight on our hands once we step onto the Salford turf. Freddy has got back-up, so we need to make sure we go team-handed and do the job properly.'

Jacob was on the blower in moments, getting his boys together, all of them eager to prove their worth. There was going to be a bloodbath and only the strongest would survive, but those that did would come out with a reputation worth as much as what they'd earn from Jacob.

Tommy looked over at Rico. 'And what's happening with this tosser?'

Jacob scratched his head and smirked over at Peter. 'It's your shout, mate. I'm easy. He's the small fry here. Throw the dickhead in the river with a brick tied around his neck, for all I care.'

Peter looked at his phone, impatient. The clock was ticking, and his main concern was getting his money back. This idiot could wait until later. He had bigger fish to fry for now.

Rico was curled up in a tiny ball waiting on his fate. The men left the room in a hurry and all Rico could do was thank his lucky stars that he was still breathing, still alive for now.

Chapter Twenty-Nine

Molly stood at the bedroom door and closed her eyes for a few seconds before she walked over to the bed and patted Zara's shoulder. This was hard for her to do. How could she add more stress to this woman's back? It would break her for sure.

She took a deep breath. 'Zara, you need to wake up. Something has happened, love.'

Zara opened her eyes wide and for a few seconds she didn't know where she was, staring around the bedroom. 'How long have I been asleep?'

Molly stared deep into the woman's eyes. 'It's your Brian, love. I went over to your house like I promised I would. When I walked into the living room he was on the floor. He was hurt, Zara, badly hurt. I rang an ambulance, and they have just taken him to the hospital as I was coming over here.' Molly choked up, her hand resting over her heart.

Zara looked back at Molly as if she was in a trance, in a world of her own.

Molly carried on. 'I asked Brian what had happened, and it was all mumbo-jumbo. All he kept saying was they took Rico. "Bad men," he said. "Bad men."'

Zara let out a scream from the pit of her stomach like an injured animal. 'No!' she roared. 'Not my baby, not my bleeding baby. Molly, how badly was he hurt?'

'Zara, you need to calm down. I was going to jump in the ambulance with him, but I told them you would follow them up. Oh Zara, my heart bleeds for you, woman. It's one thing after the other. If you want, I'll ring you a taxi. Don't even think about driving yourself, you're in no fit condition.'

Zara was howling, her heart shattered into a thousand pieces. Her poor son, he'd only just come out of hospital, and someone had jumped him. What for, though? Bri was the sweetest of all her boys. Her mind was racing.

Molly went downstairs with Zara, rang a taxi and the pair sat waiting anxiously.

Zara strained a drag from her cigarette. 'Nobody messes with my family. I will do what it takes to protect them. On my life, I'll go to jail for these bastards. I promise you now if anything happens to my boys I won't rest until I've settled the score.'

These were strong words. Molly had known Zara for a long time and she'd seen her swing at folk for shouting at her boys. Nobody ever went knocking on the Makin door to report bad behaviour if they knew what was good for them.

Zara rushed through the hospital doors and went straight to the reception desk, banging her palm on the window. 'My son has been brought in, Brian Makin, can you tell me where he is? I'm his mother.'

The receptionist took a few details from her and pointed through the double doors into A&E. The NHS was under pressure for sure and, looking about the area, she could see the staff were overworked. A male doctor was walking past and she grabbed him by the arm. 'My son's been brought in, Brian Makin, can you tell me where he is, please?'

The doctor quickly checked the white board behind him and pointed to a corridor to the right of her. 'He's in number three. Please knock before you go in as the doctor might still be with him.'

Zara's heels clipped along the corridor. She stood outside the room for a few seconds before she went inside. Her heart was racing, and her palms were hot and sweaty. The door opened slowly, and she feared the worst as she saw two doctors around her son's bed.

'I'm his mother, please tell me he's going to be alright?'

No words were spoken for a few seconds. The medical team had a job to do and there was no time to sit down with distressed relatives, explaining every injury, when every second counted. Zara knew to remain quiet, she could see her son's head now, his bruised face, the deep cuts under his eye.

A nurse came into the room and guided Zara to a nearby chair. 'Your son is a very lucky man. Twelve stitches he's had in his stomach, and we have managed to stop any internal bleeding. It's a knife wound, I'm afraid. He's going on a drip now and all I can tell you is that he's in the best hands. Fortunately, the blade used to stab him just missed any vital organs by centimetres.'

The doctor came to talk to her directly. 'He's responding well to treatment, and we have done all we can for him. He's a lucky man, a very lucky man indeed.'

'Can I stay here with him? I won't make a nuisance of myself. I just want to be by his side when he wakes up. I have another son in hospital too and my head is a mess with all of this. I need to be here with them both, in case they need me.' The doctor nodded and, after speaking to the nurse again, he left the room.

Zara watched as the woman attached a drip to her son's arm. Once she left the room too, she scraped her chair over to the edge of the bed. 'What on earth has gone on, son? If you can hear me, please speak to me. Is Rico involved, have they taken him? Who did this? Is he safe? You need to tell me so I can get him home safe.'

Brian rolled his head about, every word leaving his mouth sending pain surging down his body. 'Mam, I don't know the guys who did it. They wanted the money, money they said Rico had. He couldn't find it, said it had gone. Jacob, I heard the name Jacob, that's all I know.' He barely got the last words out before a deep sleep took him.

Zara had seen the nurse lining up the morphine and she hoped, at least for a little while, he'd feel no pain.

The door opened and a shaft of bright light came into the room. Ben came marching towards the bed. 'I've not long left Tyler and just been back to yours. Your neighbour filled me in on what has happened. Jesus, Zara. What's going on?

Two boys knifed up, the other gone AWOL. Someone is out to get this family.'

She broke down, shoulders shaking. 'Ben, what the hell is happening? Look at him, look at my boy. He said they've taken Rico. What the fuck have I done in this world to be treated like this? All three of them are in danger. I can't take much more of this, on my life, I can't take any more.'

The door opened again, and the shadow of a man blocked the light. Ben squeezed her shoulder. 'I couldn't stop him coming, Zara. Said he wanted to see his boys, wanted to see you.'

Slowly, she lifted her head, a rush of adrenaline soaring through her veins. Ben held her back, fearing what she might do. 'Max Bloody Makin. Why are you here? Nobody asked you to come. We've survived without you for years so take your sorry arse, turn around and piss off right back out of that door.'

Max had expected more abuse than this. His voice was soft as he stepped nearer to her. 'I'm here for my boys. It's not the time or place to be having this conversation. When we have time, I will sit down with you and answer any questions you have. I know I've not been there for them, but I'm here now and that's what matters right now.'

Zara sagged. She knew she couldn't sort this mess out on her own, she needed Ben and Max to help find Rico. Her own beef could be put on the backburner for now.

'Fine, there will be no trouble here today from me. My boys are what I care about, and I need help finding out what the hell has gone on. Rico is missing and Brian told me the men were looking for some money in the house. Jacob, he said one of them were called.'

Ben went to the door. 'I'll go back upstairs and see Tyler, see if he can shed some light on it. He'll know the crack, for sure. I mean all these grafters know each other, don't they?'

He walked out of the room and Zara felt spooked. If Ben was gone, it left only her and Max in the room. All the years that had passed, she had a script ready in her head, just on the off chance she would ever bump into him, but now she was sat in the same room as him her mind had gone blank.

Max held his youngest son's hand and leaned into kiss his cheek. 'Look at my boy, look at what they have done to you.' Regrets came creeping into his mind, the years gone by that he'd not been around. He was their father, the man they should have looked up to, but he'd left them, thought about his own happiness and his own life. He sat down on the other side of the bed and looked smaller than she remembered him. She watched him from the corner of her eye.

He coughed to clear his throat but still kept his eyes looking down at the floor. 'I'll sort this out, Zara. While there is a breath left in my body, I'll find these bastards and make sure they hurt like my boys have. I'll put the word out and, you mark my words, names will be at my door by the end of play today. I still have a lot of friends around Manchester.'

'You've been gone a long time, Max, a very long time. Things move on.' She was talking in a civil tone to him, but her pain was clear.

Neither of them spoke for a few minutes, both looking at Brian sleeping.

It was Max who broke the silence. 'I still think about you, Zara, about how it could have been if I hadn't messed it all up. We were happy once. Do you remember how much laughing we did together when we were younger? I know I left and never came back, but the truth is I could never look you in the eye again after I'd let you down like I did. I was a young foolish idiot who should have known better. Sandra was a liar, she was always whispering shit in my ear when you weren't about, and that day it happened me and you had been arguing all day over something or nothing. I was feeling sorry for myself, and she took advantage of that.'

'Bullshit, Max, you knew exactly what you were doing. In my bed, with my best friend, how low can you get? I'm glad you left Manchester because the way I felt I would have done something I would have regretted. I was broken, Max. Never thought I would pick myself back up from the floor, but I did. I rebuilt myself and I promised myself I would never ever let any man get close to my heart again. You ruined my heart, you and that slapper. So, go on, how long did you two last when you pissed off?'

'It didn't even last a month. She cried to come with me, said her life around Manchester would be a misery with you on her case, so I let her tag along for a bit. My head was all over and, every time I looked at her, I wanted to punch her lights out. She was the reason I wasn't at home with my family.'

'Stop blaming other people, Max. You were a grown man, not a baby. You let your dick rule your head, that's what you did.'

Max didn't deny it. 'I was not in a good place for a long time. I'm not going to lie, I hit the bottle, tanned the weed like it was nobody's business. I was stoned for years, didn't know what day it was from one day to the next. I always thought I would get enough money together and come back to try and sort things out, but each day that passed it got harder and harder.'

'What, not even sending a Christmas card to your lads? A birthday card? No, Max, I'll never buy that story. Any man that can walk away from his children is a lost case in my eyes.'

'I can't defend myself, Zara. I'll take everything you have to give me. I deserve it.'

'I know you do, and more, if I'm being honest. I feel nothing when I look at you now, numb. I always thought I might still have feelings for you, but seeing you here today has done me a favour. All I'm interested in is making sure the boys are alright. Rico could be lying in a ditch some- where dead, and I haven't got a clue where he is.' She started to sob again.

Max stood up, then froze. Did he go and comfort her? Put his hand on her shoulder? Touch any part of her? He walked slowly around the bed, and gripped her in his arms. 'It's all going to be fine. I won't rest until Rico is home safe.'

Ben rushed back in looking flustered. 'Right, get your arse in the car, Max. Tyler had a phone call in jail from this guy Jacob Watts and he was giving it the big one to Tyler, telling him to speak to Rico about the money he'd had away. He was trying to reach Rico when he got jumped. Jacob is a main head, a Moston kingpin. We need a few heads with us if we are going to tackle him and his firm. You might need to bring the metal out.'

Max didn't blink. Guns were part of his life, and he had always had access to them. Zara shot a look at Ben. If this was what it took to get her boy back and keep the other two in here from being harmed again, then so be it.

Max rolled his neck about, and his ears pinned back. 'I'll be back soon, Zara. No need to tell you to keep your mouth shut is there? You know the score.'

She ignored his comment and addressed Ben. 'Just bring him back safe, that's all I ask. Do what you have to do.'

Zara walked into Tyler's hospital room. Mike was at his bedside, and he sat upright when she came in. He could tell by her face something was wrong and waited until she sat down before he spoke. 'I think your Tyler is coming through the worse of it. He was eating a bit of food before this nap.'

'Mike, Brian is back in hospital. Some heavies went through my door and battered him within an inch of his life. And they've taken Rico. Tyler spoke with Ben before, and he's given him a name. I hope it's not too late.'

Mike swallowed hard and looked about the room. 'I've thought about what you asked me, and I'll do it. I'll help get Tyler out of here. We have to plan it well. We could have him out of the country as soon as he's well enough to travel.'

Zara smiled. 'You'd do that for me?'

'I would do anything for you, Zara. Seeing you hurt like this makes my heart break. And if there are guys out there who are out for your other two boys, then you're right – Tyler won't be safe whichever nick he gets sent to. I hope this shows you that I'm here for the long haul. I've already started to plan it out in my head. I'll be off shift soon and another officer will be here, so stick to his rules and do what he tells you. He'll be doing everything by the book and visiting will be limited so be prepared for that. Look – he's waking up again.'

Tyler opened his eyes. He was usually a rock but tears filled his eyes as he spoke. 'Mam, I tried ringing Rico before this happened to me. These are proper bad guys we are talking about and if he's not coughed up the money he'll be up shit street. I'll try and phone about and see what the word on the street is, but while I'm lay in here like this there is fuck all else I can do. Look at me, Mam, how the hell have I let my life come to this? I should have been home protecting my brothers, both of them.' Tyler pulled the white sheet over his face, and she could see his shoulders shaking.

Mike was called outside by another officer arriving, and he looked concern as he left the room.

Zara moved closer to her son, pulled the sheet down from his face. 'Son, you have always looked after us all. You've let nobody down. Your brothers are grown men and they have to look after themselves. Rico is a bleeding idiot. Fancy messing with men like that, he should have known better. He had enough on his plate looking after your stuff – why did he have to go trying to get a piece of someone else's action?' She rested her head on his chest and his pale hand stroked her head.

Mike returned and the colour seemed to have drained from his face. He eyeballed Zara to follow him back out of the room.

Her heart was beating like a drum. 'Please tell me Rico is alright, don't you dare say anything has happened to my boy.'

Mike looked about and made sure he could hold her in his arms for a few seconds before he delivered the news. 'It's Tyler's friend, Smidge, he's just passed away.'

The words seemed to sink in slowly at first and then, all of a sudden, her legs buckled underneath her.

Mike quickly pulled a chair over and led her to it. 'I'll get you a drink of water.' The water fountain was a few steps away from where they were, and he could still keep a close eye on Zara. He picked up a white plastic cup and filled it with ice-cold water. 'Here you go, have a few sips of that.'

Zara's hands were shaking like a leaf, water dribbling down the side of her mouth. She wiped it away. 'The poor lad, his poor family. We can't tell Tyler yet, it would finish him off. He's not in a good place at the moment and this news would send him over the edge. Bleeding hell, I can't believe it. His poor mother, is she there with him now, Mike?'

'Yes, his family was around his bed when he took his last breath.'

Zara's eyes clouded up with tears, the thought of losing any of her sons running through her mind. 'Will you tell her how sorry I am? Tell her how much our Tyler loved Smidge, and tell her our thoughts are with her. I'll go see her as soon as I know my boys are OK.'

Mike nodded his head. 'I will, I'll tell her.' He gave Zara a few more minutes and then urged her into an empty room he'd spotted next to them. Once they were inside, he sat down and let out a laboured breath. 'My mate has a villa in Spain. He's always telling me to come over and it's in the middle of nowhere. I think Tyler would be safe there for now until we sorted things out. The guy is one of my ex-army pals and he's sorted, he'd never say a word to anyone.'

'Mike, that sounds ideal, but I can't think straight at the moment. Ben and Max are going looking for Rico. Once he's back safe then we can plan what we are doing with Tyler. I know you're only trying to help but for now I can't think of anything else but Rico.'

Mike screwed his face up, couldn't hold his words back. 'Max? Your ex? Why is he back on the scene with Ben? I thought you said Tyler's dad hasn't been around for years?'

'I did, but he's heard what's been going on and come back to Manchester. He came in to see Brian just now. Honest, I nearly died right there on the spot, gobsmacked I was.'

'So, is he here for you or the boys?' His concern was clear.

'Mike, I've told you before, me and Max have been done for years. Seeing him here today has only made me think how far I've come without him. He's not the man I used to love anymore.'

'As long as he knows his place, that's fine by me.'

Zara bit back the words she wanted to say. Right now, all the men in her life were causing her grief. But she couldn't tell him that. She needed him in her camp, needed to keep him on her side. She felt a pang of guilt then remembered: men had been using her all her life. Two could play that game.

Chapter Thirty

Max and Ben sat in a car facing the most notorious boozer in Blackley. The Grove was a small pub set on a main road. They'd had a tip-off that Jacob was in there having a few cold ones with Tommy and Peter. Maybe they should have gone there with a bigger team, two vans full of men at least. But what they lacked in man-power, they made up for in fire power. Max bent down and opened the black bin-liner near his feet, checking the shotgun lying inside. Ben swallowed hard and kept his eyes on the pub. He was tooled up, but no firearms, no way, that wasn't his game. 'So, how do you want to play this? Go in and talk to them, or go in and drag the bastards out?'

Max ran a single finger down the barrel of the cold shotgun, his nostrils flaring. 'First, we go in to get a pint and have a look how the land lies. We'll wait for him to go to the toilet, and I'll do the rest. You're kitted up, right?'

Ben reached under his seat and pulled out a silver claw hammer. 'I've got this and a machete. It's all I need to make sure whoever steps up doesn't go anywhere.'

'Ready when you are then, Benny-boy. Get me my jacket from the back seat. I'll slide my little friend inside the lining so nobody can see it.'

Ben passed the coat over and Max made sure that the shotgun was out of sight. 'Showtime,' he growled.

They locked the car up and went inside the pub. The place was quiet and as soon as they walked in all eyes were on them. Max kept his eyes straight and spoke to the barmaid. 'Two pints of lager, love.'

Ben slowly turned his head, and he clocked the men straight away. Jacob was playing cards, laughing and joking. He didn't look like a man who'd just put a price on someone's head. Max and Ben stood at the bar until they had got their drinks, then found a nice quiet corner to sit in. They could see everything from where they were sat and now they were playing the waiting game.

Ben kept his voice low. 'There's a side door to the left of you. Get the fucker in the bogs and drag him out by that door into the car. I'll make sure these other pricks go nowhere and as soon as I can I'll be out that door with you. Make it quick, no time to be fucking about.'

'Don't tell your granny how to suck eggs, bruv. I've been in this game a long time and I know what I have to do.'

Ben picked up his pint and supped a large mouthful. Tick tock, tick tock.

At last Jacob made a move to go to the toilets. The vein at the side of Max's neck started to pump and, when he saw Jacob walk past him, he was up out of his seat like someone had poured boiling water over him. Ben gulped, pulled the silver claw hammer out of his jacket and was ready to rumble too. Any second now he would hear his brother screaming at Jacob, ramming the barrel of the gun to the side of his head.

And there it was.

Ben was on his feet the moment he heard the first shout, already swinging the hammer around in the air as he saw Tommy and Pete scramble towards him. 'Sit the fuck back down, lads. I swear if either of you move another step it's goodnight Vienna for you.'

Noises continued from behind him, loud banging. Ben screamed at the top of his voice, his eyes bulging from their sockets, 'Fucking sit down, I said!' He smashed a few pictures on the wall behind him, swinging the hammer at full force. Without Jacob to command them, Tommy and Pete hesitated. The pause was long enough.

Ben ran to the car and jumped in the driver's seat. Max was piling into the back with Jacob. He had the barrel of the gun rammed down the back of his mouth and his hands handcuffed behind him.

'Fucking drive,' Max screamed. Ben was an excellent driver and, in the past, he'd been worked as getaway driver on a few jobs. He'd always preferred that to the violent stuff. The wheels spun and the smell of burning rubber filled the air. A few passers-by stood gawping, trying to make out what was going on. It all happened so fast.

Max pulled the shotgun from Jacob's mouth and surged a clenched fist into his back. 'Start talking now, you prick. Rico Makin, where the fuck is he?'

Jacob was wriggling about, hands cuffed behind his back, unable to move. 'Fuck off,' he screamed. 'The little shit has got my money and I want it back.'

Ben sneered at him through the rear-view mirror and put his foot down. He needed away from the scene of the crime. The dibble would be all over the place in seconds. The Grove pub was a regular trouble spot and the blue lights wasted no time when aggro was phoned in from there.

Max dragged Jacob up by his hair. 'We can do this the easy way or the hard way, pal. You have my son and I want him back. If he owes money, then we can talk about it after I know he's alright. I'm a fair man and I stick by my word.'

Jacob turned his eyes and looked out of the window. He was a wise man and knew when he was backed into a corner. 'Go to Longsdale Road, second lock-up on the right.'

Ben heard the directions and headed straight there. Max was on red-alert, and never letting his guard down for one second, always aware this man could strike at any time. 'How much are we talking?'

Jacob spat a mouthful of blood out onto the back of the car seat and licked at the large gash in his bottom lip. 'One hundred and fifty Gs. Not pennies, is it?'

Max's eyes opened wide as Jacob carried on. 'He said he had thirty and the two dickheads he was working with had sixty each.'

Max did the sums in his head and frowned. 'What, he got thirty and the others got sixty?'

Jacob smirked. 'Exactly what I said. So, don't think for one second your lad is taking the shit for them. He told me he was just the driver. It was them who messed up my grafter.'

Max shook his head, a grudging respect building between him and Jacob. They both worked by the same rules. Max started to understand where this geezer was coming from and spoke in a softer tone. 'Our Rico is still a bit wet behind the ears and, if Tyler would have been out, he would have never got involved. He's fucked up, I admit that, but I'm his dad and I can't stand back and watch him get tuned in. You know the score, don't you?'

Jacob had kids of his own. 'They learn the hard way, don't they? I've drummed it into my kids what not to do. But, like your lad, they think they know it all the first chance they get to go solo. I'd be doing the same thing as you if my boy was in trouble. I've already chinned a few men because of him when really I should have let him crash and burn, but you just can't do it, can you?'

Max felt a rush of guilt riding through his body, guilt that he'd not been around to help his sons fight battles they were not ready for.

Jacob knew what these men would be walking into and prepared them. 'He's had a good arse-kicking, your lad has. It's what he deserved, but he'll live.'

The door opened to the lock-up and Max stood behind Jacob. Ben rushed past them.

'Rico, Rico,' he shouted. Was he going to find the dead body of his nephew? Was he going to have to destroy Jacob Watts for taking his relative's life?

'Rico, it's me, Ben. Are you alright?' The shape under the table moved slightly. Ben bent under the table and stretched his arm out. 'It's me, kid, Uncle Ben. You're safe now, your old man's here with me. We're going to take you home.'

Rico squeezed his eyes shut, the light from outside blinding him. With every movement he made, Ben could see he was in pain, dried blood stuck to his cheeks, bruises blooming everywhere. Rico crawled from underneath the table and sat up against the wall with his knees drawn up to his chest. He was scared, still unsure of what lay ahead for him. He looked behind Ben and, as he saw Max, tears started streaming down his face.

His dad looked like a tank, fearless, his protector, just like he'd always imagined him to be. 'Dad,' he blubbered.

Max pushed Jacob away from him and went straight to his son. He dragged him to his feet and held him in his arms. 'You're going to be alright, son. I'm here with you now, everything is going to be alright.'

Jacob shouted from behind him. 'It is if I get my fucking money back, don't forget that.'

Max turned his head slowly, still digesting every mark on his son's body. 'I could just end you, couldn't I? Fucking throw you into a river and nobody would ever find you again.' He still had the shotgun at his side.

Jacob gulped, realising that his fate was in this man's hands. He changed his tone. 'I'm ready to put this behind us, but I need some cash back. My boys won't rest until their pockets are lined and to be fair I won't either. I can shake hands when that's sorted, and we can all walk away from this.'

Max knew Jacob was talking sense and spoke to Rico. 'So, have you got his money or what?'

'It was under my bed, Dad. On my life it was there. My mam must have moved it.'

'There you go, Jacob. He's not spent it. You can have it back, so no harm done.'

Ben paced the room, still unsure what to do with Jacob. This man wasn't letting this go, no way. Max had just shoved a shotgun down his gob, dragged him out of the pub in front of his wingmen, and hadn't yet found the guys who had most of his money. Max might believe they could shake hands on it all, but he was sure they needed to think about this more. He jerked his head at Max. 'Word, bro.'

Max backed off to the side. 'What you thinking?'

Ben swallowed hard, sweat forming on his brow. 'This is not going to end well for any of us. We know Jacob has power in the area and, although he's saying it will be sorted, we both know it doesn't always work like that. Blood money is called that for a reason. If we leave him still standing then we'll be forever watching our backs, sleeping with one eye open. And then there's Rico. Jacob's never going to leave him alone, never in a month of Sundays.'

Max closed his eyes for a few seconds and then stared at his brother. He was a realist and knew Ben was talking sense. A decision had to be made. 'Ben, I'm taking Rico to the car and then it's back home for our kid, back under his mam's roof where he belongs. Lock this gaff up and do what needs to be done.'

Jacob looked puzzled, realising it was not all cut and dry like he'd first thought.

Ben watched his brother and nephew leave, then pulled the door shut behind them. He'd always disliked the heavy side of this world. Never carried a shooter himself. He wasn't looking for glory, status, he never craved the power. But that didn't mean he didn't clean up when he had to. Without a word, he walked over to where Max had put the shotgun down.

Screaming, banging. A gun shot.

It was always the quiet ones you had to watch.

Rico lay in the back of the car, shaking from head to toe. 'Horrible fuckers, they were. Kicked the living daylight out of me. I thought I was a goner.'

Max sat next to his son and his head dropped low. 'Brian is in hospital. They left him for dead. And I don't think you know Tyler is in hospital too. He got done in behind his door in jail. Smidge too. They left them both for dead.'

Rico was on the edge of having a panic attack. 'I know, I can't believe it. He can handle himself, how has he ever left himself open and let some clowns get the better of him?'

Max shrugged. 'Shit happens in the nick, son. Even the strongest fall sometimes.'

Rico screwed his face up. 'Yeah, well the wanker was seeing my woman behind my back. Call it karma.'

Max flipped and turned to face him. 'That's your brother. Nothing comes between you, ever, especially not a woman. Do you hear me? Nothing.'

Rico swallowed hard and sat in silence for a few minutes. He'd been put in his place. 'When did you get back to Manchester?'

'The other day. I'm back for good and just in time to save your sorry arse. What the fuck is wrong with you stepping on someone else's turf? Don't you fucking know shit about how things work?'

'Yeah, course I do. I've been managing Tyler's graft since he went in and it's doing alright. I had a tip-off for some extra dollars and got involved. A bit of action for myself. Don't tell me you wouldn't have done the same, because my mam has told me some stories about you and your past and what you got up to.'

Max let out a laboured breath. 'I made mistakes, granted, but I never had local fucking heavies turning up to my door kicking ten bells out of me and our Ben. We need to sit down and sort all this shit out. Tyler is out of the picture for a few years, and we need to make sure he's got a graft waiting for him when he's out.'

Rico snarled over at his father, 'Whoa, where has the 'we' come from? I don't need you managing anything. I can do it myself. Yep, I fucked up, but it won't happen again. Once bitten twice shy and all that crap.'

Ben scrambled into the driver's seat, speckles of blood all over his hands and face, and flicked the engine over. He nodded at Max. That was all it took to let him know the job in hand had been sorted out. The car spun off. Rico stared out of the car window, not knowing how fine the line was between life and death.

Chapter Thirty-One

Tyler sat up in his bed using Zara's mobile phone, constantly texting. Zara was reading a women's magazine and she kept reading things out from it. Mike was due on duty again and, once he was back, they were all going to run through how they were getting Tyler out of there. Tyler was on the mend and any day now the nick would be on at the doctors to let them take him back to the big house. They had to move fast or the chance would be gone for good.

'Mam, send a big bunch of flowers to Smidge's mam for the funeral. They won't let me attend but I want to show them that I care about them all.'

Tyler burst out crying and Zara flung the magazine to the floor.

'Come on, get it out of you; it's good to cry, you need to cry.'

'What will I do without him, Mam? It's always been me and Smidge. It's my fault he's not here today, fucking my fault for even involving him in my shit.'

'Stop saying that. If it was the other way about, you would have backed him too. You two were as thick as thieves. He will never be forgotten, ever.'

Tyler sucked back his tears and closed his eyes. 'I will avenge him. One day I will make those bastards pay for taking my best friend's life. Mark my words, as God is my witness, they will pay for this.'

Mike walked into the room and looked at Tyler and then Zara. The officer who was on duty wasted no time in changing shifts.

Mike looked flustered, couldn't wait to speak to them. 'Right, I spoke to my mate, and we have a villa for you to go to. It's safe and nobody will bother you. It's in the middle of nowhere and you can live a quiet life.'

Zara held her hand over her heart, her voice low. 'When… when can he go? The other screw was only saying before that, now Tyler is responding to medical help, he could go back to the hospital ward in the jail. How are we going to get him out of here?'

'I've got it figured out. But that's why we need to get this plan underway; it needs to be sooner rather than later.'

Tyler sat up in the bed and examined Mike in more detail. He was willing to risk everything for Zara – lose his job, his good name – it didn't make sense.

'And then what?' Tyler asked.

Mike raised his eyes to the ceiling. 'You live your life and keep under the radar. You can never come back to Manchester, never contact home directly, never ring your mam or brothers on their numbers, because the cops will be monitoring every call they receive.'

Tyler rubbed at his skin as the hairs on his arm stood on end. All he had in the world was his family. He loved them with all his heart. Could he ever be without them?

Zara's mobile started to ring on the bed and, after a quick glimpse at the screen, Tyler passed it to his mother. 'It's Ben again. Bleeding hell, you've not spoke to him for years and now it's like your best friends or something.'

Zara blushed and Mike looked concerned as Tyler carried on. 'I hope he's not trying to get in your knickers, Mother. You know what Ben is like: he's a proper womaniser.'

Zara went beetroot. 'Don't be bleeding daft, son. I'm with Mike and you know I'm a loyal woman. I never burn the candle at both ends. One woman, one man is my motto.'

Tyler let out a sarcastic laugh and eyeballed Mike. 'So, what's the story with you and my mam? It's all a bit too much too soon, if you ask me. A few dates and you're willing to put your neck on the line for her. It's a big ask and not one I can get my head around.'

Mike sat down next to Tyler. Zara was listening even while she was on her phone texting.

'I knew from the very first moment I saw your mam that she was different. I've dated lots of women in the past, and I'm not going to lie to you, I've dabbled with other inmates' visitors, but none of them have interested me like your mother has. Don't get me wrong, I've spent a few months with some of them, but it never went any further. I see a real future with Zara. I see the bigger picture and how happy we can be. And, for that happiness, I will do whatever it takes.'

Tyler nodded his head, but said nothing.

Zara said, 'We have to get all your stuff together, anything you will need while you're on the run.'

Tyler's voice was stern, meaning every word. 'I need all my money. You're going to have to get it all together and bring it to me. I want the car selling and the money from that too. If I'm going to be in another country, I need money to set me up. Money talks and I want to make sure I have plenty of it.'

Zara nodded. 'I'll sort it. How much are we talking?'

Tyler shot a look over at Mike and then at his mother. 'About one hundred and twenty grand, give or take a few quid. Harvey knows where and who to collect it off so there shouldn't be any problems. Once the cash is here, I'm ready to go, so Mam, get cracking and sort it out.'

'Message received and understood,' she choked, trying to think only about getting him to safety, not about how much she was going to miss him. She couldn't let him see how much this was hurting her.

Mike sat chewing his fingernails. 'Zara, can I have a quick word outside, please?'

Tyler smiled over at her. 'Leave me your phone, Mam, I need to sort a few things out while you are gone. First things first, I'm getting the word out that Rhino is a grass. I've had time while I've been in here to work out how Brendan and his lads got to me and Smidge, and when the time's right, I'll make sure Rhino pays for what he's done.'

Zara scooped her handbag from the floor and hooked it over her shoulder. She could nip for a quick ciggie while she was out and settle her nerves.

Mike made sure they were alone, and kept his voice low. 'You do still want us, don't you, Zara? I mean that Ben guy is constantly on the phone to you and…' he paused, 'you seem distant. I haven't touched you in weeks and, before you start kicking off, I do know you have had lots on your mind. But still, I've had no texts from you except about Tyler. If It's just for Tyler you are keeping me here, then fine, I'll still do what I said I would, but don't play me for a fool. Because I've been there, done that, and I will never do it again.'

Zara swallowed, aware he was right in what he was saying. She checked nobody was watching, then stroked his face. 'Babe, I'm so sorry for neglecting you. I've been a hundred miles per hour lately and you're right, it's been crap for you. I'll tell you what, after your shift today let's have a quiet one. Have a nice date and a few drinks.'

Mike looked deep into her eyes. How could he say no to her? Any anger he had seemed to leave his body and he was back in the love bubble again.

Ben sat at home, staring at his phone, waiting on a reply from Zara that never came. He'd told her him and Max had dropped Rico off at hers, and that Molly had been straight over to nurse him, while Zara was torn between Ty and Brian's bedsides. This was it – the boys were safe – now it was time for Zara to put herself first. He'd told her as much, but she'd gone silent. He dragged his fingers through his hair. Max came into the room and clocked his brother was stressed.

' 'Sup with your mush?'

Ben let out a laboured breath and plonked back down in his seat. 'Nowt, our kid, just a bit of business I need to take care of.'

'Well, if you need me, I'm there. You've had my back for long enough and I can't thank you enough for everything you've done for me lately. Without you I would have never been back in touch with my boys, with Zara, and for that I'm forever grateful.'

Ben scuffed at the floor with his foot, not meeting Max's eyes. 'You don't have to thank me. I did what I did because I could see the lads were struggling after Tyler got sent down. They needed a father figure. They needed one of us back in their lives – turns out they got us both.'

Max scratched his arms. 'I think, given time, a few more months, me and Zara could be back on. The way she looks at me, the feeling I get from her, I think she's still in love with me. I know she says she isn't, but I know her inside out and she can't hide her feelings from me. There's a reason why she never remarried. So, bro, keep your fingers crossed for me and all that. I might be back in the big bed after all.'

Ben let out a fake laugh as he left the room.

Max reached over for the remote but instead saw Ben's phone, a message alert lighting it up. Curiosity got the better of him. He tapped in Ben's date of birth, knowing it was his passcode, and started to scroll through the messages. As he heard footsteps coming down the stairs, he flung the mobile back on the sofa. The door opened and Ben came back into the room looking flustered.

'I forgot my phone. I always take it with me.'

Max kept his eyes on the television. 'Yep, I'm the same. It's the only bit of peace I get when I'm on the bog.'

He watched Ben leave again then immediately went outside to the car and brought something in. Slowly, with soft steps, he headed up the stairs. He froze for a few seconds before he booted the toilet door open. Ben's eyes were wide with fear as the shotgun pointed straight at his head.

'What's going on, Max, what the fuck?'

Max sneered at his younger brother and let out a menacing laugh. 'Do you think I came down in the last shower, bro? You've been sleeping with Zara. Don't try and blag it, because I've read the messages. My own flesh and blood screwing my ex. I didn't have you down for that, Ben, thought you had loyalties?'

Ben struggled to pull his jeans up. 'Nah, you've got it all wrong, she wanted me, and I told her no. She wanted revenge for what you did to her. I'm not daft, I knew what she was about.'

Max sucked on his front teeth and shook his head slowly. 'You could never lie to me, our kid. The truth is written all over your face. They are my boys and Zara is my woman. I told you years ago that one day I would have them all back.' He paused. 'That will never happen with you about. Plus, I need a scalp for Jacob Watts' boys to get off my back. You did the deed – now pay the piper.'

Ben could see the look in his brother's eye and knew there was no more arguing. He had always thought his time would be up early, that he wouldn't make old bones. But he'd never thought it would happen like this. His own brother. He held his hands in the air, said a silent prayer.

The shot was fired, and Ben fell back on the toilet seat, his eyes still staring forward.

Chapter Thirty-Two

Tyler continued to amaze the doctors with the speed of his recovery. The next day, he managed to go upstairs to the floor above and see Brian on his ward, 'escorted' by Mike, who was glad to have a chance for a practice run at his plan.

Tyler was relieved to see his little brother was still in a side room. He was here to say his goodbyes and wanted to do it in privacy.

'I've let you down, Bri, I'm so sorry. If I had been at home, none of this would have happened. Rico is a loose cannon, and I should never have named him. He wasn't up to the job of looking after things while I was in jail. I thought it was safer to have a Makin running the show, but I was an idiot. I should have kept him away from that life, like I've tried to keep you clean. That way I might have kept you both safe.'

Brian was tearful as Tyler told him about Smidge's death. 'He was too young to go. This world ages you – makes you think like you've seen it all when, in reality, you've seen too much. I know drugs, they've been my life, given me – and all of us – a living. But in the end they only ever bring misery to people's lives. Dealer or user, we're all their victims. Maybe all this is karma for the life I chose, a message to me to stop what I'm doing. And, in fairness, being behind doors for hours on end – in the nick or in here – makes a man think, think long and hard. This isn't the life I want anymore. I want peace, and I'm never going to get that here. I know, wherever I go, I'll have to look over my shoulder all the time, but if I go now, like Mam and Mike have sorted, at least I've got a chance. I wish I could take you with me, Bri, wish we could all go and start again somewhere new where nobody knows us, but I need to do this on my own. Once I get there, if I get there, I'll see if it's sound, and when it's all died down maybe you can all come and join me. But until then, at least I'm keeping you safe the best way I can – clearing off so none of you think you have to live up to my name.'

Brian gripped his brother's hand and squeezed it with all his might. 'You have always been there for all of us. I know you're no angel, but you did it all for us. I'll find a way in time to come and see you. Trust me, we'll all find a way. I just want you safe now and away from Manchester. You've carried the burden of looking after us for as long as I can remember and now it's time to look after yourself.'

'Mam is bringing me my money tonight, so any time soon I'll be gone. I'm going to leave some dough with her for you all, enough to get you by, enough so if anything happens you have money to fall back on. I've just spoken with Rico.' He paused. 'The guy is still bitter about Clara. I told him she means nothing to me, but he's spat his dummy out and said I betrayed him. So I'm not counting on him to look after you and Mam. I need you to do that, our kid.'

Brian nodded. Was this how Tyler had felt when he had to step up? Was he ready? Was anyone ever ready?

Mike came into the room . 'I'll have to take you back down now. I've got the wheelchair outside. Do you want me to bring it in?'

'Yeah, thanks Mike.'

Brian and Tyler were alone again for a last moment. They shared a hug, one that told them both how much love they had for each other. Tyler pulled away and took his brother's face in his two hands. 'Brothers for life, yeah? I'm only ever a phone call away, remember that, our kid. I'll get a burner phone as soon as I'm in the clear. You'll be hearing from me.' Tyler choked back the tears and turned as the door opened. He never looked back.

Back in his bed, Tyler lay clock-watching. Tonight at midnight he would make his escape and head for a new life. Mike had swapped shifts to get the night watch and they'd been going over the details like clockwork.

Zara sat blubbering with her head held in her hands. 'I feel like I let you all down if the best I can give you is a ticket out of here. I've failed you, kid.'

'Mam, stop it, will you? For fuck's sake, I don't need to hear this. It's nobody's fault how we all turned out. You are a brilliant mother, always have been. We chose our path and nothing you could have done would have changed that. We are men now, making our own way in life.'

'Yeah, but look at the state of you all. Each of my boys is battered and bruised.' She winced as she said it, feeling each cut and bruise as if it were on her own skin.

'And you taught us that, if we fall down, then we get back up bigger and stronger and learn from our mistakes.'

She tried to smile. 'I did, didn't I? I was never one to let you lie down feeling sorry for yourself, was I? And I need to take my own advice now. I know it, son.'

'You made me strong, Mam. I get that from you. Whenever I came home after a fight, you always sent me back out and told me not to come home until I'd won.'

Zara smiled. 'I know you're a battler, lad. But right now I need you to be safe, need you away from harm.'

'And come tonight I will be. I'll get myself sorted, Mam. I'll be better, stronger than ever. Nobody will ever, ever, get one over on me again. Lesson learned.'

Zara dug in her bag and passed him a plastic bag filled with money. 'It's all there, I counted it myself.'

Tyler dug his hand in the bag. 'That's for you. Call it a safety net,' he said as he passed her a tight roll of notes. 'And it's not all for the boring stuff. There's money for a few nights out too and a couple of curly blows. I know what you're like.'

Tears fell from her eyes and all she wanted to do was hold her son in her arms, smell his hair, touch his warm skin. She looked at his fingers and kissed the end of them. These were the hands she'd held when she was teaching him how to walk, the same hands she held when it was the first day of school, the same hands she held when he woke up in the night after a nightmare. She softly kissed his fingertips. 'I'm going to miss you more than you'll ever know, son. I'll miss our chats, miss having a brew together and, most of all, miss knowing you're sleeping safe under my roof.'

'It's not forever, Mam. Nothing is forever, until the Reaper comes.'

Zara knew when to keep quiet and this was one of those times. It was hard for them all, hard to say goodbye.

———

The midnight hour struck and Mike, who was stationed outside on a chair, opened his eyes as his phone alarm vibrated. A power nap, he called it, although nap was stretching it – he'd shut his eyes almost as soon as he came on shift – figured he'd need his rest as he wouldn't sleep a wink for the rest of the night. He stretched his arms above his head and stood up. Looking one way then the other, he patrolled the area to make sure Tyler's escape route was not jeopardised. Taking a deep breath, he made sure he was ready. He knew what he was risking, but he was driven by equal parts love and fear. A dangerous mix.

He walked into the dimly lit room and whispered, 'Tyler, it's time to go, wake up.' There was no reply and Mike edged further inside the room, still muttering under his breath. 'Tyler, I said wake up. Coast's clear. You need to make a move or we will mess everything up.'

Mike froze on the spot, eyes focused on the bed. Small steps forward and, through the gloom, he saw the bed was empty.

He rushed outside and rummaged in his pocket for his phone before he stepped back into the room. 'Zara, he's gone. He's not here.' Mike dropped his phone onto the floor and stood with his back against the cold wall. 'Fuck, fuck, fuck,' he growled through gritted teeth.

This was bad. He just didn't know how bad yet.

Chapter Thirty-Three

Tyler lay flat in the back of the car. It was dark and all he could see was pinpricks of light through the blanket that covered him. He was clutching something close to his chest, never letting it leave his side.

His voice was low as he spoke to the driver. 'Fill the tank up and then we can get the fuck out of here.'

Clara kept her eyes on the road. 'I meant to do it before, but I was rushing about, getting my clothes packed. I told my mam I'm going working away and she never bleeding batted an eyelid. I told you she doesn't care about me, didn't I?'

'Pull over at the services and do what you have to do.'

Clara indicated to leave the motorway, aware every move she made took her further down a path she couldn't turn back from. Was she ready for a life on the run?

But Clara was in deep now and there was already no turning back. She'd helped him escape from the hospital and, if the police got wind of her part in all this, she would be charged with harbouring a criminal, or aiding and abetting.

She jumped out and filled the car up with petrol. Tyler browsed the phone his mother had given him. They both knew he'd have to ditch it as soon as word broke that he'd escaped, but she'd said she had to know he'd made it out OK.

He was relieved he'd got out of hospital before Mike came looking. He had never trusted that screw. He could have turned at any time. And it wasn't fair on his mother to be tied to a man like Mike just because he'd helped him escape. Tyler always preferred to do things his way, and he had made sure nobody knew where he was or where he was going. It had been easy to work out Mike's patterns and slip past him, harder to find a place to head for. But that's why Clara was along for the ride. She would stay with him forever, if he let her. As long as she knew he had money, as long as he was buying her gifts.

He heard her heels clattering across the tarmac as she went to pay. She was probably buying half the shop up ready for their journey. Tyler listened out for Clara's return, edging the blanket down off his eyes so he could look up at the silver moon. That's what his mam had always told him when he was nipper, after his dad left – 'We're all under the same moon, wherever we are.'

The car door opened, but it wasn't Clara standing there.

'Money, I want the money, and nobody will get hurt.' A voice muffled only slightly by the balaclava covering the man's face. A cold silver barrel shoved into his mouth.

Tyler patted one hand along the seat. 'Here, it's here.'

The man grabbed the bag and stood looking down at him. It was long enough for Tyler. He pulled his other hand from under the blanket, clutching a silver pistol so small it almost looked like a toy in his hand. He'd laughed when Clara had delivered it earlier, rolled up in a tea towel and shoved in with the fake passport he'd got his contacts to make up. He'd felt like a pantomime villain holding a gun so ridiculous. He wasn't laughing now. He knew that voice anywhere. It meant there was no messing about. He pulled the trigger and sat up to watch the man fall to the ground.

Tyler knew he had to be quick. His attacker was still moving and he would only get one chance to finish him off. He ripped the balaclava from the guy's face. 'Dad, you've outdone yourself this time.'

Max was clearly in pain, blood bubbling from his mouth. Tyler bent and pulled him up by the scruff of his neck. 'I knew you were up to no good. I told them all not to trust you. Once a shady bastard, always a shady bastard.'

Max gasped for breath. 'I have debts, son, big gambling debts. They are going to kill me. I have to get money from somewhere. I was going to talk you round, get a loan, but once I realised you were out of here, you left me no choice.'

Tyler spat in his father's face. 'Rot in hell, you're no father of mine. I was going to finish you off cleanly. But you deserve nothing more than to bleed out right here.'

Clara arrived back and her chatter stopped abruptly as she came round the side of the car and saw the body. 'Tyler, what the hell? Oh my God, is he dead?'

Tyler stood over Max, whose breathing was getting slow and shallow now. 'He's always been dead in my eyes. Get in the car, we're going.'

———

Zara stood waiting for Mike on the corner of the street a few minutes away from the hospital. The police were all over the hospital now and sirens filled the air. The weather was bad, and Zara zipped up her thin coat and leaned back in the shadows. A cloud of grey smoke came from her mouth, and she kept checking her phone. Where the hell was Ben? He'd told her he and Max had dropped Rico off ages ago and that he was coming to see her. She'd tried to put him off after she got the call from Mike to say Tyler was missing – dreading Mike and Ben turning up at the same time – but now they'd both gone silent.

She heard rustling behind her. She turned quickly, spooked. Her eyes strained looking down the dark alley-way behind her. It was probably rats rummaging through the rubbish scattered about there. She pulled her jumper up over her nose as the smell of rotting refuse assaulted her senses. She took another drag from her cigarette.

The blow came from nowhere. Zara was upright one minute, then a blinding pain and the next minute she was on the floor with a woman stood over her, half a brick in her hand.

Her attacker smashed it into Zara's head again. 'Slut! Life-wrecking bitch!' she screamed.

Zara was trying to shield her face. The woman bent down and looked Zara in the eyes. 'I was happy with Mike, and we were fine until you started to show your face in the jail. He was mine and we could have had a future together. You're a tease, you never wanted him, you just didn't want me to be happy.' The woman's voice went higher as she poked her finger into Zara's chest. 'He told me he loved me then just stopped ringing me. I knew there was someone else and made it my business to find out who. Imagine how I felt when I saw it was you, you bleeding tart.'

Zara stared at her attacker, her eyes not focussing as blood ran into them from her forehead. Her voice was quiet but clear. 'Jane,' she whispered. But the woman had already turned on her toes. Zara could hear her footsteps running back down the alleyway. She was gone.

Chapter Thirty-Four

THREE MONTHS LATER

B rian sat at home, still not used to the silence, even though it felt like a lifetime since Tyler had gone. There was no noise in the house anymore, no laughter. Rico had tried to rebuild his brother's empire, but he couldn't make it work. Nobody feared him like they feared his big brother. Even Brian wouldn't graft for him. Instead, he'd been volunteering with a charity – warning kids about what laughing gas could do. He got a kick out of telling kids like he'd been that there was more to life than balloons. Other ways to get that buzz.

Where Rico's name had turned to mud, Tyler's reputation had only grown since he vanished. Everyone asked Brian how his eldest brother had escaped but, though the police still claimed to be hot on his trail, they'd stopped visiting the house, stopped asking Brian and Rico endless questions or expecting Tyler to show up. In fact, the last time he'd seen the dibble was the obvious plain clothes policeman standing at a distance on the day the Makin men were buried. There had been no arrests for either Ben's or Max's murders – the investigating officers seemed glad the gangland feud had burned itself out without innocent victims and had left it at that.

Zara had insisted on no church service, no crem funeral for either man. She'd expected Max's extended family to step in and demand the full works – horses with black feathers, a procession behind the coffin. But they'd gone quiet. Word was Max hadn't come to rescue his boys – but instead had been fleeing trouble in his new life. She figured the rest of his family were as glad to see the back of him as she was. As for Ben, he'd always been a loner at heart. Instead, she, Rico and Brian had gone alone to the cemetery. Zara had left a single white rose on Max's coffin, a red rose on Ben's. Then she'd walked away without a tear.

'I was so young when I first became a Makin, I don't think I ever knew adult life without bearing the name,' Zara had told her youngest that day. 'I always felt like I needed the name to tell people who I was. First it was Max protecting me, then Tyler. This is the first time in years I've not hidden behind someone else, son. And let me tell you what: it feels good. I'm no one's wife. I'm me. Mother of boys, I answer to no one, and I sleep sound at night. Alone.'

It looked like it was going to stay that way. Mike Patterson had gone quiet. He'd realised he'd put everything on the line getting mixed up with Zara and Tyler – and knew he was lucky to mess with the Makins and get out alive.

Brian had never seen his mum so content with her own company, so happy in her own skin. She had an angry scar from where Jane had attacked her, and he'd expected her to go ape at Jane's trial – shouting and threatening like she always had before. But when the judge gave Jane a suspended sentence due to her poor mental health, Zara walked out of court head held high, no shame, no fear.

Yes, life was quieter in Collyhurst than Brian had ever known it. Without Rico trying to run Tyler's patch, Brian had assumed the Moston crew would take over, but Jacob Watts' family seemed to have gone into retirement too. He'd seen one of the Watts kids on the local news talking about ending gun violence, and wondered if maybe, just maybe, with the generals killed off, the foot soldiers had asked themselves what they were really fighting for. Certainly Rico barely left the house these days, shut away in his room gaming instead of fighting in the real world.

Brian never thought he'd get tired of the peace, until the day Zara told him funds had started running low. Perhaps peace was a luxury only the rich could afford.

'Mam, we can rebuild our lives, you know, put our names back on the map. Tyler will guide me. Send me word somehow about what I need to do. I know he trusts me more than Rico and I can get things moving around here again. Rico will have nothing to do with it. He's a bleeding recluse now, anyway. What do you say? Nothing stupid, just what we always did best – local boys selling decent gear to local customers.'

Zara looked him in the eye. She'd only recently started wearing her hair up again, rather than covering the scar with a fringe. 'To do that, son, we'd need money and plenty of it. I've not got a pot to piss in and we don't have a money tree growing at the bottom of the garden, do we?'

Brian took a deep breath to speak but she stopped him dead in his tracks. 'You and Rico could both get a proper jobs and earn money legally. I'm done with waiting for my boys to get hurt by other kids playing at being gangsters. I can't cope with that life anymore. Plus, you'd be starting at the bottom, clawing your way up just to get a patch to run.'

He shuffled about in his seat. 'Mam, I need to tell you something. It's been lying heavy on my mind, and it is not something I am proud of.'

'Nothing shocks me anymore, son, nothing at all. Out with it, then.'

Brian pulled a box out from by his side and emptied it onto the floor. Money, wads of money scattered across the carpet.

Zara's eyes lit up. 'Where the hell did you get that from?'

Brian walked over and sat by his mother's side. 'It's the money Rico stole from Jacob Watts. I found it under his bed and took it because I knew one day he would fuck up and leave us all on our arses.'

Zara was lost for words. Then she found her tongue. 'You crafty sod. I thought Ben had swiped it all. I thought we'd lost any chance of getting our hands on it when the coppers cleaned out his gaff after he was done in. But all this time you, my sweet-faced baby boy, have had it stashed. When were you going to tell me?'

'I dunno, Mam. It was just there, and I took it. Then I realised it was driving me nuts. I'm not like Tyler: I don't want to spend it stocking up on Class As to resell. I was always happy with the weed. And I'm not like Rico – desperate to spend it on labels and girls and flashy stuff. So I figured, who really deserves it? You. You're right, Mam. You don't need Tyler's instructions or another bloke telling you what's what. So here – you decide what we do and where we go.'

It was like the sun had come out from behind the clouds. Zara was quiet for a long time, thinking. She stood up and looked at her reflection in the mirror, then finally she spoke. 'What is it I've always said? "You get knocked down, then you pick yourself back up and come back stronger than ever".'

'Your words, Mother,' Brian smiled. 'Those who fight but walk away live to fight another day.'

Zara grinned. 'And our day will come around soon enough, son, don't you worry about that.' She nodded at her reflection and stood tall, shoulders back. 'I will come back bigger and stronger than I ever was. And, mark my words, so will my boys.'

Acknowledgements

Thank you to James for his support.
My children: Ashley, Blake, Declan, Darcy and
all my grandchildren.
Thanks to Gen, Megan, and Alice as well as all
the crew at HarperNorth.
Finally, thank you to all my readers and followers.

Harper North

Book Credits

HarperNorth would like to thank the following staff and contributors for their involvement in making this book a reality:

Fionnuala Barrett
Samuel Birkett
Peter Borcsok
Ciara Briggs
Sarah Burke
Alan Cracknell
Jonathan de Peyer
Anna Derkacz
Tom Dunstan
Kate Elton
Sarah Emsley
Anna Gamble
Simon Gerratt
Monica Green
Natassa Hadjinicolaou
CJ Harter

Megan Jones
Jean-Marie Kelly
Taslima Khatun
Sammy Luton
Rachel McCarron
Molly McNevin
Alice Murphy-Pyle
Adam Murray
Genevieve Pegg
Agnes Rigou
Florence Shepherd
Eleanor Slater
Emma Sullivan
Katrina Troy
Daisy Watt
Sarah Whittaker

For more unmissable reads,
sign up to the HarperNorth newsletter at
www.harpernorth.co.uk

or find us on Twitter at
@HarperNorthUK

Harper
North